BELLA ANDRE

Can't Help Falling In Love

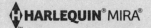
HARLEQUIN® MIRA®

Recycling programs
for this product may
not exist in your area.

ISBN-13: 978-0-7783-1558-2

CAN'T HELP FALLING IN LOVE

Harlequin MIRA/August 2013

First published by Bella Andre

Copyright © 2011 by Oak Press, LLC

Printed in U.S.A.

www.Harlequin.com

Dear Reader,

Firefighters are strong, courageous and willing to take on the danger that everyone else runs away from. Even better, they also happen to be some of my favorite heroes in romance novels. In *Can't Help Falling in Love*, Gabe can't make the mistake of falling for another fire victim. Megan can't love—and lose—another man with a dangerous job. They have every reason to stay apart. But they can't help falling for each other.

Just like Megan, I couldn't help but fall for my firefighting Sullivan. Especially when a little matchmaking in the form of a seven-year-old girl had me grinning like crazy whenever Summer appeared on the page.

I hope you enjoy this sizzling romance…and I can't wait for you to fall in love with Gabe, too.

Happy reading,

Bella Andre

One

It was a beautiful Saturday afternoon in San Francisco. The air was cool, the sky was clear. Couples were walking hand in hand through Golden Gate Park, tourists were discovering the wonder of clam chowder in sourdough bread bowls at Fisherman's Wharf and kite-surfers were out en masse in the bay, zigzagging around the yachts and sailboats with their bright sails.

Unfortunately, for the two dozen people who lived at 1280 Conrad Street, a fire had turned their perfect Saturday into a nightmare.

The fire trucks and firefighters arrived first, the news trucks close on their heels. To the casual observer the fast-moving men in their turnouts who were yelling information and coordinates at one another, the radios that were turned up loud in their hands and the hoses that snaked across the road and the sidewalk looked like utter chaos. In truth, the men of Station 5 were a well-oiled machine.

Earlier that afternoon, firefighter Gabe Sullivan had been enjoying a fund-raising concert his brother Marcus's girlfriend, Nicola, had put on at the fire station. Everyone had been beside themselves with glee at the chance to pay big bucks to attend the very intimate acoustic concert with Nicola, who went by the name Nico when she performed. Her show had been amazing, as usual, and Gabe was still beyond impressed that his oldest brother had scored a woman like her. She wasn't just beautiful and sexy, she didn't just have amazing musical talent: she was really sweet, too.

Nicola had just come to the end of her third encore when the call came in. Ten minutes later, the fire-fighters from Station 5 had arrived on scene, hooked up their hoses and began to evacuate the building and work to put out the fire.

Wearing his full turnouts, Gabe helped an elderly couple down the stairs of the old San Francisco apartment building and out onto the sidewalk. They looked to be in good health, but their nervousness about the fire was giving them trouble with the stairs. With a gentle hand on their elbows, he worked to keep their pace up so that he could get them completely out of the building and away from the fire as quickly as possible. They'd just made it to the sidewalk when the gray-haired man started coughing. Gabe steered them over to the ambulance parked a few feet behind the largest fire truck.

Gesturing for one of the paramedics to come over to them, he told the couple, "We're going to get you checked out for smoke inhalation. If you have any questions about anything, make sure to—"

His words were cut off by an explosion of flames and smoke out a second-story window.

After ten years as a firefighter, Gabe knew no fire was ever routine. No flame ever played the same game. And sometimes the simplest call could turn into the most complicated. The most dangerous.

Over his radio Gabe could hear concern in the voice of his station captain. "Everyone out!" Todd barked to the crew. "This fire has accelerated. We're switching to defensive operation. Repeat, evacuate the building."

Gabe still had his hand on the elbow of the gray-haired woman and she turned to him with a look of horror on her face.

"Megan and Summer are still inside. You have to get them out!"

He could tell from her rapid breathing and dilated eyes that the woman must be on the verge of going into shock, so he spoke to her in a clear, steady voice to make sure he got the information he needed.

"Who are Megan and Summer?"

"My neighbors, a mother and her little girl. I saw them go into their apartment a while ago." The woman looked at the other tenants who were gathered around the fire trucks and watching—horrified—as their homes and possessions went up in flames. Flames that were raging more out of control by the second. "Megan and Summer aren't out here." She was clearly panicked and gripped his arm harder than her earlier frailty had suggested she was capable of. "You have to go back inside to save them. Please!"

Gabe wasn't a firefighter who believed in superstition. He didn't have a routine he lived and died by. But he did believe in his gut.

And his gut was telling him there was a problem.

A big one.

"Which apartment are they in?"

She pointed to the third-story windows with a shaking hand. "Number 31. They're on the top floor, corner unit." The woman looked terrified. The stress of the situation was clearly becoming too much for her.

"It will be all right," her husband soothed her. "He'll find Megan and Summer." He was speaking to his wife, but his eyes held Gabe's, along with the silent message: *Don't you dare let my wife down. She loves those girls like they are our own.*

Seconds later, Gabe found both the captain and his partner, Eric, marshaling the crowd of people out on the sidewalk and street. Reporters were now swarming the street, only adding to the confusion.

"We've got to go back in. A neighbor just told me a mother and daughter could still be inside. Third floor, corner apartment."

They all glanced up in the direction Gabe was pointing. All that could be seen was dark smoke billowing above the rooftop.

Todd looked from Gabe to the fire raging inside the building. "Make it quick, guys. You've probably got ten minutes, tops," he said, and then turned and gave instructions to the rest of the crew to focus their fire-hose streams up toward the apartment.

In the same way that the loud boom from the explosion had rocked through the crowd, now a momentary hush fell over the assembled masses as Eric and Gabe moved in tandem to pull another hose into the building. Masks on, their earpieces activated, they moved up the stairs as quickly as they could through the smoke that hung thicker than the fog San Francisco was so famous for. With their breathing apparatus on, they were okay. But a civilian wouldn't last long in these conditions without frequent hits of oxygen.

Forcefully pushing his fears for the mother and daughter aside, Gabe concentrated on moving from the first floor to the second, and then to the third. All the while the roar of the fire increased, and the heat notched up higher and hotter. A door on the second floor blew out and shook the landing.

Gabe and Eric dragged the heavy hose through the thick smoke and debris. Despite the steep, tight flight of stairs, and the immense physical challenges, they arrived at apartment 31 in a matter of minutes.

Gabe tried the door, but it was locked. He prayed that the fact the fire hadn't yet blown out this door meant the people inside still had a chance.

Sliding his ax from its holster, while Eric waited several feet behind him, Gabe pounded on the door, yelling, "If anyone is by the door, I'm about to knock it down with an ax. Back away." Even though he shouted at the top of his lungs, his voice was muffled by the protective mask.

Jesus, the smoke was heavy—nearly thick enough to cut with a knife—and the heat was probably approaching eight hundred degrees Fahrenheit.

Would they find anyone alive inside?

"You got it?" Eric yelled, then took a few quick hits of oxygen.

Nodding, Gabe cocked the heavy tool back and landed the top of the ax head right against the doorknob. A hollow door would have split apart in seconds, but this old wood door was thick enough that he had to do a dozen sustained hits to get it to budge. When he felt the frame start to loosen up, he kicked at it, putting all of his two hundred pounds of muscle behind the effort.

Finally, it swung open and he was suddenly inside the apartment.

Sliding his ax back into its holster, he reached for the hose and started to drag it inside, but it wouldn't move.

"It's stuck. I need more hose," Gabe shouted to Eric.

He looked behind him and saw Eric yanking on the hose with all his might. "It's caught on something, damn it! I've got to head down and figure out where it's hung up."

They both knew how dangerous this situation had suddenly become—leaving his partner behind was not something a firefighter ever did unless there was a dire emergency.

No question, if a mother and daughter were stuck inside apartment 31, this was one of those times. They didn't have a choice; they needed that extra length of hose.

Gabe and Eric exchanged a look that held a world of meaning. If one, or both of them, didn't make it out alive, they'd had a good run together full of honor, laughter and countless pots of firehouse chili.

"Hurry," Gabe yelled to Eric.

Lives were on the line tonight. And the sixty seconds it would take Gabe to help Eric with the hose might mean a child would die.

Eric ran back down the stairs through the smoke as quickly as he could, and when Gabe looked up at the apartment's ceiling, the flames were already rippling above his head. Gabe cracked open the nozzle on the hose and started blasting the roof in an attempt to douse the blaze. He could feel the oppressive heat coming down on him as he moved farther into the room. Judging by the black-and-white soot already covering the furniture, this apartment was clearly one of the hot points of the fire, possibly the room where it had begun.

He stilled as he thought he heard someone calling out, crying for help. With the hose still stuck, he had no choice but to drop it, and make a move in the direction of the sound, a white interior door with a mirror on it. The door was closed, so Gabe kicked it open with his steel-toed boots.

A new flood of smoke rushed through the door, impairing his vision for a split second. But even though at first glance he couldn't see anyone in what was a small bathroom, he knew exactly where to look.

He ripped back the shower curtain and found a woman crouched in the old claw-foot bathtub, holding her daughter in her arms.

He'd found Megan and Summer. Thank God his prayers had been answered and they were alive.

"Megan, you've done good. Real good," he told her through his mask.

The woman's eyes were so big, and so scared. She was clearly terrified. Gabe's chest clamped down on itself and the emotion of the situation got to him for a second. But it was a second he couldn't afford right now. Not when all that mattered was getting Megan, Summer—and himself—out of the apartment building alive.

"I'm going to get you and Summer out of here. Now."

Megan opened her mouth and tried to say something, but all she could do was cough, her eyes closing as tears seeped out onto her face.

Realizing now that the little girl was unconscious, Gabe pulled off one of his gloves to check her pulse. Giving more silent thanks that it was still steady, he put his glove back on, then reached to take her.

Her mother's eyes shot open and they played tug-of-war for a moment before she let the girl go. Her lips moved in a silent plea: *Please.*

He knew better than to let her fear, her terror, stop him from doing what he needed to do to get them out alive. And yet, her eyes held him a moment longer than he should have let them. The love she felt for her daughter was so obvious, so apparent, and Gabe felt her desperation. In that brief look, Gabe felt as if he'd known her forever, rather than just a handful of rapidly ticking seconds in the middle of what had become a war zone.

"I'm going to take Summer and we're going to crawl out of here. Can you do that?"

She nodded and he gripped her arm to help her slip over the edge of the tub. She was shaky, but she was clearly a fighter. After helping her out of the tub and down to the floor where the smoke was thinnest, he pulled a second air mask out and moved to put it over her face so that she could take some clean hits of oxygen into her lungs. She tried to push it away, tried to get it over her daughter's face, but he'd anticipated this movement and shook his head.

"You need to take it first." He spoke loudly and firmly so that she could hear him through his mask. "Otherwise, you'll be dead weight and none of us will get out of here alive."

She grabbed the mask from him, and clamped it against her face. Her eyes widened as she took her first breath and he knew to pull it back so that she could cough a few times before putting it back on, holding it gently in place as she took in the clean air she so desperately needed.

When she shook her head and glanced wildly at her daughter, he removed the mask and put it over her daughter's mouth and nose. The girl stirred slightly, coughed, then seemed to settle. It had been barely a minute since he'd found the two of them in the bathtub, but those sixty seconds had been enough for the flames to grow higher, hotter, even more hellish.

They were all flat on the floor to avoid the heat and he was about to tell Megan the next steps in their escape plan when the motion detection alarm on his belt went off. It was second nature for him to reset it before anyone on the crew could be alarmed that he was down. It was dangerous as hell up in the third-floor apartment and he didn't want anyone else on his crew up there unless there was no other option.

With visibility almost completely gone, he yelled, "We're going to crawl against the wall edge to stay low out of the smoke and heat until we find the doorway. It's hot out there but if you keep moving, I promise you we're going to get out okay." Gabe would never make a promise he couldn't keep.

He would damn well keep this one.

Slowly, they made their way along the molding at the bottom of the tiled bathroom wall to the doorway. Gabe hoisted Summer under his left arm as he crawled along the floor with only one hand free, barely noticing the burning muscles in his right triceps and biceps.

Gabe kept frequent checks on Megan as they continued through the doorway into the living room, which was even hotter than the bathroom had been. He prayed the heat wouldn't have her passing out. Just in case, he helped her along every few seconds by wrapping his free arm around her waist and pulling her forward. She wasn't limp in his arms, which was a very good sign, but he could feel how weak she was becoming, that she was fighting to stay conscious with everything she had.

Finally, they made it to the tip of the hose and he realized Eric had never made it back up to the apartment. Gabe hoped like hell his partner was okay.

Preparing himself to deal with the possibility that the reason Eric hadn't been able to get back up the stairs to the apartment on the third floor was because the stairs had burned up, or collapsed while he'd been helping Megan and Summer, Gabe called out to Megan, "You're doing great. All we need to do is grab the hose and follow it back down." There was no time to try to radio his captain with his coordinates. Everything he did from here on out would depend on a decade of fire training…and instinct.

He took her hand in his and placed it over the rigid pressurized hose. When he was confident that she had it, he moved behind her to help push her along, lifting her when her legs collapsed every few feet or when she was coughing too much to move on her own.

It was damn hard going through the heat and smoke, and he admired the hell out of her. He should have been carrying two dead weights out of the apartment building, not just one little girl. But somehow Megan was holding it together. Despite everything, she was holding focus.

One leg, one arm, after another, she put everything she had left into moving forward. The weight of his safety gear and oxygen tank combined with holding Summer under one arm was extraordinary. But he hadn't spent the past fifteen minutes hiding in a bathtub holding on to hope that someone would find him. He had it worlds easier than Megan did.

"Turn around," he yelled to her when they reached the landing at the top of the stairs. "We're going to go down backward. And we're going to keep moving, no matter what."

He moved behind her again, going lower on the stairs to catch her in case she fell. Her little girl was stirring in his arms and he prayed she wouldn't wake up in the middle of this fiery hell.

A loud booming noise sounded and he looked up to see part of the wall beside Megan's front door falling down in sheets. The oxygen that had been reintroduced from the bathroom had combined with the heat and heavy smoke inside the apartment to create rapid combustion.

Grabbing Megan, he moved with her and her daughter as quickly as he could down several steps. She had her head lowered and her arms over her head to protect herself from falling Sheetrock.

"Keep moving!" he yelled.

As the seconds ticked by, they made it down one more step, and then another, but it was slow going and fraught with peril. Beneath his feet, Gabe could feel how thin the well-worn steps were. They could crumble at any second.

They'd made it down two flights of stairs before he heard his crew yelling over the deafening sound of the miniexplosions that kept going off all around them.

Gabe knew time was running out. It was time for a last burst of speed.

He pushed himself to the brink as he descended the last few steps, still maintaining a firm grip on Megan and Summer.

When he was almost at the bottom of the stairs, he finally saw what had stopped Eric from coming back upstairs. A huge ceiling beam had fallen down over the rail and it had sent the whole area around it up in massive flames. Judging from the water and smoke pouring off it, he guessed Eric had been focused on putting that fire out before it destroyed the entire staircase, leaving Gabe and his victims stranded upstairs.

Somehow he needed to get around the beam, but it was still too big and too hot for him to get past without putting Megan down first. Damn it, he didn't want to leave her there alone where anything could happen to her while he took Summer outside.

Just then, thank God, through the smoke he heard voices yelling, "Give them to us," and a moment later Eric and Todd were pulling both mother and daughter from his arms and taking them to safety.

Amazingly, it wasn't until that moment that Megan lost consciousness, her strong grip at his arm going limp as Eric took her from Gabe.

As he yelled, "The mother just passed out," to his partner, Gabe's attention was so focused on Megan that he waited a moment too long to hurdle the smoking beam himself.

He heard the loud *crack* a split second before a chunk of ceiling came flying down straight onto his forehead. He hit the ground as hard as the beam had hit him. Darkness swam before his eyes.

The last thing he heard was the motion detection alarm on his belt going off.

Two

Megan Harris woke with her daughter in her arms. They often snuggled at night after a late movie or if Summer had had a bad dream, but something felt different. Not just the bed, but the itchy spot on the inside of Megan's elbow and the way her throat felt raw and abused.

She smelled smoke in her hair, in Summer's hair, and she scrunched up her nose at the scent of fire that felt as if it was seeping from their pores.

Suddenly, it all came back to her. She woke all the way up with a gasp, her eyes flying open. There were two narrow beds pushed together side by side in the hospital room, but Summer's bed was empty. At some point during the night her daughter had chosen to climb in with her and snuggle up close.

The fire.

Oh, God, the fire.

She'd almost lost—

No. Summer was right here, in her arms.

Megan pulled her daughter closer and Summer shifted to look up at her.

"Mommy?"

"Hey there, baby." Her words came out rough and ragged. As if she'd actually swallowed fire. Which she pretty much had. Megan kissed her little girl on the forehead and each cheek, following those kisses up with a puckery smooch on her soft little lips. "How are you feeling?"

Summer gave a little wiggle. "Okay, but I want them to take this itchy tube out of my arm." She lifted up her left arm and looked at Megan's. "We match."

Smiling through tears of joy and gratitude, Megan agreed with her daughter. "We do," she said, then held up four fingers. "How many fingers am I holding up?"

"Six." Her daughter's crooked grin told her she was teasing. "Four." Summer held up one finger. "What about me?"

"One," Megan said with a kiss to the fingertip. "How about we call the doctor and see if they need us to keep our IVs in or if we can be set free?"

A smiling, middle-aged doctor came in shortly after Megan hit the call button, clearly pleased to see them awake and doing so well. The doctor quickly checked their vitals, smiling as she wrote on their charts, then removed their IVs. "You're welcome to stay here awhile longer if you'd like, but I'm happy to say it doesn't look like either of you have any of the serious aftereffects of prolonged smoke inhalation, probably because you're both young and healthy."

Megan shot a glance at Summer. She didn't want to freak her daughter out, but she needed to ask the doctor a very important question. "Summer was unconscious for a while. Are you absolutely sure she doesn't need to see a specialist to make sure everything is okay?"

The doctor shook her head, and smiled again at both Megan and Summer. "No. Everything looks great." She turned her focus to Summer. "You're in awesome shape, kid."

Summer grinned back at the doctor. "I'm the fastest kid in my class when we go out to the track. Even faster than the boys."

The doctor laughed. "I have no doubt you are. So," she asked Megan, "do you know what you'd like to do? Would you like to stay here for another day?"

"Thanks, but I think we'd both like to head home." A moment too late, she realized she didn't have a home to go back to.

The doctor gave her a sympathetic look. "I'm sure you'd like to get washed up and changed." Before Megan could remind her that they didn't have any clean clothes to change into, the doctor brought over a bag. "The hospital keeps a stash of clothes for people in your situation. I'm so sorry about what happened to you, but I'm very glad you're both doing so well."

Tears threatened again. She was in a *situation*. How she'd hoped that her *situations* were behind her.

Well, she thought as she ruthlessly pushed more tears away, she and Summer had survived the first "situation" five years ago and they'd survive this one, too. Heck, they already had survived, hadn't they? Now it was just down to details.

If there was one thing Megan knew how to deal with, it was details. Her work as a CPA meant she was a master at taking the often messy financial details of her clients' lives and transforming them into clean, well-organized accounts and spreadsheets. She'd simply have to do that for herself now. She'd heard enough accountant jokes to last several lifetimes, but she loved her work. It gave her great pleasure to make sense out of chaos, and to watch numbers line up in perfect rows and sums. And after what she'd been through with Summer's father, Megan loved the security of a job in which gray areas simply didn't exist. The figures had to add up every single time, and for every disparity, there was an accompanying reason that would clear up the problem.

Thankfully, she was religious about backing up her clients' files to an off-site server. She'd be okay there, at least, once they'd found another place to stay and she was ready to get back to her job.

Before leaving the room, the doctor reminded them to take it easy for a few days and to check back in with her if they had trouble breathing, had coughing spells or felt dizzy and confused.

The police came in a few minutes later to take her statement about the fire. She tried to keep her voice strong and steady while Summer was listening, but her voice caught more than once. Each time, the two police officers would stop their questioning so that she could compose herself.

When they were finally alone again, Megan told her daughter, "I'm going to take a shower and then you can go on in and clean up."

Summer nodded, reaching for the remote control and turning big, pleading green eyes on her. "May I watch TV?"

Even though Megan was usually strict about not watching TV during the day, she quickly decided that something mindless would be a very good thing for her daughter right about now. She nodded, ruffling Summer's short blond hair before scooting off the bed. "Just for a little while."

"Yay!"

As Megan headed into the bathroom toward what was going to be the best shower of her life, she was glad to know that, where her very resilient daughter was concerned, it looked as if she was going to be okay.

Only, as she stood under the warm spray that was slowly washing away the black smudges of smoke on her skin—along with what she realized were the charred ends of her hair—she didn't have any idea how long it was going to take her to feel okay, too. Not with the visions of what might have happened to them running through her head one after the other— mental pictures of their ordeal that were blurred with the dark edges of a thick, black fog.

And yet, despite how exhausted and drained she felt, she hadn't forgotten about the heroic firefighter who had pulled them out of their flaming apartment. He'd risked his life for theirs. Once she and Summer were back on their feet, she would go find him. Not just to say thank you, but to find a way to repay him for the incredible gift he'd given them.

The precious gift of life…when death had been so horribly close.

Closing her eyes tight, as if that would keep the dark visions at bay, she lifted her face to the water and let it wash away her tears of shock—and joy that she got to live another day with the little girl who meant absolutely everything to her.

As they walked through a nearby Target store a couple of hours later, Megan was amazed to find that, despite the horrors of the fire they'd lived through, Summer had returned almost immediately to her normal energetic personality.

Megan wished she could rebound so fast. As soon as they'd walked into the store, they sat down on the plastic red chairs in the small cafe and made a to-do list. There was so much to think of, so many things to tackle.

Despite what the doctor who had attended them had said, Megan had already made an appointment with Summer's regular pediatrician. She knew her daughter wouldn't be crazy about going to the doctor again, but Megan couldn't take any risks with her. And, to be perfectly fair, since fairness was of utmost importance to six-year-olds, Megan had scheduled an appointment for herself, too.

They were wearing mismatched clothes that didn't fit quite right. She needed to get all new IDs. The tips of her hair had singed badly enough in the fire that she now desperately needed to get a haircut if she wanted to look at all presentable. And she badly needed to find out if her neighbors were okay. When she'd asked around at the hospital, no one had mentioned anyone else from her building being admitted. She prayed it was because everyone else had gotten out unscathed.

Of course, making this very overwhelming list after filling out approximately two zillion forms for the insurance company wasn't exactly helping her state of mind. She was used to plenty of paperwork, but this had been over the top.

She'd purchased their small but charming apartment last winter and had been fixing it up in her spare time. Now all she had to show for her hard work was a promise of money from the insurance company. After they did their assessments, of course. Until then, they'd given her enough cash to get by on until she could contact her bank for a new ATM and credit card. They'd also informed her that she had been checked into a Best Western hotel near the hospital until she could make other arrangements.

As soon as she bought a new cell phone, she'd call her parents and try to break the news of the fire to them without giving them a heart attack. No doubt they'd be on the next plane out from Minneapolis to come take care of her and Summer. Of course she wanted to see them, wanted to feel their warm arms around her, but at the same time…well, she wasn't looking forward to a repeat of five years ago when David died.

No doubt about it, they were going to put the pressure on her to come "back home." They'd use this fire as the perfect example of how much safer she and Summer would be in the small town she'd grown up in.

Megan unconsciously lifted her chin. She was proud of how well she'd done raising her daughter by herself. And, regardless of what her parents thought, she'd learned her lessons about safety perfectly well. The men she'd dated the past couple of years were accountants like her, or teachers, or corporate engineers. She'd never again make the mistake of giving in to the thrill of being with a man who thrived on risk, who ran toward danger instead of away from it like any sensible, reasonable person would.

Summer tugged her toward the food and Megan broke another one of her rules, this time about junk food as they bought hot dogs and nachos and big cherry Slushies. But although Summer polished everything off, Megan couldn't do more than take a couple of bites.

Knowing how much her daughter liked new clothes—oh, who was she kidding, they both did—Megan told her, "We're just going to buy a few essentials like jeans and T-shirts today."

"But we'll need to get a whole bunch of new stuff soon, right?"

Silently thanking God that her daughter was more

pleased about getting new clothes than she was distressed about losing her old ones in the fire, they went to try on a handful of things and were on their way to the front of the store to buy them when Megan realized she'd forgotten something very important.

Yes, they needed clothes. Of course, they needed to buy some food. But despite how cheerful Summer was being about their *situation,* her daughter had just had all of her things taken away from her…including the Rapunzel doll she slept with every night.

Knowing they needed to be extremely careful with their cash for the time being, she put down one of the T-shirts she'd been planning to buy on the dressing room reshelving cart and steered her daughter toward the toy section.

"Look, I think they have Rapunzel dolls here. Why don't you go pick one out?"

Summer's eyes lit up and she threw her arms around her mother. "You're the best mom in the whole world!" As she ran down the aisle to get the doll, Megan found herself standing in the middle of the big store with tears threatening to fall again.

When they were trapped in the bathtub, she'd hoped, she'd prayed, that she and her daughter would live to do something as mundane as go shopping together, but the fact was that as the fire had raged hotter and bigger, as the sirens had rung out louder without anyone coming to help them, she'd almost stopped believing.

When Summer returned with the brand-new doll, perfect in its shiny package, Megan quickly wiped away the evidence of the emotion threatening to spill over again. She knew she had a lot to learn from her daughter's smiling face, from her happiness over something as small as a pretty doll.

They'd lost things, but they still had each other.

All she wanted to do now was check in to their hotel room and curl up with Summer for a much-needed nap. But as soon as she arrived at the hotel, her old neighbor and friend, Susan Thompson, pulled her aside.

"Megan, Summer, thank God you're all right!"

The older woman brought both of them in for a hug. Again, tears threatened and Megan had to hold her breath and focus on a patch of dried gum on the carpet to keep from breaking down. She wasn't normally a crier, hadn't let herself give in to tears even after David's death. She'd been too busy then trying to keep up with her two-year-old, trying to hold on to her accounting job and keep them fed with a roof over their heads, and resisting the pressure from her parents to come back home to Minneapolis immediately and never, ever leave again.

Mrs. Thompson, however, had no such qualms about crying. Her cheeks were shiny with tears as she finally let them go. "As soon as I told the firefighter you were both inside, he ran straight in to get you."

Again and again throughout the past hours, Megan's brain had flashed back to the firefighter who had found them in the bathtub, his firm, confident voice directing her. Her skin, her muscles and bones, still felt the phantom imprint of his hands, the strength of the way he'd lifted, moved, pulled her and Summer forward toward safety.

They were alive because of him.

Susan sat with Megan on the nearby faded couch in the lobby. "He had just helped me and Larry out onto the sidewalk when I looked around and realized you and Summer weren't standing there with the rest of us." Her mouth trembled. "I'd seen you come in just a little while before the fire started so I knew something was wrong."

Megan swallowed hard, reaching out to cover the other woman's hand. "Thank you so much," she whispered. "If you hadn't told him—"

Megan shot a glance at Summer, who was happily unwrapping her doll. Her daughter seemed to be totally engrossed in her toy, but Megan knew darn well that she was actually taking in every little thing around her. Every expression, every word. Megan didn't want Summer to turn what had almost happened into a fear that she'd take forward with her.

But Mrs. Thompson was shaking her head. "That firefighter was the real hero. They didn't want to let anyone else into the building, but he didn't hesitate to run in to save you. I just hope he's all right after what happened to him."

Megan looked up at her friend in horror. "He was hurt?"

Susan frowned. "You didn't know?"

"No." She couldn't remember anything after they'd made it down the stairs.

"Mommy?"

Megan knew she should be pulling it together for her daughter, that it was the most important thing for her to do, but instead, all she could do was ask, "How badly?"

Her friend sighed, looking even more upset. "They had to carry him out on a stretcher."

Megan felt just as she had when they were stuck in the bathtub—like she could hardly breathe, like the darkness was coming down over her again.

She jumped up from the couch. "I have to call the firehouse. I have to find out how he's doing." Susan stood with her and followed her to the front desk. "I need to use your phone. Please."

The young man behind the counter nodded quickly and she realized he must have overheard their conversation. "Of course. No problem."

Her hand was shaking on the receiver as she called Information for the phone number of fire dispatch. She asked them to transfer her to the firehouse in her neighborhood.

By the time the call went through, she was near-frantic. A man's low voice barely said hello before she was saying, "I'm the woman the firefighter saved yesterday. Me and my daughter. I just heard he was hurt. I need to know how he's doing. Was he hurt badly? How long will it be until he's okay again?"

The man on the other end of the line was silent for a long moment. "I'm sorry, ma'am, but I can't give you that information."

"He put himself in terrible danger to save me and

my daughter. I need to thank him. I need him to know how much what he did means to us."

"I understand how upset you are, but—" He stopped speaking and she heard another voice in the background. "Hold on a moment."

Another man came on the line. "Is this Ms. Harris?"

She was momentarily surprised the man knew her name. "Yes, this is Megan Harris."

"My name is Todd Phillips. I'm the captain at Station 5. How are you and your daughter doing?"

"We left the hospital a few hours ago," she quickly told him.

"I'm very glad to hear that. And I'm sorry about the fire in your apartment."

Megan knew the time would come when she'd grieve the loss of all her precious mementos of her daughter's baby years and of David. But the loss of their things paled in comparison to the horrifying knowledge that a firefighter had gotten hurt while saving them.

"I need to thank the firefighter in person for what he did to help me and my daughter."

She could almost hear the fire captain shake his head across the line. "I'm sorry, Ms. Harris, but—"

"Please," she begged. "I owe him everything."

Everything.

After a short silence, he said, "I'll need to check with Gabe first."

"Thank you so much."

She gave the fire captain the number for the phone

at the front desk before hanging up, but even as she and Summer finally went upstairs to their new temporary home and her daughter zombied out again in front of the Disney channel, Megan couldn't stop worrying about the man—*Gabe*—who had given up his own safety for theirs.

She was on the phone in her room, wading through more red tape with a representative from her bank, when there was a knock on her door. The young man from the front desk was there with a message.

"A fire captain called. He said he'll meet you at the hospital in thirty minutes."

Three

Out. Gabe Sullivan wanted out of the damn hospital bed. He wanted to yank the IV out of his arm, too, and was just about to do that when his mother walked in.

"Don't you dare take that out."

Mary Sullivan had already been in to see him earlier in the day, but this time she'd returned with two of his brothers and their significant others.

Nicola ran forward. "Oh, my God, I was so worried about you!"

When Marcus's pop-star girlfriend had heard that the city's fire stations were facing heavy budget cuts, it had been her idea to play a show to raise money for them. She was clearly horrified that at the tail end of her acoustic benefit concert, Station 5 had been called out to the three-story building on Conrad Street…and that he'd gotten hurt.

She threw her arms around him and he purposefully pulled her closer as Marcus looked on. The way his brother shook his head said he knew exactly what Gabe was doing. Any other time, Marcus would have had him up against the wall for getting this close to his woman, but evidently being stuck in the hospital had some bonuses. Such as the fact that Marcus was too happy that Gabe was alive to lose it over the placement of his hands just above the curve of Nicola's hips.

Still, Gabe knew he could only push things so far when Marcus wrapped his hands around Nicola's waist, growled, "Get your own damn girlfriend," and yanked her back against him.

Gabe understood exactly why his oldest brother had fallen for the pop star. She wasn't just easy on the eyes and talented, she also had a huge heart. Gabe had never been with anyone like that—someone with whom he could actually imagine having a long-term relationship with rather than just a few hours between the sheets. Jackie, the woman he'd been casually dating, had come by the hospital earlier that day. She was a sweet girl, but he didn't have the heart to keep stringing her along. By the time the visit was over, she was in tears and his head pounded worse than ever, but he knew he'd done the right thing by letting her go.

Fortunately, a moment after Nicola was pulled away, his brother Chase's fiancée, Chloe, was taking her place in Gabe's arms.

"Damn it," Chase muttered, "now he's got my girl. Nothing like being a hero to make women throw themselves at him."

Clearly, they were all so glad he was okay that they'd let just about anything slip right about now. Everyone except his mother, who was staring at him with eagle eyes.

"I just spoke to the doctor and he's informed me that you'll be staying here for another night so that they can do one more CAT scan. I'm glad about that. You took a serious hit on the head. We all need to make sure you're perfectly healthy."

"Aw, Mom," Gabe said, sounding more like a fourteen-year-old boy than a twenty-eight-year-old grown man. "I feel fine." His head ached like a son of a bitch, but he'd suffered hangovers nearly as bad as this.

"Since I can see that the beam that hit you knocked out what little common sense you have, I'm going to trust the doctor." He barely stifled his groan at being stuck in a small hospital room for so many hours on end when his mother added, "And so are you."

Chase was doing a pretty good job of trying to act as if the bandage on Gabe's head wasn't that big a deal. But Marcus, who had stepped into their father's role when he'd passed away more than twenty years ago, was clearly concerned.

"How did this happen, Gabe? I know you've always been smart out there. But from what the news reports have said about the fire, the building wasn't safe to go into at the point you did." His brother's expression tightened even further. "Not even close to safe."

Gabe wasn't surprised that Marcus was the one

to call him on what he'd done. Marcus had always dropped everything to help them when they needed it, and even though Marcus now had someone really special in his life, Gabe knew he would never stop worrying about each and every one of them.

Although the rescue had almost ended in disaster, Gabe wouldn't have done a damn thing differently. Not when he could still see the helpless little girl in her mother's arms, her big eyes pleading with him to save the person she loved most in the world.

"The building wasn't empty." It was the only explanation necessary for a firefighter.

"You could have died, Gabe."

He held his oldest brother's gaze. "You're right. I could have." He waited a beat before saying, "But I'm still here."

Marcus blew out a hard breath. "How many goddamned lives are you going to burn through playing hero?"

"Marcus!" their mother exclaimed.

Wanting to break through the tension in the hospital room, knowing this was just all part of being a firefighter's family, Gabe said, "It's okay, Mom. This is Marcus's way of showing he cares."

Fortunately, Nicola helped thaw things out in the room by laughing at Gabe's statement. When Marcus glared at his girlfriend, she merely grinned at him and said, "We all know you're like one of those hard candies with a gooey center, Marcus." He turned the full force of his scowl at her, but when she went up on her toes and kissed him, he stopped scowling.

Before Marcus—or anyone else—could start in on Gabe again, he yawned big and loud. One sibling after another had been in and out of his hospital room all day. The nurse had even said at one point, "How many of you are there? My patient needs his rest." Of course, when Ryan had flirted shamelessly with the woman, she'd agreed to bend visiting hours as much as she could for the Sullivan clan.

Picking up on his signal, his mother began to shoo them out, kissing him on the cheek before leaving. "If the doctors give you the all clear and let you go home tomorrow, I'll be by your house with food."

He could take care of feeding himself, but he knew helping him like that made his mother feel better about what had happened…or, more to the point, about what had almost happened. She'd never been crazy about the dangers that came with his being a firefighter, but she'd supported him, anyway.

"Not if," he said, "when." And then, with another hug for her, he added, "Thanks, Mom."

They left and he had just closed his eyes for a few minutes when another knock came at his door. His captain, Todd, stepped into the room.

"How're you feeling, Gabe?"

"Good, Captain."

He moved to sit up straighter on the bed and Todd shook his head. "You're fine just like that. I know your skull must hurt like hell." He took a good long look at Gabe. "I'll be sure to tell the guys at the station that you're looking good. Better than most of them look when they haven't been hit with a falling beam," he joked, then nodded back to the doorway. "Are you ready to see Ms. Harris and her daughter, Summer?"

No, he thought, *he'd be better off never seeing those eyes again.*

He'd thought about Megan and her daughter one too many times for comfort. Not just because he was mentally reviewing the rescue, trying to look for what he could have done differently, how he could have gotten them out faster and more safely—but because he hadn't been able to forget her strength, how hard she'd fought to stay conscious and what a fighter she'd been every single second of the harrowing journey from her burning apartment to the safety of the street.

Still, he understood that fire victims often felt compelled to say thank you to the men who had saved them. Especially in a case like this, where they'd barely held death at bay.

"Sure." He began to nod, but a sharp shooting pain stopped him.

Catching his grimace, Todd said, "I'll ask Megan and her daughter to come back later."

Megan fit her, Gabe had found himself thinking one too many times. *Megan* was pretty and strong all at the same time. It would be better to think of her as Ms. Harris. Although, he had to wonder, was there a husband? And if so, where had he been during the fire and why wasn't he here with them now?

"No," Gabe said, "it'll be better if I see them now."

He knew how it would go. She'd say thank you,

he'd tell her he was happy to see her and her daughter doing so well, and that would be that. No more being haunted by her eyes, or by remembering the surprising strength she'd shown as she'd crawled across the floor of her apartment and down the stairs.

A couple of minutes later, Todd walked back in with Megan and her daughter. Ignoring the pain in his head, Gabe sat up higher and forced a smile on his face.

And then, his eyes locked with Megan's and his smile froze in place.

My God, he found himself thinking before he could shove the thought away, *she's beautiful.*

The last time he'd seen her face it had been through a thick haze of dark smoke and the knowledge that one wrong move meant their lives were over. Her eyes were just as big and pretty as he had remembered. Her limbs looked as lean and strong as they had when he'd been helping to move her along the floor, but now he could see the softness in her, the sweet curves of her breasts and hips in her T-shirt and jeans. He couldn't stop staring at the startling green of her eyes, the silky dark hair falling across her shoulders and the way her pretty young daughter was a carbon copy of her, the only difference being their hair color.

She seemed just as stunned as he, and for a long moment, the two of them just stared at each other in silence until her daughter ran over to him and threw her arms around him.

"Thank you for saving me and Mommy."

The little girl's arms were just as strong as her mother's. Trying not to wince as a bolt of pain shot through his forehead, he said, "You're welcome, Summer. How old are you?"

"I turn seven on Saturday."

She beamed at him and right then and there he lost a piece of his heart to the pretty little girl with the two missing front teeth.

"Happy birthday." He'd make sure to send her a gift from the station.

Movement caught his eye. Megan was coming closer to him and, yet again, once he looked up at her, he couldn't seem to pull his gaze away. Without realizing what he was doing, he scanned her left hand for a wedding band and found it bare.

"Mr. Sullivan, I can't even begin to thank you for what you did."

He would have asked her to call him Gabe, but he knew his name would sound way too good coming from her full lips. Already his brain was starting to spin off into a fantasy of what it would sound like to hear her say his name in distinctly different circumstances, circumstances that would involve one less child and one less fire captain in the room…and a hell of a lot fewer clothes. He might have a bitch of a headache, but everything else was working just fine.

As it was, he couldn't take his eyes off her gorgeous mouth, which was wobbling slightly. She clamped her lips tightly together as she quickly brushed her fingertips over her eyes.

"I'm sorry," she said with a small laugh that

held no actual laughter in it. "I promised myself I wouldn't cry."

"She keeps doing that," Summer told him in a stage whisper as her mother worked to win the battle with her tears.

He whispered back, "It's perfectly normal."

"We wanted—needed—to come and say thank you." Megan's eyes moved over his bandages before she added, "And to make sure that you were okay."

His voice was much gruffer than usual. "I'm okay."

"I'm so glad."

"How are you both? You inhaled a lot of smoke."

She gave him a small smile that did crazy things to his insides. "We're both fine." She put her hand to her throat. "The doctor said I'll only sound like a frog for a few more days."

"You've got to hear her *ribbit*," Summer told him. "She sounds exactly like the frog we have in my class at school. Do it for him, Mommy."

This time Megan's soft laugh was closer to a real one. "I'm sure he doesn't want to hear me *ribbit*, Summer."

The power of her smile, the way her eyes lit up and a sweet dimple appeared in her left cheek, rocked all the way through him. He could get drunk on her smiles—was already feeling as if he'd been knocked off center by just one.

If Megan were someone he'd met at a coffee shop or bar, if she were one of his siblings' friends—if she were anyone but someone he'd rescued from a fire—he would have been working on ways to get her to not only stay longer, but also to charm her phone number and a date out of her.

But the only reason she was looking at him with her heart in her eyes was because he'd saved her and her daughter's lives. He knew better than to let himself fall for her and her pretty little girl.

His expression hardened at the memories of what an idiot he'd been in the past when he'd ignored professional boundaries and—stupidly—got involved with a fire victim.

"Of course he wants to hear it," the little girl said, and then, when he remained silent, turned to him and said, "Don't you?"

In the end, Gabe couldn't let the kid down. "Sure," he finally said in a tone that implied just the opposite. "Why not?"

But Megan read him loud and clear, pulling her daughter away from him and into her arms.

"We didn't mean to bother you," she said in a slightly defensive voice.

He didn't tell her they hadn't been a bother. It was better for her to think they had. That way they wouldn't come back. That way he wouldn't see either of them again.

At his curt nod, she said, "I appreciate you letting us come to see you today," then took her daughter's hand to pull her out the door, thanking Todd for facilitating the meeting as she went by.

"Do we have to go already?" the little girl protested. "I bet he has some really cool stories about all the scary things he's done."

In an instant, he saw in Summer the same desire for excitement and adrenaline, to live every single ounce of life, that he'd always had.

Megan turned back to him, wary now. "I'm sure Mr. Sullivan needs to get some rest." She forced her lips into a false smile that made his chest feel like a hundred-pound weight had just landed on it. "Say goodbye now, honey."

Summer frowned, with a minipress of the lips that perfectly mirrored her mother's. And then instead of saying the goodbye her mother had insisted on, she said, "Do you think maybe we could come by the fire station sometime? You know, so you could show us around?"

Megan didn't give him a chance to say a word, saying, "Summer," in a clear warning that had her daughter sighing in resignation.

"Goodbye, Mr. Sullivan."

He wanted to smile at the sweet little girl, wanted to let her know that the way he was acting didn't have anything to do with her, and everything to do with knowing better than to let himself fall into something that would only end up hurting all of them in the end.

Instead, all he could say was, "Goodbye, Summer."

Four

Two months later...

Megan wrapped an oversize towel around herself and stepped out of the bathroom to get changed into her clothes. The apartment they were renting until they could find the perfect new place to buy was small enough that she could see into the kitchen as she headed for the master bedroom.

"Summer, what are you working on?" she asked, trying to hold on to her patience as she took in the flour on her daughter's cheeks and hair...flour that was, no doubt, all over the kitchen floor, too.

They were still setting up house, putting together a full set of furniture and dishes and clothes. Megan was also calling the insurance company every day about the second set of claims she'd had to fill out when the first set were inexplicably lost. Soon, they'd promised her, it would all be worked out. Her fingers were cramping from crossing them with hope for so long.

In the past two months, whenever Summer did something that made her mad, all Megan had to do was remember how small and fragile her daughter had been during the fire, how much she'd longed for the scrapes and mishaps Summer always managed to get into, and the little frustrations would disappear. Only, these past few days, it seemed that Summer was more and more intent in her efforts to rile her up—and Megan was holding on to her calm by a very thin thread.

"Making muffins," Summer hollered back. "They're just about ready to go into the oven. Can you turn it on?"

They'd been baking together since Summer was old enough to stand on a stool at the kitchen counter and play with flour and sugar and sprinkles, and Megan loved how creative her daughter was with both ingredients and decorations.

Of course, Summer had yelled loud enough for the next apartment building over to know exactly what was going on in 1C. Although Megan had always loved looking out over the streets of San Francisco, she would never again live anywhere but on the first floor. Her nightmares about being trapped on the third floor and having to crawl down what had seemed like endless stairs were starting to disappear over time. Still, after the fire she'd now take safety over views anytime. If she missed the views, well, that was just something she'd have to deal with. Anything was better than getting trapped in another *situation* like that again.

"Okay," she said slowly as she tucked the towel tighter beneath her arms and stepped barefoot into the kitchen to turn on the oven. "But what brought this on at—" she stopped to look at the clock on the oven "—six-fifteen in the morning?"

They were both early risers, but her daughter wasn't normally quite so industrious this early, especially not on the first day of winter break.

Summer gave her a wide smile, the one she always used on people to charm them into giving her exactly what she wanted. Megan liked to think it didn't work on her. Not too often, anyway.

"We can bring them by the fire station." Summer widened her smile. "For the firefighters to eat for breakfast."

The first few weeks after the fire, Summer hadn't stopped asking questions about fire, about fire engines…and about Gabe Sullivan. Megan had answered the technical questions as best she could with the help of the internet and some books from the library. But she'd done her best to sidestep her daughter's inquiries about the firefighter who had saved them. Particularly the ones about going to see him again.

In the hospital, she'd seen honest emotion in his eyes when Summer had hugged him. But then he'd closed up on them, so suddenly and so completely she'd actually felt a little hurt by it.

She knew better than to take it personally, though. Especially when she knew his head had been hit pretty darn hard during the rescue. And her emotions had been really close to the surface that day, so close they kept bubbling over. She told herself that had to be the reason she'd felt bad about his behavior.

Unfortunately, Summer wasn't the only one who thought about him all the time. Megan thought about him every day, too. About how grateful she was for what he'd done for them. About how selfless he was to have risked his life for them. And sometimes, late at night, when she was alone in her bed, she might have even thought a couple of times about how good-looking he was and how big his muscles were.

Not that those thoughts were worth anything, though. Even if he hadn't all but kicked them out of his hospital room, she could never be with a man like him. Not after she'd learned the risks—and the pain—of being with a man who was addicted to danger. She'd learned those lessons the hardest way possible when her husband had died five years ago.

Megan wanted a future with a man who would definitely be home every night. She refused to ever spend another day, another night, waiting for the phone to ring, for the knock to come at the door with the news that she'd lost a partner she'd counted on to be there.

It didn't help when Station 5 sent Summer a birthday gift the week after the fire. It was a little fire-fighter doll with yellow pigtails, a big smile and a small pet Dalmatian that came with a fire-engine-red leash. Summer dragged that doll and her dog everywhere, sleeping with them under her arm, cuddling up on the couch with them at night. Even now, the doll and stuffed dog were standing watch on the kitchen counter.

"I'm sure they already have plenty to eat for breakfast," she told her daughter in a gentle voice as she grabbed the tray to slide the batter into the oven.

"Not as good as my muffins, though," Summer reasoned.

Megan couldn't argue with that. Summer's chocolate-banana-blueberry muffins were legendary. It was a combination that shouldn't have worked, but ended up blowing your mind instead.

Lord knew, her daughter hadn't gotten her cooking prowess from her. Nope, that was all David, who'd had a surprising knack with food. Summer was so much like her father, all the way down to the light blond hair, that sometimes Megan felt as if he were still alive.

"We'll talk about it after I get dressed. Let me know when the timer dings so that I can take the muffins out before they burn."

"Okay, Mommy," her daughter chirped, knowing she was on the verge of getting her way. And really, Megan thought with a small sigh, she was all out of excuses for why they couldn't go and say hello to the firefighters at their local station.

Okay, so they'd drop the muffins off, admire the shiny fire engines and then head off to the park for a couple of hours. She wouldn't let herself get all tied up in knots over the possibility of seeing Gabe. Actually, he'd never told them to call him anything but Mr. Sullivan, even though he couldn't be much older than she was. In any case, what were the odds that he would be on shift this morning? Or that he'd even remember them?

Megan caught a glimpse of herself in the mirror over her dresser and found there was no way to ignore the lies she was piling up one after the other. Just thinking about the firefighter had her tied up in knots and there wasn't a darn thing she could do about it.

If he was on shift, he'd remember them. Because there'd been an undeniable connection, a palpable spark, between the two of them.

She stepped away from her mirror and pulled open the closet. Whether she was lying to herself or being brutally honest, one fact remained: she had absolutely nothing to wear to a firehouse on a cold Saturday morning in December.

Summer skipped ahead of Megan, who was carrying the Tupperware container full of warm muffins. At least half a block ahead, Summer disappeared into the open doors of the fire station. She recognized the station as one of the oldest in the city, in a truly beautiful building. Megan knew her heart shouldn't be beating so hard. Yes, they'd been walking up a hill, but she was in good shape from the yoga DVDs she worked out with in the mornings.

And then her daughter walked outside with *him* and Megan's heart pretty much stopped beating altogether. Her feet stopped, too, leaving her to stand awkwardly on the sidewalk holding the muffins with her mouth hanging halfway open.

He'd been gorgeous in the hospital bed with bandages on his head and a sheet covering most of his body. But now...

Oh, *now*.

There weren't words—at least, not in her overwhelmed-with-lust brain—for a man like this. *Tall, dark and handsome* barely scratched the surface. *Gorgeous, beautiful...* each of those adjectives were too pedestrian for his strong shoulders, his lean hips, his bright blue eyes set off against the square jaw and full, masculine mouth.

Megan had to forcefully remind herself that she shouldn't take a running leap and jump this man. Her dormant libido might have—stupidly—taken this moment in time to spring back to life, but that didn't mean anything in the grand scheme of things. At some point when she was all alone in her big bed, she'd find a way to take care of her newly raging sex drive. But there was no way she would risk her heart or her daughter's on a man who might not live to see tomorrow.

That thought sobered her up enough to push her past the embarrassment of her superobvious reaction to his good looks.

Willing her feet to get moving again, she finally walked the last few yards toward him, making sure to keep her shoulders back and her chin up so that he wouldn't think she was any more of a loser than she already felt like, drooling over him like that.

"Are you doing okay?"

He nodded. "I'm great."

Relief flooded her as she said, "Good. I'm really glad to hear it." Being this close to him made her brain go all fuzzy, and it took her longer than it should have to remember what she had in her hands. "Summer made these for you."

She handed him the container of muffins and he smiled down at Summer. "Thank you." He lifted the lid and inhaled, clearly surprised by how good they smelled. "These look like they're going to be great. The rest of the guys here will be begging me for them."

"You can share them and I'll make you more!"

Megan had known this was where things would go, that if she relented and let them come to the station even once, it would turn into repeat visits.

Just as she was thinking this, he turned back to her, his expression carefully blank. There were no smiles for her, only her daughter. Clearly, he wasn't any happier to see her again than she was to see him.

Good. Maybe they could keep this visit short.

Summer tugged on his sleeve. "Thank you for the doll. She's my favorite present I got for turning seven. Her puppy is so cute, too."

Her solemn thank-you had Gabe squatting down to be at eye level with her. "I'm glad. Seventh birthdays are really important."

Summer nodded. "Now, can you show me the fire engine and all the buttons you push for stuff, Mr. Sullivan?"

Nope, short wasn't going to happen, Megan thought with a barely suppressed groan. But when that smile came back for her daughter, Megan felt her insides go to mush again despite all the tall, strong walls she'd put up to protect herself against his far too powerful allure.

How long had she been searching for a man who looked at her daughter like that? Like he thought the sun rose with Summer, just as her name indicated it should? As though she were important, rather than just some bothersome kid Megan happened to have had with some other guy?

"Sure thing." He shot a questioning glance at Megan. "If it's okay with your mom, that is."

She was about to reply when she noticed the fading scar on his forehead that ran from his left eyebrow into his hairline, and her legs weakened. His forehead had been bandaged the last time she'd seen him at the hospital and she knew that was where the beam must have hit him after he'd gotten them down the stairs. She wanted to say something, wanted to thank him again and apologize for putting him in that position, but she knew it would come out all weird and wrong.

Instead, she simply said, "Of course it's okay with me. Summer loves big machines and finding out how they work, don't you?"

Just like her father had. Only his machine of choice had been an airplane, rather than a fire engine.

Gabe took Summer's outstretched hand and walked her over to the shiny historic fire engine in the back corner of the station.

Normally, Megan would have followed them, but

she wasn't sure being that close to him for a prolonged period of time would be a good idea. Not
when her hormones were still in crazy overdrive.

Walking farther into the fire station, she quickly
found herself at the center of a group of big, strap-
ping men. Only, for all the testosterone in the room,
despite the preponderance of broad chests and narrow hips and square jaws, her hormones didn't flutter and her libido didn't jump to life.

Only one particular firefighter had that effect on
her.

Shaking the useless realization out of her head,
she made it a point to meet everyone and to thank
them for what they'd all done as a team for her and
her daughter. She noticed a few raised eyebrows
when she pointed out her daughter over by the antique engine. The other firefighters looked at one
another as if they were in on a secret.

Summer and the man who made her heart go
boom! were laughing together over something and
for a moment Megan wanted to pretend they were
more than strangers, that her daughter had a father
figure to teach her things, to be proud of her, to tell
her he loved her before tucking her in with a sweet
kiss good-night.

"Am I smelling blueberry muffins?"

Todd, the captain, came around the corner just
then and she smiled at the very nice middle-aged
man who had so graciously taken her in to meet
Gabe in the hospital.

"Summer made them," she said before moving

into the front room to pick up the container with the muffins.

Turning around, Megan bumped into a pretty young woman. "Oh, hi, sorry, I didn't mean to almost knock you ov—"

She stopped in the middle of her sentence, a look of complete surprise on her face. What was one of her old friends from college doing at the fire station?

"Sophie? It's me, Megan Harris." She smiled and added, "I was Megan Green back in college."

"Megan!" Sophie's arms came around her and they hugged. Sophie pulled back. "I can't believe how long it's been since I've seen you. Six, seven years?"

They'd both worked part-time in the Stanford library and had spent enough hours shelving and cataloguing books together in the dark stacks that they'd become friends. They probably would have become even closer friends during college were it not for Megan getting pregnant with Summer. Once she and David had married, she'd temporarily left school to follow her navy pilot husband to his new base assignment in San Diego.

"You look great," she said to Sophie.

"So do you!" Her old friend looked confused. "I haven't seen you here before. Are you working with the station on something?"

Megan felt bad about not having kept in better touch. "I was just about to ask you the same thing, actually. We—" She stopped to try to figure out what to tell Sophie. Megan wasn't sure she wanted to go into the whole thing right then. "We got to know some of the firefighters here recently and my daughter wanted to bring muffins over."

"Your daughter?" But Sophie quickly answered her own question by saying, "How could I have forgotten that you got married and had a baby? She must be six or seven by now, right?" When Megan nodded, Sophie asked, "Where is she?"

Megan pointed to the corner where the antique engine was. "Summer is over there with Gabe. He's one of the firefighters."

Megan was surprised when Sophie frowned. "Wait a minute. Your daughter's name is Summer?" Her eyes went wide. "Oh, my gosh, are you the mother and daughter Gabe saved a couple of months ago?"

At nearly the exact same moment, Megan realized she'd missed a very important clue along the way. Sullivan was such a common surname that she hadn't thought to link Sophie and Gabe together.

"Are you his sister?" When Sophie nodded, for a moment Megan couldn't believe how small the world had turned out to be: the man who'd saved her and her daughter's life was Sophie Sullivan's brother.

"Yes, your brother saved us. He's Summer's hero for life." She added softly, "Mine, too." Smiling, she told Sophie, "She baked him muffins this morning and I believe she's just about to convince him to let her drive that antique fire truck around the block."

She worked to keep her voice light. God forbid Sophie ever realized how ridiculously attracted Megan was to her brother. Talk about awkward.

"You should see all those buttons and knobs!" Summer ran over at full speed across the cement floor. Gabe was nowhere to be seen for the time being. "It's so awesome! I love firefighting! Thanks for finally letting me come here!"

Megan caught her daughter's hand as she gestured excitedly and chattered about the wonders of the fire truck. "Honey, this is a friend of mine from college. Her name is Sophie."

Sophie bent down to Summer's level and said, "Oh, my gosh, you're just as pretty as your mom. It's so nice to meet you, Summer. Your mom and I had a lot of fun together at college."

Summer beamed her biggest smile at Sophie. "You're pretty, too."

Sophie laughed. "Do you like to spend time at the library?" When the little girl nodded, Sophie said, "What kind of books do you like?"

The little girl thought about it a minute. "All of them."

Sophie shot Megan a delighted look. "Perfect." She quickly explained, "I'm a librarian at the branch just around the corner. I'd love for you two to come in and see me sometime soon. Especially since I'm always looking for good readers to help with story time for the little ones."

Summer raised her hand. "I can do that. I'm a really good reader."

"I'll bet you are, with a mom as smart as yours."

Just then, tingles moved up Megan's spine. She looked up and saw Gabe heading toward them.

Megan wished she weren't quite so aware of him…and that he wasn't so darn attractive, period. It was a good thing Sophie and Summer were talking about their favorite picture books and didn't require much participation from her, because Gabe's nearness seemed to suck her brain cells dry.

Just then, a memory of Sophie talking about her family came to Megan. In addition to having a twin, Sophie had so many brothers that Megan had been amazed by all of their varied and interesting professions. A photographer. A winery owner. A pro baseball player. And a strong, courageous firefighter. If only she'd remembered all of Sophie's brothers' names, then maybe she would have pieced two-and-two together before now.

She was surprised to find he didn't look totally pleased to see Sophie. Which was confirmed when he said in a slightly curt voice, "Hey, Soph, what are you doing here?"

His sister simply grinned at him, clearly not at all put off by his gruff greeting. "I thought I'd bring you something healthy for breakfast." She lifted a bag and opened it up so he could see inside. "Whole-wheat morning buns. No added sugar or preservatives."

He grimaced. "I've already got some really great muffins waiting for me, but thanks, anyway."

Shrugging, she closed the bag and said, "Can you believe that Megan and I know each other from college? Amazing, isn't it?"

He looked between the two of them, even less

pleased than he had been just moments before. "Amazing." His voice was flat. And distinctly irritated.

Megan was glad her daughter had been pulled away by the rest of the members of the fire crew, who were telling her she was the best muffin maker who ever lived. Otherwise, even Summer couldn't have missed Gabe's abrupt shift in demeanor.

This time around Megan wasn't at all hurt by his hard mask. Not when she'd sailed right past hurt straight to mad. Whatever his problem was, he didn't know the first thing about her, and she didn't deserve to be the recipient of his bad attitude.

Yes, she owed him her thanks—*forever*—for what he'd done for her and Summer. But she could be thankful privately in her thoughts, without him staring her down as if she had a contagious disease.

"Thank you for showing Summer the engine," she said to him in her most polite, distant voice, before turning to his sister with a warm, genuine smile. "I'm so glad we ran into you, Sophie."

"Me, too. I can't believe I didn't know you were living so close by."

Megan shook her head. "I'm afraid I didn't do a good job of keeping in touch with anyone after David and I got married and moved to San Diego."

"How is David?"

Realizing there was no way Sophie would know about what had happened, she said, "He died in an accident."

"Oh, no." Sophie looked horrified. "I'm so sorry, Megan. I had no idea."

Wanting to reassure her friend, but not wanting to say too much with Gabe still standing there taking in every word, a glower on his too-handsome face, she said, "It was a few years ago now."

Sophie looked to where Summer was still the center of Station 5's attention. "You've raised her all by yourself?" Before Megan could reply, she added, "Or did you remarry?"

"Nope. Just me and Summer." She forced a smile that she hoped looked somewhat real. "We've been doing great."

"Until that fire burned down your apartment. It doesn't seem fair."

"Honestly, we're doing just fine," Megan said again, as much for Gabe's benefit as Sophie's.

Sophie put her hand on her arm. "I wish things could have been different for you."

"Soph," Gabe bit out in a frustrated voice, "how many more times does she have to tell you she's fine?"

He was clearly trying to warn his sister to back off a bit, and while Megan would have appreciated it another time, she knew Sophie was just expressing her feelings and emotions the way she always had. Straight from her heart.

Sophie simply scrunched up her nose at her brother before turning back to Megan. "You know what? Our mother is having her big annual holiday party this weekend near our old stomping grounds in Palo Alto. Please tell me you and Summer will come to meet everyone!" Before Megan could reply, Sophie added, "Don't you think everyone would just love them both, Gabe?"

He was looking past them as he said, "Sure," with shockingly little interest, just as he had in the hospital when Summer had asked him if he wanted to hear Megan's frog impersonation.

Well, it was pretty damn clear to all of them what Gabe thought about this plan, wasn't it? She could feel Sophie's eyes moving between them, trying to figure out what the deal was…and why he clearly couldn't stand the sight of Megan.

In the awkward silence, Sophie finally said, "Actually, a couple of my brothers really love kids."

Oh, God. Sophie wasn't trying to play matchmaker, was she?

But before she could stop Sophie from saying anything more, her friend said, "Chase and Marcus are taken and their girlfriends—well, fiancée in Chase's case—are fantastic. So that leaves Zach and Ryan and Smith. They're all free. At least, as far as I know."

She remembered that Smith Sullivan, the movie star, was Sophie's brother. And so was Ryan Sullivan, the pro baseball player. It had always occurred to her that the Sullivan family was way too potent for its own good. But watching Smith up on a big screen in a dark movie theater and Ryan on the mound had never made her all tingly the way Gabe's dark gaze was doing right this second as he frowned at her for daring to breathe in his presence.

Sophie continued talking while Megan processed... and worked to keep taking one slow breath after another.

"They'll all adore you. I have no doubt my brothers will end up fighting over you. Don't you agree, Gabe?"

"Zach and Ryan are two of the biggest players on the planet." He shook his head. "Smith is even worse. God knows what would happen to a kid in his movie-star world."

Sophie waved away his concerns with a hand in the air. "I think all of you are awesome. And they're only players because they haven't met the right woman yet."

Megan noticed Sophie said nothing about whether Gabe was a player or not. She hadn't offered him up as potential boyfriend material, either. Probably because he had a girlfriend.

A girlfriend that Megan was absolutely sure she would hate. Just because.

"Please tell me you'll come, Megan? You and Summer would be such a welcome addition to the party."

Truthfully, Megan didn't want to have to spend any more time around Gabe than she already had, but the devil that very rarely sat on her shoulder suddenly popped up and had her saying, "We'd love to come." She got way too much enjoyment from the way Gabe's stance tightened even further beside them. "What can we bring? I'm sure Summer would love to bake something really special for your mother's holiday party."

After Megan and Sophie exchanged phone numbers and email addresses, Sophie promised to send her all the information for the party.

With the deed done—and knowing she'd need every single second until Saturday night to make sure she was ready to completely lock down her foolish longings and hormones around Gabe at the party—she said, "Well, I think Summer and I should go and let everyone get back to work."

She called out her daughter's name and overrode her pleas to stay "just a little bit longer" because she was "having the best day ever" hanging out with the firefighters.

At long last, Summer finally took her mother's hand and Megan was able to escape back out to the sidewalk, her heart beating even faster now than it had earlier that morning, even though they were walking downhill on the way home.

All because this time she knew for sure that she was going to see Gabe Sullivan again.

As they stood in the driveway of the fire station watching Megan and Summer head down the street, Gabe said, "You're not actually going to try to set her up with Zach or Ryan, are you?" The thought of either of his brothers touching even one single hair on Megan's head had Gabe seeing red.

His sister shrugged. "I don't see why not. She's

very sweet and smart, don't you think? Besides, she's had such bad luck with the fire that some fun might help Megan and Summer take their minds off things a little bit."

He wasn't going to answer that. Because he sure as hell wasn't going to let his sister know that he thought Megan was just about the prettiest thing he'd ever set eyes on.

"They'll chew her up and spit her out."

His sister crossed her arms over her chest. "She lost a husband and has raised a child all by herself. And it seems like she's recovering really well from losing everything in that fire. I think both of those things prove just how strong she is." Another shrug. "Who knows? Maybe she could be the chink in Ryan's or Zach's armor."

Hell, no. Not when she'd already gotten under his skin. He didn't need her getting under his brothers' skins, too.

"I know what you're doing, Nice."

Normally, her nickname fit her. Not today. Today his little sister was clearly intent on messing with his mind by inviting Megan and her daughter into their inner circle.

Sophie gave him an innocent look, her eyes a little too big. "Megan is a friend from college. I like her a lot. I want to see more of her."

"So you're saying inviting her to the party has nothing to do with me?"

His sister pinned him with a gaze that told him

she knew exactly what he was feeling for her friend. "You tell me, Gabe. Does it?"

He grabbed the bag of whole-wheat nastiness from her. "Thanks for breakfast. I've got to get back to work."

Before he could turn and walk away from the sister he normally liked quite a bit, he caught her smile. And knew exactly what she was thinking.

Sophie thought he was going to fall head over heels in love with Megan and her cute daughter.

She was wrong.

So wrong.

Five

Pffft!

Megan and Summer were pulling into their underground parking garage on Saturday evening after running a few errands when their car bumped over something. The hiss of the air was loud enough for them to hear even through their closed windows.

Megan knew the loud sound coming from beneath her car could be only one thing. A flat tire.

The tire repair shop would be closed by eight o'clock on a Saturday and there was no way they could drive the thirty-five miles to Palo Alto on a spare. Which meant she and Summer wouldn't be able to attend the Sullivan party tonight.

Of course she still wanted to see Sophie so they could catch up. But seeing Gabe Sullivan again?

Just thinking about him had her body going cold with shivers and warm with flames at the exact same time. Which was precisely why she needed to keep her distance.

Gabe had nearly given his life to save her and her daughter, for which she would be forever grateful. But there was no way she could think of him as a *man*.

No, to Megan, he could never be anything but a courageous firefighter. Which meant the party at the Sullivan house was the very last place she should be tonight, because just one look at him sent her hormones racing for reasons that had everything to do with desire…and nothing at all with gratitude.

"Honey," Megan told her daughter, "with this flat tire, I'm afraid we won't be able to leave the city tonight, after all." Considering Summer had been talking about Gabe and everything he'd shown her at the firehouse all week, Megan knew she shouldn't sound too cheerful about the tire popping…even if she had never been so happy about having a flat in all her life!

Despite her daughter's enormous energy levels, Summer was normally quite even-keeled about things like this. Unfortunately, given the look of utter mutiny on her daughter's face, this looked like one of the times when Summer was going to pitch a full-on fit.

"I want to go!"

"It's going to be a bunch of adults." Megan didn't get what the problem was. Or, rather, she didn't want to get it. "I don't understand what's so important about this party."

"You know *exactly* what's so important about this party," Summer accused before stalking off to her room and slamming the door. "We should have already been there by now, but you kept making us late with your stupid errands that we didn't even need to do tonight!" she added from the other side of the closed door.

Megan had to take several deep breaths to try to keep her temper in check.

It didn't work. Not when she'd been riding on nerves all day just thinking about having to go to this party and see Gabe again.

"Don't you dare slam that door on me, missy!" Megan yelled back. "You'd better open it up right now."

A few seconds later, the door opened a crack. Megan was about to push it open the rest of the way and demand an apology, but she stopped herself just in time.

They were both making a big deal out of nothing. In a little while, everything would go back to normal, and they'd be snuggling under a blanket on the couch watching a movie.

She walked back to the kitchen and picked up her phone to let her friend know she wouldn't be able to make it to the party, which was likely already in full swing. Expecting to get Sophie's voice mail, she was surprised to hear her friend answer.

"Megan, are you and Summer having trouble finding the house?" Sophie asked.

"Actually," Megan explained, "we won't be able to make it, after all."

"Oh, no! Why not? One of you didn't come down with a cold, did you?"

Megan suddenly wished she'd thought to fake a cough. Only, she didn't believe in lying. And she certainly didn't want to teach her daughter to do something like that. "No, we're both perfectly healthy. My car isn't faring quite as well, though. I've got a flat tire and I won't be able to get it fixed until Monday."

"Can I call you right back?"

Megan agreed and hung up the phone. As she waited for it to ring again, she got a bad feeling about things. A bad feeling she tried to tell herself was ridiculous.

"Great news!" Sophie said a couple of minutes later when she called back. "Gabe hasn't left the city yet and he'd love to come pick you guys up."

Megan leaned her head into the wall and closed her eyes. "That's really nice of him, but I'd hate for him to go out of his way. We're really sad about missing the party, but—"

"He lives really close to your place," Sophie assured her. "It's no problem at all. Can I give him your address?"

No!

"Summer and I are going to not only need a ride to Palo Alto, but also a ride home, as well. It's too much to ask of him, especially with such short notice," Megan insisted.

Instead of letting her off the hook, Sophie said, "I'd really like for you both to come. And you should know that my brother Gabe is the nicest guy in the world. He loves helping people like this."

Considering he'd almost lost his life saving hers and Summer's, that was the understatement of the century.

Megan barely held back a resigned sigh as she said, "Okay." And then, knowing she was doing a terrible job of being grateful, she added, "Thanks, Sophie. Summer will be really thrilled to hear that we're back on."

It was dark enough outside for Megan to see her own reflection in the kitchen window as she hung up. She wasn't surprised that she looked shell-shocked. Worried, too. But there was something else in her expression, something that shouldn't have been there at all.

Anticipation.

She turned quickly from the window. "Good news, Summer," she called out with forced cheer. "Looks like we're going to the party, after all."

Summer let out a happy squeal and then ran into the kitchen to cut up the fudge she'd made that morning into bite-size pieces for the party.

Sophie had sounded positively gleeful over Megan's flat tire, Gabe thought as he double-parked his truck in front of the apartment building and got out to pick up his two impromptu passengers. In fact, while she was at it, his sister had given him hell for not having already offered to take Megan and Summer to the party.

The worst part about it, of course, was that Sophie was right. He should have offered.

But he hadn't, because he didn't trust himself around Megan, didn't trust their attraction not to flare up and burn both of them.

He knocked on their door, only to have it flung open before his knuckles could make contact more than once.

"Mr. Sullivan!" Summer threw her arms around him.

He hugged her back, looking up into the apartment just as Megan came around the corner…and completely took his breath away.

Clearly surprised to see him, she said, "Oh. Hi. I didn't hear you knock." Her eyes were soft as she looked at him with her daughter. "Thanks for coming to pick us up on such short notice."

There were half a dozen things he could have said—at least a handful of replies that would have made sense. But even though he knew better than to go there, all he could get out was, "You're beautiful."

And she was. So damn beautiful that his heart couldn't decide between stopping in his chest or racing out of control.

She'd put on just enough makeup for her eyes to look huge and sparkling. The slick of lipstick on her mouth made his water, and the slight curl she'd added to her hair made him want to slide his hands through one of the locks to see if it felt as much like the dark silk it resembled. The dress she was wearing hugged her figure so perfectly, he could barely stop himself from staring in awe at the way the dress curved out at her breasts, in at her waist, and then flared to cover hips that looked so soft, so touchable. It was the first time he'd seen her in heels and what they did to her legs should be illegal.

Somehow, he stopped drooling over her in time to watch her try to contain her shock at his unexpected compliment. And then her smile.

"Thank you."

Holy hell.

That smile.

The sweet yet innately sensual way her full lips curved up affected him just as much as it had in the hospital room. He'd seen her determination and tears and forced politeness...but her sweet, genuine smile was what undid him every time.

He felt Summer tug on his arm and barely managed to drag his gaze away from her mother. "You're gorgeous, too, kid," he told the little girl, who did a little pirouette to show off her sparkling green dress. "And whenever you say Mr. Sullivan, I think you're talking about my grandfather, so why don't you call me Gabe?"

"Okay, Gabe! Can we go now?"

"Sure, if your mom is ready."

He looked at Megan, who nodded, then went to grab her purse and a bright red tray of something that smelled like rich chocolate fudge. He knew, without a doubt, that his family was going to go absolutely crazy over Megan and Summer. Lord knew, he'd have to watch his brothers like a hawk around Megan. She was too pretty for one of them not to make a move.

"Thanks for picking us up," Megan said softly as they walked down the hallway and out to his truck. "I know we're out of your way."

"It's no problem at all." And it truly wasn't. Even if he had to work overtime to try to control his reaction to being this close to her again.

He held the passenger door open, and as he helped them climb up into his truck, the extra few inches of leg he caught sight of when Megan's skirt shifted up her thigh had his body reacting immediately.

Fortunately, as soon as he climbed in behind the steering wheel, Summer launched a rapid-fire line of questioning.

"When did you decide you wanted to be a firefighter? What's it like having so many brothers and sisters? Was it hard to become a firefighter? Why is your fire hat red?"

He pulled out into traffic and headed south out of the city to drive to the suburban home he'd grown up in. The rush of questions from the seven-year-old girl sitting in the middle of the extended cab should have been the perfect way to keep his focus from landing on Megan again and again. Especially since the beautiful woman sitting beside him remained almost perfectly still and silent. He couldn't tell if she was nervous being around him again, but she definitely didn't seem to want to talk to him the way her daughter did.

Still, through the entire trip, despite the mouth-watering smell of the large plate of fudge Summer had made, Gabe was all too aware of Megan's faint scent, something flowery and clean, along with her gorgeous curves beneath her knee-length velvet dress and those toned legs that he'd been unable to keep from admiring as he'd followed them out to his truck from her apartment.

When he finally pulled up outside his mother's house and stepped out onto the sidewalk to open the passenger's side door, Gabe took in a hard breath of cold, crisp air. "I'll see you both inside in a few minutes, after I park the truck."

Megan nodded but didn't make eye contact with him as she helped Summer jump down from the truck.

It hadn't taken more than five minutes to find a space for his truck down the block and walk into his mother's house. So then, how the hell could his brothers have found Megan so quickly?

Ryan and Zach were flanking her on either side, and as she laughed at whatever they were telling her, she looked beautiful. So beautiful it made something inside Gabe tighten up whenever he looked at her.

He was going to kill his brothers. If they so much as laid a hand on her, they were dead men.

And then, almost in slow motion, he saw Zach's patented load-for-launch move as his brother reached up to brush a lock of hair away from her eyes.

Gabe was halfway across the room, his hands in tight fists, when his mother stopped him with a hug.

"Honey, I'm so glad you're finally here." She looked across the room to where Megan was being entertained by his brothers. "And I'm so glad you brought Megan and Summer with you. They're both just lovely. Absolutely lovely."

Gabe tried to get his blood pressure to return to normal. He had no claim on Megan. Maybe Sophie was right. Maybe someone like Megan was just what Zach needed to make him see the light and change his ways. He loved his brother, but there was no question that when it came to women, Zach was a player through and through.

The thought of Zach and Megan dating only made Gabe's blood boil hotter.

Feeling his mother's eyes on him, he somehow managed to hold it together enough to grit out the words, "Looks like another great party, Mom."

"As long as all of you are here, I'm happy. Well, minus one, unfortunately, but I know Smith tried his best to get back."

Smith hadn't been able to clear his shooting schedule to fly to San Francisco. To his credit, Gabe was fairly impressed with how many family functions Smith managed to attend. They were neck and neck, actually—for every movie Smith couldn't get away from, Gabe dealt with a fire that had to take priority over seeing his family.

Megan's laughter pulled his gaze back over to her despite his best efforts to look elsewhere. He was torn between wanting to get an emergency fire call so he could get away from temptation…and not wanting to ever stop looking at her.

Judging by the way Zach was hanging on her every word, his brother clearly felt the same way.

"Megan said the sweetest thing to me when we met." His mother's hand on his arm had him working to yank his attention back to her. "She thanked me for raising such a wonderful man who made such a difference in her life." He watched his mother swallow hard. "I almost started crying right there in the kitchen thinking about what would have happened to her and her little girl if you hadn't been there."

He knew better than to let himself think about that scenario, about what might have been if he hadn't gotten to them in time. Instead, he reminded himself that the one time he'd made the mistake of getting involved with a fire victim he'd saved, things had gone terribly wrong. All these years later, he could hardly believe what Kate had done when he'd broken up with her, that she'd—

"Gabe, honey, are you all right?"

At his mother's hand on his arm and her soft but concerned question, he shoved the memory back down. Still, he needed to get his mother to understand that Megan wasn't any different from any other fire victim, and that there was nothing special between them. His mother didn't know what had happened between him and his ex, and he wasn't going to freak her out by telling her about it now when it was ancient history.

"I was just thinking about what Megan said to you," he told his mother. "She's still processing the incident. It's perfectly normal."

"I suppose so," she said softly, "but I didn't expect her to apologize to me."

He frowned. "She apologized?"

"She feels responsible for you getting hurt. She said if she had moved faster, if she'd just been able to hold it together better, that you wouldn't have been where you were when the beam fell."

"That's bullshit."

He didn't realize he'd sworn aloud until his mother looked at him with raised eyebrows, but he couldn't stand the thought that Megan blamed herself in some way for anything that had happened.

"She was incredibly strong. She should have been unconscious long before then, but she was fighting for her daughter's life." He closed his eyes for a brief second and he was right back there in the smoke. "You should have seen her."

"I know if I had been caught in a fire with any of you, I would fight with everything I had to make sure you stayed safe. It's what being a mother is all about."

He gave his mother a hug, and when he finally let her go, her eyes were slightly damp as she told him, "Sophie is thrilled they've reconnected. I hope to see more of her."

Only his brother Zach knew that he didn't date fire victims anymore—and the reason why. Which was probably why Zach thought it was safe to make a play for Megan, because he knew dating her would break one of Gabe's hard and fast rules.

But his mother had never believed in matchmaking, thank God. So he tried not to read anything into her statement as he said, "I'm sure Sophie and Megan will be seeing quite a bit of each other in the future now that they've reconnected." He purposefully made Megan's appearance in the Sullivan household about the fact that his sister and Megan had been friends in college.

"What can I get you to drink, honey?"

Man, did he ever need something to take the edge off. The problem was, even though this wasn't his official shift, the station was short staffed over the winter holidays and he'd agreed to be a backup on the roster. Which meant there'd be no alcohol for him tonight.

"Go ahead and entertain your guests, Mom. I'll take care of my own drink."

"Okay, and if you wouldn't mind starting a fire in the fire pit outside, I'd really appreciate it." Outside it was cool and dry, typical Northern California weather for this time of year. Only in the mountains around Lake Tahoe, which was hours away from Palo Alto, would there be snow.

Any one of his siblings could have started the fire for her, but he knew she liked to have him do it because she—correctly—assumed he was more concerned with fire safety than the others.

"No problem."

She kissed him on the cheek and moved back

into the throng of old friends, but instead of heading over to the bar for a soda, he made a beeline for the woman he'd planned on staying away from the rest of the night.

Six

Why was Gabe looking at her like that?

Megan felt the slightest bit fuzzy from the glass of champagne she'd guzzled way too fast, but she wasn't even close to drunk. So then, why was she all but wobbling in her heels as Gabe moved through the crowded living room toward where she was standing with his brother? As soon as they'd arrived, Mary Sullivan had guided Summer into the rec room downstairs and introduced her to the other kids. Sophie and Gabe's mother was incredibly sweet and nurturing, yet Megan also sensed she must have a backbone of steel to have raised eight kids so well.

Megan had been tempted to stay down there with the kids all night, but when Mary had offered to make her a drink and to introduce her to the rest of the family, there had been no way Megan could refuse. After Gabe had finished parking the car and walking inside, she'd felt him watching her while she'd been talking to Zach and Ryan—and maybe she'd let herself laugh a little louder than normal, if only to make sure he didn't think she was at all interested in him.

"Call me tomorrow about your flat tire and I'll take care of it for you." Zach Sullivan followed up his words with a grin that had her flushing.

But not because she was attracted to him. Okay, so she was human, and out of all the Sullivan men, Zach was undoubtedly the best-looking on a technical scale that measured height of cheekbones and distance between the eyes. When she told him she could just take her car to the normal place down the street that she usually brought it to, he mentioned, oh, so casually, that he was the owner of Sullivan Autos…and that he insisted she bring her car to him from now on. All repairs and maintenance would be on the house.

Really, these Sullivan men were too much. And yet, for whatever teeny-tiny flutter that had happened as a result of Zach's undivided attention, there was an earthquake going on inside her from nothing more than Gabe's hot eyes staring a hole in her from across the room. An earthquake causing ruptures inside, threatening to break open parts of her that she'd sworn to keep locked down.

She opened her mouth to thank him for the offer, but before she could, Gabe moved between the two of them. "Can I get you another glass of champagne, Megan?"

Her heart stuttered and when she lifted her glass and said, "I've still got plenty, thanks," her hand might have even been shaking a bit. She was barely aware of Zach moving away to leave her and Gabe alone.

"Is Summer down in the rec room?" Gabe asked.

Despite all the champagne, her mouth was almost too dry to answer. "Yes, your mother introduced her to some of the other kids. I stayed down there with Summer long enough to see that she was already making friends."

"Good." His gaze was dark. Intense. "We need to talk." He gestured to the backyard. "Somewhere private would be best."

Even though he was easygoing with her daughter, Gabe had always been intense around her. Still, he seemed more serious than usual right now. Something was wrong, she was sure of it. Only, she couldn't figure out what. Not, of course, that she'd been able to figure him out at all, yet.

She headed through the French doors that led to the empty back patio, with Gabe close enough behind her that she could feel his heat keeping her warm as they stepped out into the cool air. She moved farther into the darkness, away from the crowd of people drinking and eating and laughing together.

He took off his leather jacket. "Here, this will keep you warm."

When he slipped the jacket on over her shoulders before she could refuse it, she couldn't help but be warmed not only by the jacket, but by the gesture, as well. She loved the way a little bit of smoke always seemed to cling to him, a scent that was utterly unique to him.

"What do you need to speak with me about?"

"Fighting fires is my job, Megan," he began with no preamble, no small talk whatsoever. "I'm trained to deal with dangerous, possibly deadly situations. When firefighters get hurt, it's either their own fault for not taking the proper precautions, or it's a natural consequence of the fire that no one can control." He searched her face, and when he clearly didn't see what he was looking for, he said, "You shouldn't be apologizing to my mother about what happened to me."

She couldn't mask her surprise. "But it's true. If I could have—"

He cut her off. "I should have had two dead weights to carry out of there, but you never stopped fighting to get out of your apartment and building. Not for one goddamned second until you knew your daughter was safe."

There was enough outdoor lighting from the decorative lanterns hanging from the oak's branches for her to see the expression on his face.

Out-and-out respect.

For her.

"You were amazing, Megan. And I don't want you to feel guilty about my part in the fire. Not ever again."

Beyond surprised, she finally said, "Thank you for saying that, although I don't think I can help the way I feel."

"Neither can I."

They stared at each other, the air between them doing that thing with the sparks and the electricity again. Suddenly she didn't know if they were talking about the fire anymore...or the sensual tension in the air between them.

"I shouldn't have brought you out here," he suddenly said. "It's too cold without a fire. I'll see you inside in a bit after I get a fire going in the fire pit."

Clearly, that was his way of dismissing her. And Megan knew she would be wise to leave before any of the sparks ignited between them. But, darn it, she didn't like leaving on his terms. And she definitely didn't like it when he turned away as if she was already gone, and started piling his arms with nearby firewood.

No woman wanted to think that she could be forgotten that quickly. Even one who had sworn not to want the attention of the man in question.

Knowing she was often too stubborn for her own good, she headed to the woodpile and picked up several good-looking pieces of firewood.

Gabe didn't look happy to see that she was still there. "Weren't you going inside?"

Quickly guessing that most women Gabe dealt with probably jumped at every command out of that gorgeous mouth, she knelt by the built-in fire pit he was uncovering. "I figured I'd help you get the bonfire going." She admired the brickwork. "This is fantastic. Summer is going to beg me for one just like it in our backyard. She's a huge s'mores fan."

"Your apartment has a yard?"

She shook her head. "Not the temporary apartment we're in now. But once we find the perfect new place, I might put one in." Although, even as she said it, she knew she wouldn't, knew she would be too worried about fire spreading from the fire pit to her home.

"I hope you find the perfect house soon, Megan." He was silent for a moment before adding, "I've been to a thousand fires in a thousand people's homes, but it's not the same as having it happen to me. I'm sorry about what you must have lost."

She didn't look up from where she was positioning the logs into a perfect pyramid. "I am, too."

She hadn't wanted to say as much to Summer, believing instead that her daughter needed her to be strong. She hadn't wanted her clients to worry that she couldn't handle their workloads, so she'd simply reminded each of them that she had backup records in a secure, fire-safe location. Her parents were bound to worry no matter what she said, so of course she'd been tight-lipped about her feelings to them, too. And as for her girlfriends, well, the truth was she hadn't had a lot of time for going out with the girls between working and taking care of Summer. Some of the other mothers at school were friendly, but she hadn't felt a strong connection with any of them. That's why it had been so nice to run into Sophie again.

"Fortunately, most of our pictures were in online storage, but the things I saved from when Summer was a baby, from her first day at school, her first lost tooth…I wish all of those things weren't gone." She made herself shrug and pull her lips up at the corners as she took the matches he handed her. "But they are and we're doing pretty great, all in all. I got lucky with that kid of mine."

He was nodding and looking into the fire that she'd just kindled as he said, "You sure did." The flames took off and he grinned at her. "Nice job with that fire, by the way."

He'd grinned at Summer plenty of times, but never directly at Megan. The force of that smile, so utterly genuine, without any of the knowing charm that his brothers Ryan and Zach laid on, had her wanting to take two steps closer to him and kiss him.

As if he could hear her silent yearnings, in an instant his smile fell away and his eyes darkened again, filling with that heat that she couldn't help but be drawn to, heat she was dying to get closer to, to see if it could warm all those places inside her that had been cold for so long.

"I should get back inside to check and make sure Summer's doing okay."

His eyes were still hot, still intense, when he nodded. "Go."

She was halfway to the French doors when she realized she was still wearing his jacket. She turned, moved back to where he was staring after her and lifted it from her shoulders. "Thank you."

His fingertips moved across her knuckles as they made the transfer and she was glad for the excuse the cold weather gave for the goose bumps suddenly appearing on her skin. Only she needed to know it wasn't the outside temperature that had caused them.

She didn't wait for him to say, "You're welcome." She simply turned and hightailed it back to safer ground.

The bonfire outside drew both children and adults out of the house. The kids all went to find sticks in the backyard for the marshmallows that Mrs. Sullivan had put out on a nearby table. But the melted sugar on a stick wasn't the end of the delightful surprises in store for them.

"They have a clubhouse up in one of the trees," Summer told Megan, her eyes wide and thrilled. The party had clearly been as much fun as she'd thought it would be. "Gabe said he's going to take us up and show us around, if our parents say it's okay."

Ignoring the voice inside her head that was saying, *I want to play in the tree house, too,* Megan ran a hand over her daughter's soft hair. "Of course you can go. Just be careful."

Summer rolled her eyes. "I'm not a baby."

Megan had to pull her in for a hug. "You're *my* baby."

"Mom!" Summer pushed away. "I've got to grab a flashlight before they're all gone."

She ran across the yard to where Gabe was waiting with flashlights and Megan tried not to let her insides turn to mush as he headed off with the kids

toward adventure, laughing and joking with the energetic group.

She'd never known a man to be so comfortable
with kids. But it was more than that, she quickly realized. He liked kids, plain and simple. Even Summer's father, while he'd clearly adored his baby girl,
hadn't really known what to do with her. And Megan
always had the sense that David was counting down
the minutes to nap time so that he could get back to
something more exciting.

Megan gave herself a little shake, thinking that
she shouldn't be comparing David to Gabe, when she
saw Sophie moving quickly across the patio, out of
a dark corner and into the light for a brief moment
before heading around the side of the house.

She'd looked for Sophie when she'd arrived, but
hadn't been able to find her so that they could catch
up on old times. They'd tried to connect a few times
over the past couple of days, but between Sophie's
busy schedule at the library and Summer's winter
break from school, they'd finally accepted the fact
that the party would be their first chance to chat.

Now, however, instead of just wanting to have
some girl talk with someone she'd always liked a
great deal, Megan was a little worried about her
friend.

Knowing Summer was in good hands with Gabe,
Megan followed the path that Sophie had taken
around the yard heading to a small shed. Opening
it slowly, she looked inside and found her friend sitting on a large upturned pot.

"Sophie?"

"Oh!" Sophie started to jump up, when she realized who it was. "Megan, hi." She looked a little sheepish at being caught in the potting shed, but she smiled and asked, "Care to join me?"

Megan grinned at her old friend, closing the door behind her. There was a lightbulb in the ceiling that illuminated that tidy interior, permeated with the smell of potting soil. "Is everything okay?"

Sophie blew out a shaky breath. "Have you ever wanted something you really, really shouldn't want?"

Megan was struck by her friend's honest question. There was no pretense with Sophie. There never had been. It was one of the things she'd always been drawn to in the other woman.

Because she was hoping that they could reestablish the friendship they'd started in college, especially living as close to each other in the city as they did, Megan nodded, even though she was tempted to try to evade Sophie's question.

"I know exactly how that feels," she said, thinking about being in the backyard with Gabe, and the heat that had nothing to do with the fire jumping to life in the fire pit.

Only, her admission didn't seem to make Sophie feel any better.

As the other woman looked at her hands, Megan followed her gaze to neatly trimmed nails with no polish. Sophie was wearing a simple navy knit dress that covered her arms and most of her legs. She had on no makeup, no jewelry, and yet where other women would have been plain, Sophie was undeniably beautiful. After having spent a good half hour on her hair and makeup, not to mention trying on all of the new dresses she'd bought since the fire, Megan suddenly felt a little overdressed.

She found an empty pot and turned it upside down, sitting across from Sophie. "Do you want to talk about it?"

It didn't take a genius to figure out that Sophie was upset over a man. Only, Megan was a little ashamed she couldn't possibly have known who, since she'd barely been able to focus on anyone but Gabe all night.

"No," Sophie said with a shake of her head. "I just need to get over it. Especially since I'm now officially the worst friend in the world for inviting you to a party and then disappearing off into the potting shed to mope."

Megan had to laugh at the funny expression on Sophie's face. "I've always liked gardening."

"Come on," Sophie said, standing up and extending her hand to Megan. "Let's go get a couple of glasses of bubbly and you can fill me in on the past seven years."

Megan could see that Sophie wasn't at all over what had sent her off to hide in the potting shed, but she clearly didn't want to talk about it. Not yet, anyway. Maybe when they'd gotten closer, she'd open up.

Then again, Megan knew exactly what it was like to have a secret crush on someone who was totally off-limits. It didn't matter how close she and Sophie grew as friends, Megan was never, ever going to admit that she got tingly and breathless whenever Gabe was near.

If anything, the short conversation they'd just had was more than long enough to reinforce what she already knew: that giving in to the sparks she felt with Gabe would only end up breaking her heart.

Or worse, her daughter's heart.

Seven

As the Sullivan holiday party wound down, most of Gabe's siblings gravitated toward one another in a tight group around the fire pit. Normally, Gabe would have been in there with them all, but Sophie had pulled Megan into the group and he didn't have a good enough grip on himself around her yet.

Sure, there was nothing going on between them. And there wouldn't be in the future. But every once in a while a guy needed a break from a half dozen pairs of probing eyes that just might see what he didn't want them to. As it was, his sister Lori had already pulled him aside to ask if everything was okay. Fortunately, she'd seemed to buy his excuse about a long shift at the firehouse.

Gabe kept himself busy playing pirate ship with the kids in the tree fort, and then flashlight tag in the backyard, until his mother called out that she'd put a movie on for them in the basement.

By that point, Gabe had to face up to what he was

doing. He figured he'd been called a lot of things over the years, but he could guarantee he'd never been called a coward. And he could feel his brother Zach's eyes on him, watching to see what he was going to do about Megan.

Chloe was yawning when he walked up to the fire pit. "Sorry to leave right when you get here," she said to him with a sleepy look as she and Chase got up. "I'm exhausted for some reason."

After his brother and fiancée said their goodbyes and he took one of the open seats, their friend Jake McCann strolled over to take the other. Jake and Zach had become friends in the fifth grade and Jake had hung out in their house so much while they were kids that he'd become "the ninth Sullivan." Despite how rough Jake's childhood had been—his father had been a drunk and his mother hadn't been there at all—he was a great guy…and very successful with his chain of Irish pubs. He'd been out of state working on a new chain of pubs for most of the past six months, so this was the first time any of them had seen him in a while.

"Hey, Jake." Lori, Sophie's twin, peered over his shoulder. "What happened to your date?"

Gabe watched Jake grin at the woman he'd treated like a little sister for the past twenty years he'd been hanging out at the Sullivan house.

"Had to pour her into a cab a little while ago."

Lori rolled her eyes. "You have terrible taste in women," she teased Jake, then said, "We were just about to play Truth or Dare. Come on, join us."

It didn't matter that they were all adults now; the games the Sullivans played over the years hadn't changed. They still played a nasty game of touch football on Thanksgiving in which the girls got in harder hits every year on their brothers…and everyone still wanted to know one another's secrets.

Gabe knew he was lucky to have a big family where everyone got along so well. Then again, with six brothers and two sisters, they were bound to have their fair share of fights. Fortunately, everyone got over them pretty darn fast.

Lori threw a marshmallow across the fire to her twin. "Why don't you go first, Sophie?"

Sophie caught the white puff of sugar right before it nailed her in the face, glaring at Lori as she tossed it straight into the center of the fire. As the flames caught and jumped, she said, "Truth."

His sisters' relationship hadn't been all that great for a while now. No one could figure out why, and even though their mother was clearly worried about it, neither Lori nor Sophie would say what had happened. Even when they were arguing, they were fierce in their solidarity to keep things between the two of them. They were a tight little unit that none of the brothers had ever been able to penetrate, not even Gabe, who was the closest in age and had spent more time with both of them than anyone but Marcus, who had pretty much helped raise them from toddlers.

"Why were you sneaking around tonight?" Lori asked her twin.

Sophie's eyes were big, worried, as she fixated

on the flames. She'd never been good at hiding her feelings, which was why she was nicknamed "Nice," whereas Lori, who loved causing trouble, was "Naughty."

Finally, Sophie said in a tight voice, "I wasn't sneaking around."

Lori narrowed her eyes. "I saw you coming out of Mom's potting shed."

"That's my fault," Megan offered in a cheerful voice. "I was looking for Summer and found my way there by accident."

Her first victim saved by the bell, Lori turned on Jake. "Truth or dare?"

He shook his head slowly as he held out his hands toward the fire to warm them. "If you're the one dishing out the dares, Naughty, I'll pick truth, thanks."

She shot him a wicked grin before putting her elbows on her knees, her chin on her hands, and leaning forward. "Have you ever been in love, Mr. McCann?"

Gabe noticed Sophie shiver beside him. "Cold, sis?"

"No." She shook her head hard.

He frowned. Something was definitely up with her tonight, only he'd been too focused on Megan to try to figure out what Sophie was worried about.

Jake's laughter rang out in the cold backyard. "In love?" he repeated. "Not even close. And I don't see it happening anytime soon."

Clearly bummed that she hadn't gotten more dirt out of Jake, Lori spun to face Gabe. "Your turn."

The last thing in the world he was in the mood for was this game, but it was usually easier just to play along with Lori.

"Dare." Lord knew, truth wasn't in the cards tonight, not with Megan sitting too close, looking far too beautiful in the firelight.

Lori gave him a slightly evil grin. "Sing us a campfire song."

Marcus groaned and held his hands over Nicola's ears. "Asking Gabe to sing is more like a dare for the rest of us."

Marcus's pop-star girlfriend shoved his hands away and smiled at Gabe. "I love it when other people sing."

Rather than being pissed off at Lori, Gabe decided that, if anything, he should be thanking his sister for the dare. Because after hearing him sing, there was no chance of anything happening with Megan.

He launched into a version of "Home on the Range" that had all the dogs and cats in the neighborhood joining in. At Nicola's faltering smile he decided to play it up for all it was worth, and soon she had her hands over her ears, too.

Marcus, whose voice was nearly as bad as his, joined in with a god-awful "harmony" and everyone laughed so hard, including Megan, that he forgot not to stare at her in front of everyone.

Yes, she was a gorgeous woman. But she was also fun and fit perfectly into his family.

Damn it.

Their gazes collided and both of them stopped

laughing. She abruptly pushed her chair back. "It's way past Summer's bedtime."

Gabe stood, too. "I'll drive you both back to the city."

As they said their goodbyes, he prayed no one would say anything to make Megan uncomfortable about the two of them leaving together.

They were almost back in the house when Zach called out, "Don't forget to call when you're up tomorrow, Megan, and I'll drop by to fix your tire. You've got my cell number, right?"

Gabe had run up and down hundreds of flights of stairs in zero visibility countless times over the years. But hearing that his brother had already arranged to see Megan again—under the guise of helping her with her car—was what finally had the breath clogging in his chest.

He knew he shouldn't be getting so upset about it. If he was half the man he liked to think he was, he'd be happy that his brother was finally choosing a nice girl for once. After all, hadn't he just thought how great she fit in with his brothers and sisters?

But none of that helped the knot in Gabe's gut loosen as he and Megan silently headed down to the basement, where they found Summer asleep in front of the old TV. Some of the bigger kids were still up watching a Disney movie, but she was curled up in a ball on the old couch under an afghan his mother had made a long time ago.

Megan went to scoop her up, but he said, "Let me," in a low voice that wouldn't wake Summer. Effortlessly, he lifted the little girl off the couch and walked upstairs with her in his arms.

As Megan said thank-you and goodbye to his mother, he gently laid Summer down upstairs and went to get his truck. When he got back, they were waiting for him on the sidewalk, Summer in her mother's arms, just as he'd first seen them. Summer wasn't big for her age, but he knew she had to be heavy for Megan. He quickly jumped out to help get her buckled into the backseat of his truck, using a sweatshirt as a makeshift pillow.

In the dark on the freeway headed back to San Francisco, neither he nor Megan spoke, a repeat of their drive in the opposite direction.

Earlier in the evening he'd been glad for Summer's constant questions and chatter to fill the space so that he wouldn't make the mistake of getting closer to Megan. He should be happy about her silence now, too. So then why wasn't he? Why did he wish he could get to know her better instead?

Parking in front of her building a while later, he unbuckled Summer and moved to carry her inside Megan's apartment. This time, as she turned on various lights to help him find his way through the small rooms to Summer's bedroom, he noticed how comfortable her place was. She hadn't been there two months yet, and he guessed it was only temporary, but still, he found he liked the ambience.

Gabe's apartment was in a fantastic location with lots of windows and great views from his top-floor rooms. But it had never felt like home to him. Not like this did.

"Thanks so much for the ride," Megan said once she'd gently pulled the covers up over her daughter, kissed her cheek and closed her bedroom door.

In the living room, the lights of the small Christmas tree blinked behind her, lighting her up like an angel. She looked a little nervous. Summer was down for the count. Considering that the little girl hadn't stirred once during all the transporting from the basement to the car and then to the apartment, he knew she wasn't getting up anytime soon.

"Can I get you a cup of coffee or anything?"

Anyone with a beating heart could have figured out that the offer was made out of politeness, nothing more. He knew what to do. Stick to his M.O. and get the hell away from her. No big conversations. No letting down his guard.

But for all his strength of will, and the tight hold he usually had on his self-control, tonight Gabe couldn't quite bring himself to go.

Not when he finally had Megan all to himself.

Okay, so he wouldn't leave just yet. But he'd use the next few minutes as the perfect way to prove that he could control himself around her...and that she wasn't that much of a temptation.

"Sure," he said in an easy voice, "coffee sounds great."

She looked momentarily surprised by his agreement. No doubt because he hadn't exactly gone out of his way to be friendly with her. Not like Zach or Ryan had at the party.

"It will just take me a second, if you want to have a seat."

Gabe was pulling up a stool at the kitchen counter when she grabbed a bag of coffee beans from a small pantry along the way and shook out a couple of beans. She gave him a cute little look of consternation and he had to wonder if it was caused solely by the lack of coffee beans or if having him there in her space was the real reason.

"I have more beans," she said. "Somewhere." She turned and scanned the rest of her cupboards before admitting, "I still haven't quite gotten used to our new apartment. Sometimes I think I definitely have something and then I'll realize it was destroyed in the fire and I never got around to replacing it."

Gabe had to practically sit on his hands to keep from moving to her and pulling her into his arms to console her. Instead, he said, "It can take a while to process what happened, Megan."

She sighed. "I just didn't think I'd feel so lost and rootless without my things. Because they're just things, you know?" She shook her head and smiled at him. "Summer and I are fine and that's what matters."

He was struck, yet again, by how strong she always expected herself to be, and wanted to say something more to let her know that it was okay to grieve her loss, even of little things, when she snapped her fingers and said, "Wait, I know where the beans are."

She pointed at a cupboard that went up to the ceiling. "Up there."

She was reaching for a stool that was stored between the fridge and the counter when he said, "I'll get them for you."

He could easily reach the bag of beans on the top shelf, but he hadn't realized just how small the kitchen would be when two people were in it. And somehow, by the time he turned around with the coffee, Megan was pressed back against the pantry shelves.

"Thank you."

"You're welcome."

But she didn't take the coffee from him and he didn't give it to her. Instead, both of them just stared at each other.

When he saw his own desperate need reflected in her eyes, he dropped the bag of coffee behind him onto the counter and took her face in his hands. He bent his head down just as she went onto her toes, wrapped her arms around his neck and lifted her face to his.

Their mouths met a moment later, hot and hungry, long past gentle or sweet. It was a kiss that had been on the verge of happening more than once and was now completely out of control. She tasted like sugar and champagne and something else that was entirely Megan. Her hair was so soft against his fingers and the little moans of pleasure she made into his mouth as they kissed drove him crazy.

He ran his tongue over the plump curve of her

lower lip and she melted deeper into him, her curves pliable and so damn sweet as he tasted the corner where her upper and lower lip came together before plunging back into her mouth to tangle with her tongue.

Just as their kiss had gone from zero to one hundred in a millisecond, that's how Gabe wanted to take her. Fast and hard, up against the wall, the pantry doors banging as he slammed into her to take the intense pleasure their very first kiss was already promising.

And yet, despite how much he wanted her, Gabe knew he had to put the brakes on—and fast. But just as he started to pull away, Megan's hands abruptly moved from around his neck to splay flat across his chest so that she could push out of his arms.

The words "I shouldn't be kissing you" flew from her lips at the same moment he said, "I can't do this."

Eight

He should have pulled away from her; she should have stepped out of his arms. But neither of them moved.

Not sure who he was trying to convince more, Gabe explained, "I don't date people I've pulled from burning buildings."

Almost before he finished speaking, she gave her own explanation. "I can't be with someone who could die at any minute."

It was a moment of pure honesty, their first one.

No, Gabe quickly admitted. That kiss had been their first truly honest moment together. Honest passion...full-throttle desire.

As she finally slipped out of his arms and he moved to let her go, she added, "After the way Summer's father died, I just can't."

He should have been leaving, should have left ten minutes ago so that none of this could have happened. But Lord, he couldn't regret that smoking-hot kiss. And he wanted to understand Megan's reasons as well as he did his own.

"How did he die?"

"He was a fighter pilot."

"Navy?"

She nodded, looking heartbroken, and he had a moment of serious jealousy over a dead man. What was happening to him?

"I don't date men like you with jobs like yours. Not anymore. Summer was only a toddler when David died, but it still hurt her. If I were to let her get close to another man with a job like that and one day he didn't come home…"

She seemed to realize she'd said too much about herself and quickly turned the question back on him. "And I'm assuming you don't date women you save because—"

"It never works out." He'd heard what she'd said about not letting herself date a guy in his dangerous line of work, but he could still taste that kiss, could still hear her sexy little moans as their tongues had slipped and slid against each other. Yet again, he didn't know whether it was for her or for himself when he said, "It's just not a normal way for two people to meet. It sets up expectations. Ones that can never be lived up to in everyday, real life."

Knowing he was the one saying too much now, he was glad when she took another step back from him and said, "Okay."

She gave him a smile that trembled slightly around

the edges. "I'm glad we've got that out in the open." She licked her lips. "Settled between us."

He shouldn't have been standing there thinking how cute she was when she was nervous, but damn it, that was exactly what he was doing. And he sure as hell shouldn't have been on the verge of reaching for her and kissing her sweet mouth again.

Gabe shoved his hands into his pockets to keep them from straying back to her gorgeous curves. He needed to leave—the sooner, the better. She'd make the coffee. He'd drink it. And then he'd say goodbye and go back to his place and not let himself think about her again, damn it.

If only he could have stuck to his original plan of staying as far away from her as possible. But she'd been to his mother's house. She'd met his family. She was friends with his sister, the same sister who clearly had designs on getting them together.

As if she needed something to do with her hands, too, Megan picked up the bag he'd dropped on the counter and poured beans into the coffeemaker.

"Sophie's your friend and we're bound to see each other again—"

"—so we'll just agree to be friends," Megan said, finishing his sentence. "No big deal." She gave him another one of those not-quite-there smiles as she pressed the button on the grinder. When the beans were ready for the coffeemaker, she scooped them in and said, "I mean, now that we both know exactly where the other person stands, right?"

Still wanting her more than he'd ever wanted another woman, Gabe nodded.

"Right."

She was a blur of activity, clearing off a stack of Frosty the Snowman drawings Summer must have been working on, pulling out a pretty plate and arranging some white-frosted snowflake cookies on it.

He'd never dated anyone with kids. Not, he reminded himself, that he and Megan were dating. But it was the first time he'd seen anyone apart from his mother juggle more than just her own life.

She handed him the cup of coffee. "Why don't we go sit down?"

He followed her over to the small living room on the other side of the open kitchen, noting that she wisely chose to sit on the small, velvet-covered chair rather than joining him on the couch.

She slid her heels off and tucked her bare feet up under her, rubbing them with her free hand. "My feet were killing me in those heels."

Gabe wouldn't ever have called himself a foot man. Feet were just feet. But Megan's pink-painted toes were incredibly sexy. He wanted to push her hand away and replace it with his. He already knew how sweet her mouth was, how soft her hair was. What would her skin feel like beneath his hands?

He was blowing the "just friends" thing already. What made it worse was that not only was he just as opposed to falling for Megan as she was for him, but he also understood her reasons for not wanting to be with him. She had every right to want to be with a man who wouldn't die unexpectedly on her this time around.

There was no question whatsoever that he didn't fit that bill. At all.

There was a desk in the corner of the living room, along with a couple of large filing cabinets and a bookshelf that looked as if it held reference manuals rather than novels.

Following his gaze, she offered, "I work from home. I'm a CPA."

Before tonight, Gabe might have assumed that all accountants were dry, passionless geeks glued to their calculators and spreadsheets.

Megan definitely wasn't passionless.

"Do you like being an accountant?"

"I do." She took a sip of coffee. "I like how numbers add up. I like the rhyme and reason. How they always make sense, and if there's a discrepancy, I know that as long as I look hard enough, I'll figure out what the problem is. And solve it." She blinked at him with those beautiful green eyes. "I take it you love being a firefighter?"

"I was never able to sit still when I was a kid. And I used to like playing with matches a little too much. Fire always fascinated me."

"Your mother must have loved that," she said in a tone that indicated just the opposite.

"Not so much," he acknowledged.

"I guess the fascination with fire makes sense," she said slowly, as if considering it for the first time. "Otherwise, you might not be so willing to run straight into one rather than away from it like the rest of us."

Did she know that he was fascinated with her, too? That even when he knew he should be turning away from her, he wanted to move closer?

"You have a great family, but I have to say, some of you must have been a handful. My hat's off to your mother. And," she said with a slight question to her words, "your father?"

"He passed away when I was five. She raised us alone."

His father's death was another reason he'd chosen his career. Also trained as a paramedic, many of the calls he went on were medical. He couldn't save everyone's father or mother or child, but he wanted to know, at least, that he'd done everything he could.

Megan's eyes grew big. "Eight children alone?" She put a hand over her heart in a clear gesture of sympathy for his mother. "Half the time Summer feels like too much for me to deal with by myself."

"You're a great mother."

She smiled at that. "Thank you. Although I'm not sure you'd say the same thing if you could see me yelling at her about homework or clothes on the floor or spending too much time on the phone with her friends."

He shouldn't want to see those things, shouldn't want to get any closer to Megan or her daughter. But the longer he sat with her, talking about family, the more that wanting grew.

Quickly downing the rest of his coffee, he got up

and put his empty cup on the coffee table. He noticed the window off the kitchen was open a crack and a cold breeze was coming in.

"Do you want this open?"

"No, it's jammed," she replied, coming back into the kitchen with her own still-half-full cup of coffee. "The landlord said he'd try to stop by this week to see if he can fix it."

Not wanting her to have to deal with being cold and paying for heat that just seeped outside, Gabe put his hand on it and pushed. Nothing happened. "Do you have a small screwdriver?"

She pulled one out of a well-organized drawer. "Here."

It didn't take him long to fix the problem. "A little glue or paint was stuck in under the metal." As he handed her back the screwdriver, he said, "Your old place must have had a great view."

"That's why I bought that apartment. I knew it was an old building, but I figured the view was worth it." Her green eyes shadowed. "I never thought about how safe it would or wouldn't be in a fire, though."

"Isn't having a view still at the top of the want list for your new place? Along with a backyard for a fire pit?"

"Views aren't worth quite as much as I thought they were," she replied in a soft voice. "And I'm not sure that a fire pit is such a great idea, either."

For all Megan's outward resilience, the way she'd clearly moved past losing her husband so young, how capably she'd recovered from her home going up in flames, Gabe could suddenly see her vulnerability.

Along with the fears she was trying so hard to hide.

As if she suddenly realized she was letting him look too deep, she said, "Well, thanks for fixing the window. And for the ride."

He got the hint. It was time to go.

She was right. He needed to leave before he kissed her again.

She moved to the front door just ahead of him. Opening it, she stood there as he walked out, so close. Too close.

He should have just kept going down the hall and out to his car without looking back or saying anything more, but in the same way that being in her apartment, putting Summer to bed and staying for coffee had felt so right, leaving felt just as wrong.

"Tell Summer I had a good time playing flashlight tag with her."

He was standing close enough to smell her perfume, something soft and floral that made him want to bury his nose in the curve of her neck until he figured out exactly what kind of flower it was.

"Okay."

The one word was slightly breathless, and from the way her eyes were focused on his mouth, he knew she was just as close to that edge of wanting as he was.

Just one kiss. That's all he wanted.

Needed.

Gabe had almost convinced himself it wouldn't hurt anything, that he could stop at *one more,* when she abruptly lifted her gaze and took a step back on a sharply indrawn breath.

"Just friends." She shook her head. "I like you a lot, Gabe, and that kiss in the kitchen…" Another shake of her head. "Well, we've got to forget that kiss. Because we've both agreed that's how things need to stay. Even if it's not easy, we've got to keep things totally platonic."

When she was done laying out the reminders, she put her fingers over her mouth as if to keep herself from jumping across the space between them and kissing him. The problem was, all the good sense in the world couldn't negate the magnetic pull between them.

Compelled to be as honest as they'd been in her kitchen after they'd given in to desire for way too short a time, he said, "I want you. And if you were anyone else, I wouldn't be leaving right now." Her eyes went wide at the shock of his flat-out admission. "But I already know and like you and Summer well enough to know we can't just sleep together."

"No," she said quickly, even more breathlessly, "we can't."

Wanting her more with every word they spoke about the hot sex they weren't going to have, he said, "I'd better go now."

"Yes," she whispered, "you should go."

But then, instead of leaving, he was reaching out

and pulling her against him, his hands on the swell of her hips. "One last kiss."

"God, yes," she gasped out. "One more."

And then her mouth met his and he was backing her up against the open door, pressing himself into the soft heat of her body, taking, giving, falling deeper under the spell that Megan had woven around him from the very first second he'd seen her.

Her taste was addictive, and so sweet, he couldn't stop himself from going deeper, from moving from her lower lip to her upper, from pulling her so close that he could feel her nipples pressing into his chest even through their layers of clothes. He moved between her thighs and she opened them for him as he pressed her harder into the wall, her hips moving against his groin, making him harder than he could ever remember being in his life.

Here. He could take her right here. Pull up her skirt, unzip his pants and be in her in seconds, her legs wrapped around his waist.

Somehow, a noise from down the hall broke through the fog of lust clouding his brain. He knew better than to put on a public sex show with Megan when her daughter was only a couple of rooms away.

In sync, they moved apart, both of them breathing hard.

"That was the last one," she said in a shaky voice. "The very last kiss we can have."

Somehow, he managed to turn away, to get his feet to move. But with every step that he took away from her, Gabe had a feeling that not kissing Megan again just might prove to be the most difficult thing he'd ever done.

Megan closed her front door and leaned against it, closing her eyes as she fought to deal with what had just happened. She brought her fingers back up to her lips. They were tingling, burning up from his kiss.

She couldn't remember ever wanting anyone the way she wanted Gabe. She'd had a couple of lovers since David had passed away five years ago, but none of them had imprinted themselves on her body like this. In fact, she suddenly realized the faces of her past lovers were cloudy in her memory.

After David, it wasn't as if she'd sat down one day and made the decision to stay away from men with dangerous, deadly jobs. She hadn't been thinking about other men at all, actually. She'd been trying to raise her daughter on one income with only so many hours in the day while going back to school to get her degree in accounting.

It had been more of a gradual realization as she'd surfaced from her grief that she couldn't go through all that again. Yes, she understood that a businessman could get hit by a car and die. But she was a numbers girl and it didn't take a statistician to calculate that the odds of an early death were a heck of a lot lower for a man who sat behind a desk nine to five than they were for a fighter pilot.

Or a firefighter.

Still, she couldn't help but remember the way

he'd carried Summer out of his mother's basement and then into their apartment a little while earlier. It had been utterly different from the way he'd carried her daughter out of the burning building. He'd been one hundred percent firefighter then. Tonight, he'd looked more like a father taking care of his sleeping daughter.

Her hands shook slightly as she locked the front door and turned off the lights in the kitchen and living room before heading to the bathroom to get ready for bed. She knew better than to make the mistake of thinking of Gabe as anything but an off-limits firefighter. They shouldn't have shared those two kisses. But, since they had, at least they'd been smart enough to stop.

A few minutes later, as she crawled into her big, empty bed, she refused to let herself imagine what it might have been like to have Gabe there with her, his strong muscles pressing her down into the mattress as he came over her.

Into her.

No, she thought as she buried her face beneath her pillow to try to block out the far-too-potent images, she couldn't let herself imagine that.

Nine

"Mommy, what's the name of the place we skied at in Lake Tahoe last year?" Summer asked as they sat down to bowls of cereal the next morning.

"Heavenly Ski Resort." Megan had hoped to make it up to the snow again this year, which was four hours away from San Francisco, but things had been so crazy since the fire that she hadn't had a chance to think about holiday plans.

"I love snow."

"I know."

"I mean, I really, *really* love snow! And I wish we could see some soon."

Megan grinned at her daughter. Summer not only loved snow, she loved sun and wind and rain. She was an equal-opportunity outdoor girl. Although more than once Megan had thought that her daughter preferred the more extreme weather simply for the thrill of it.

Because of the fire and the time it had taken to

find and move into another apartment, they'd had to cancel Summer's birthday party. They'd taken a few of her friends out to pizza, but Megan knew it hadn't been the same as a full-blown party with games and homemade cake. She couldn't throw a party together with such little notice, but they didn't have anything planned for the next couple of days. An impromptu ski trip was the perfect birthday gift.

Besides, it suddenly occurred to her that if they didn't get out of town, Summer might very well request another trip to the fire station to see Gabe.

And Megan *definitely* couldn't see him again anytime soon.

Not until she was holding much firmer reins on her self-control.

Despite it being high season in Lake Tahoe, Megan figured they were due a little good luck. She picked up the phone. Summer watched her with wide, excited eyes as she was connected through to the Heavenly Ski Resort.

"Hi. I know this is last-minute, but I was wondering if you might have a room that we could rent? You just got a cancellation for tonight?" She gave her daughter a thumbs-up. "And tomorrow night, too? Fantastic!"

By the time she'd given the reservations person her credit card information, Summer had run back to her room and was gathering up her new winter clothes.

Megan stood in her doorway and asked, "Is that what you were hoping for?"

Her daughter almost tackled her with a hug. "Yes! Yes! Yes!"

Funny, Megan thought as she hugged her back, Summer had never been *this* excited about skiing before.

"Oh, no," Megan thought aloud, "I forgot all about the tire. I doubt anyone will be open to fix it on a Sunday." Summer's mouth turned down so fast that Megan knew she was in for the second part of yesterday's partial tantrum when she remembered, "What a minute. Zach Sullivan said he could fix it."

She'd had no intention of calling him to come over to fix her tire today, even though he'd offered more than once. Now she found herself going to find his cell phone number in her purse.

How, she wondered, had she gone from zero Sullivans in her life to three in a matter of days?

Zach immediately made good on his promise to change her tire, and when she'd made him a sandwich as a thank-you, he'd spent their impromptu lunch regaling her and Summer with all of the great things his brother Gabe had ever done. Megan couldn't help but feel that between Sophie and Zach, Gabe's siblings were doing whatever they could to push her and the firefighter together.

Of course, neither of them knew her reasons for needing to steer clear of him.

Five hours later, as Megan and Summer pulled up to the Lake Tahoe ski resort, Megan couldn't stop thinking what a great idea this trip already was.

During the drive from the city, they'd sung along with songs on the radio and then they'd finally had a chance to talk about second grade, everything from the teacher to Summer's friends and even a little bit about boys.

While they checked in, Summer kept scanning the hotel, for what, Megan didn't know. "Look," she said when the man behind the check-in desk switched their room from the second to the first floor, then gave her the schedule of activities, "there's a horse-drawn sleigh ride tonight at six." It was late afternoon already and skiers were coming in looking exhilarated from a day in the snow. "This is going to be so much fun."

"Kids only, Mom."

Megan frowned. "Oh. I hadn't noticed that. Well, maybe they can make an exception for me."

Summer didn't say anything for a moment, but she scanned the lobby extra hard. At long last, Megan had to acknowledge that something fishy was going on. Hadn't there been more than one sign that something was up?

"Summer, what aren't you telling me?"

Her daughter pressed her lips together as though that would mean she didn't need to say. Deciding she'd get to the bottom of things after they settled in, Megan was just about to pick up their bags and head to their room when she heard a familiar voice.

The same deep voice she'd been daydreaming about all day long.

"Megan? Summer?"

Oh, God.

Now she knew what was up. Megan didn't have time to shoot a glare at Summer before turning to Gabe.

"Hi."

She was going to *kill* her daughter!

He was clearly surprised to see them standing there in the lobby. Just as surprised as she was.

Summer, on the other hand, didn't seem the least bit surprised. *Relieved* was more like it.

"Hi, Gabe!"

He turned his frown into a smile for her daughter. "Hey, pretty girl. You going skiing tomorrow?"

She nodded happily. "Actually, I'm hoping to learn how to snowboard."

This was the first Megan had heard about it.

"Do you know how?" Summer asked him.

Oh, no, Megan could see where this was going. She tried to shoot Gabe a look to let him know he shouldn't agree to anything right now, that even a "yes" was too much at this point. But he was already nodding.

"Will you teach me?"

No! You're busy on your own winter vacation. There are plenty of professional snowboard teachers we could pay to teach her.

When Gabe looked up at her, Megan used every ounce of mental telepathy she could. He looked like he was trying to figure something out, like he was weighing facts before coming to a decision.

When he gave her a short nod, she nearly fell over in her relief that he understood.

"Sure I will."

"What?" The sharp question was out before Megan could stop it. She turned to her daughter. "Gabe is not going to teach you to snowboard."

"But he just said he wanted to!" Summer's chin was out now, a picture of stubbornness.

Megan put her hands on her hips. "First of all, you didn't even ask me if you could snowboard. And second—" She was about to lay into her daughter about organizing this whole "accidental" run into Gabe when it hit her just how much it would embarrass Summer.

Not that she was going to let her get away with it, of course. She just didn't need to do it in front of Gabe. Or in front of the check-in desk for the whole hotel to hear about.

"Megan, I agree that Summer should have definitely asked you first if it was okay," he said in a perfectly reasonable voice, "but if it is, I'd like to teach her how to snowboard."

Summer practically glowed at his words. Megan hadn't seen that glow since David had been around when she was a toddler. How she'd loved her father.

And that glow was the *only* reason Megan finally said, "Okay."

She wasn't prepared for Gabe to say, "What about you? Do you know how?"

"No."

His grin was slow and way too powerful, if the

way her heartbeat ratcheted up another zillion beats was anything to go by. He shouldn't be looking at her that way after they'd agreed they'd had their very last kiss at her front door the night before.

They'd agreed, darn it!

"Want to learn?"

Someone had to be the voice of reason here. Someone needed to stand firm and think things through. But, oh, why did it have to be her? And why did he have to be such a ridiculously good kisser?

She forced the word "No" from her lips.

Only, for some reason, her repeatedly sharp replies weren't having the right effect on him. He shouldn't still be smiling at her, shouldn't be nodding as if he knew exactly what she was afraid of. Not of learning a new sport, but of being with him all day. As if he knew she didn't have it in her to tough it out and not give in to kissing him during a day on the slopes.

She shouldn't have read it as a challenge. But her daughter hadn't come by her personality by accident. Megan was just as stubborn. Heck, that stubbornness had been a large part of why they'd survived David's death so well, why their transition from losing everything in the fire to getting back to living their normal lives had been relatively smooth.

Which was why there was no stopping her own chin from jutting out, and the words, "You know what, I'm sure snowboarding can't be that big a deal," from escaping her mouth. Just like resisting him wasn't going to be a big deal. No problem. She'd just shut down every part of her that was female, every cell connected to attraction and arousal, and she'd be fine.

A young woman started ringing a bell in the hall where the big fireplace was. "The kids' group is meeting here for the sleigh ride in five minutes."

Summer grabbed Megan's hand. "Mom, please, can I go?"

She was still extremely upset with her daughter for orchestrating this whole trip just to see Gabe again. But it didn't make sense to spend the next two days punishing her for wanting to be around the nice man who'd saved their lives.

Really, how could she blame Summer just because Gabe was irresistible to girls of all ages? Especially twenty-seven-year-old single mothers who knew better.

"Can you keep an eye on our things for a minute?" she said to Gabe, before taking Summer's hand and heading over to the kids' group leader.

"My daughter would like to join the sleigh ride, please."

"Wonderful," the woman said, then turned to introduce herself to Summer.

Before the fire, Megan wouldn't have been particularly worried about letting her daughter head out into the snow on a sleigh with a bunch of kids. But now, she needed to confirm that first-aid procedures were in place, and the exact number of adults who would be present.

Once everything was explained to her satisfaction, and after making sure that Summer would be meeting her at eight o'clock, sharp, in the same spot in front of the fireplace, she gave her a kiss, then headed back over to her bags.

And Gabe.

"You're not going on the sleigh ride, too?"

"Kids only." She gestured to their things. "Thanks for watching our stuff. I'm going to head to my room now." She'd order room service and buy a book on her e-Reader. Something mathematical and dry. It would be a perfectly mellow night. She was really looking forward to it.

Seriously. It was going to be great.

"Have dinner with me, Megan."

Having dinner with Gabe was the last thing she should do. Well, next to snowboarding with him tomorrow, anyway.

"Look," she said in what she hoped was a friendly, normal voice, "we both know it's better if we don't." When he didn't look convinced, she said, "We agreed, remember?"

"I'm not going to kiss you in a crowded restaurant, Megan."

She felt her breath go, tingles immediately landing on her mouth, with nothing but the word *kiss* from Gabe's lips.

While she was still trying to figure out how to breathe normally, he continued, "And we both need to eat."

"You must have friends you were going to see tonight."

"Nope, they're staying out for night skiing," he said, and then, "We'll talk. That's it. And tomorrow we'll have fun out on the mountain."

As oxygen finally hit her lungs, she realized how crazy she was being. Especially since he was the height of sensibility, actually having to remind her that he wasn't exactly going to throw her down on the table in a crowded restaurant and ravish her. Heck, he made it sound like the thought hadn't ever crossed his mind. Just food and snowboarding, that's all he was thinking about.

"Okay. How about we meet back here in thirty minutes?"

"Thirty minutes sounds good."

She went to go ask the sleigh ride guide if she could please bring Summer to the restaurant when the ride was through. When Megan came back to pick up the two small bags she and Summer had brought with them—their snow gear had all been destroyed in the fire and they were going to rent for the next couple of days—Gabe grabbed them.

"I've got it," she told him.

He said, "I know you do," but he didn't let go of her bags.

She supposed she could have seen it as some sort of macho move on his part. But, instead, she realized it was simply good manners.

He was heading to the elevators when she said, "I'm on the first floor."

He frowned for a moment before nodding and following her to her room. She refused to let herself be nervous about being alone in her hotel room with Gabe for the split second it would take him to bring her bags in. He'd help her with her things, she'd clean up from the drive and they'd have a nice, perfectly platonic dinner, followed by a friendly day out on the snowy mountain tomorrow.

Still, it was incredibly awkward the way they'd shown up at the very same ski resort he was at on the same exact day he was here. Somehow Summer must have found out about his holiday plans at the party last night. Megan was about to say as much when a group of loud teens shoved past them.

They were both inside her room a few moments later. It wasn't a small room, but she couldn't help but think it wasn't big enough for her and Gabe at the same time.

"Thanks for carrying the bags. The bed's fine," she told him, trying not to let her thoughts wander back where they'd been the night before, when she'd been unable to stop herself from fantasizing about what it might be like to share a bed with the hunky firefighter. She turned a too-bright smile on him. "I'll see you at the restaurant in a little bit."

He stared at her for a beat too long before nodding and closing the door behind him.

Gabe was known in the firehouse for his determination. He'd always had a knack for quickly sifting through data and then making good decisions on a course of action. But now, for the first time in his life, he felt as if he'd gotten onto a runaway train.

One where he saw Megan through the window and he was leaping on board without thinking.

Megan was his ultimate temptation, plain and simple, and he wasn't fool enough to think he'd be able to hold out against her allure much longer. Fortunately, he'd promised her he wouldn't kiss her at the restaurant. And making a pass at her in front of her daughter on the slopes was out of the question.

Both of those things meant the pressure should be off. At least for the time being.

Eventually, however, Gabe had a feeling that if they didn't get a handle on the situation, just like the flashover point of a fire, the force of their attraction was bound to blow apart their good intentions to stay away from each other.

Facts were facts: he had no business asking her to dinner tonight. Snowboarding lessons for her and Summer weren't much smarter.

The situation was cut-and-dried. They'd laid it out to each other the night before. They were both off-limits to each other.

And yet…every time he had a chance to walk away, he found himself needing to move closer to her instead.

Ten

Megan hated the nervous butterflies in her stomach.

It wasn't a date. It was just dinner…with a really hot guy. They'd talk about Summer, the state of the slopes, favorite runs to ski. Nothing more than two people who had been thrown together enough times to accept that they should be friends.

She smoothed down the long-sleeved dark green wool dress she'd thrown into her bag at the last minute. It wasn't high fashion by any means, but at least she felt pretty. And sometimes a girl needed a little armor to make it through the night in one piece, which was why she'd redone her makeup after her quick shower.

Gabe was waiting for her by the fireplace and her stupid heart actually skipped a beat when he smiled. Hoping her expression didn't betray her, she smiled back.

"You look great, Megan."

"Thanks." She took in his jeans and dark blue, long-sleeved shirt. "So do you."

The growing heat in his eyes was response enough for her to realize she'd already gone off course on the whole "nothing but friends" thing.

She put her hand over her stomach. "I'm starved. Let's eat!" Okay, so maybe that was overly cheerful, and maybe she wasn't actually hungry at all after she and Summer had pigged out on Cracker Jacks and beef jerky all afternoon in the car, but keeping everything completely nonsexual was the key to making it through dinner in one piece.

Yes, she could do that. Heck, by the end of the evening she vowed to win an award for being the least sensual woman on the planet.

Gabe followed her into the restaurant, where he told the host, "Two for Sullivan."

His low, slightly husky voice made thrill bumps rise across her skin.

They were, unfortunately, shown to a table in a dimly lit corner. One quite obviously set up for romance with a flower and a candle. She wasn't usually all that picky about where she sat, but she couldn't stop herself from looking for another option. Wouldn't you know it, all the other tables were full.

She realized, belatedly, that Gabe had pulled out the chair for her and was waiting with a small smile for her to take it. She got the sense he knew exactly what she was thinking, especially when he said, "Don't worry, I'm going to keep my promise," in a low voice as she finally sat down.

Her face flamed as the young waitress waited for Gabe to take his seat. She handed them menus and told them about the specials.

The girl was just turning away when Megan grabbed her arm. "Wait. I need a drink. Please." Racking her brain for something that had a ton of alcohol in it, she said, "A Long Island iced tea."

"Um, okay," the girl said, and Megan realized in horror that she was still holding her arm.

"Sorry!"

The girl shrugged. "I'll tell your server you're thirsty."

Megan felt hot all over—not the good kind of hot, but at what an idiot she was making of herself around Gabe.

"So you're a big drinker, huh?"

She looked up at him in surprise, before realizing he was teasing her.

"No." She licked her lips, making herself hold his gorgeous gaze. She was only getting herself into trouble by trying to act like this dinner was no big deal.

By trying to feign not wanting him.

"I only drink when I'm nervous."

"Do I make you nervous?"

She refused to look away. "You know you do."

He didn't look away, either. "If it makes you feel any better, you make me nervous, too."

Bad. This was bad. They were both heading down the wrong path.

So even though she had trouble taking her next

breath, she made herself say, "Tell me about the snow. How was it out there today?"

He continued to stare at her for several long moments. *Please,* she silently prayed, *please follow me away from temptation.* They both knew platonic was the only thing that made sense.

Finally, he said, "The snow is good. Perfect powder after the recent storm. Should be great conditions to learn to board tomorrow."

"About that. It's really sweet of you to agree to teach Summer—"

"—and you—"

"—and me to snowboard. But I know you came here to—"

"—have fun with friends on the mountain. That's what we're going to do tomorrow. Be friends, having fun."

But, thought Megan a little wildly, what if she had a little too much fun? What if she lost all control and couldn't bear to be "just friends" for another second?

The waitress came with her drink and took their dinner order. As soon as the woman left, Megan knew it was time to say, "I'm beyond mortified about what Summer did. I haven't actually figured out how she got wind of your trip here. If you're upset with us, I completely understand."

He shrugged, not looking too concerned about the machinations of a seven-year-old with a case of hero worship. "I'm sure she overheard me talking to someone at the party. And I'm not upset about seeing you."

"But she shouldn't have done this, shouldn't have made us barge in on your vacation like this."

"She's a really sweet kid."

"I know that, but..." She shook her head. "Summer's too young to understand the reasons why two people might not want to be together."

"Do you think she's hoping you and I will start dating?"

Megan felt her face grow terribly hot again. "I'm afraid so. She already thinks you're the greatest because you sent her that firehouse girl and Dalmatian for her birthday. She likes it even more than her Rapunzel doll with the long—"

"—hair," he finished for her. "With two little sisters, I know way more about fairy tales than any guy is supposed to."

He was so charming that she had to clear her throat to get back on track with the difficult—but necessary—conversation they were having. "Anyway, I'll find a way to explain to her that you and I are just going to be friends. I just wanted to apologize to you for screwing up your vacation. I swear I had no idea you were going to be here and I've already decided that Summer is going to be grounded for life when we get back home."

"Megan."

She'd dropped her eyes to her lap by the end of her apology, but the way he said her name had her lifting them to his face.

"I'm glad you're here."

"That's really nice of you to say, but—"

"Really glad."

The *really* stopped her protests cold. He didn't look like a man who was lying to preserve her feelings.

And, oh, she liked it too much, knowing he was glad they were in Lake Tahoe with him. It would have been so much easier if he had been upset with them, if he'd felt as if they'd stalked him, or something. Then he'd steer clear of them, rather than offering dinner invitations and arranging to take them snowboarding in the morning.

"Still," she had to say, "I wish Summer had been honest with me about what she was doing."

"Would you have come in that case?"

Megan had to smile and admit, "No. We definitely wouldn't have come."

"You should have seen the stuff I pulled when I was seven."

Glad for the shift away from the two of them, she took a sip of her drink and relaxed a bit. "I can't even begin to imagine—a thrill seeker like you surrounded by five older brothers that I'm guessing weren't exactly angels."

"You'd lock Summer in her room until she's eighteen if I told you some of the things we would attempt." He held up his bottle of beer. "How about a toast to a brilliant seven-year-old who knew just what she wanted and pulled it off without a hitch?"

Even though she was shaking her head, Megan couldn't help but laugh, realizing how right he was considering it was just the two of them having a "romantic" evening together.

She raised her glass. "She is pretty darn smart, isn't she?"

They clinked their drinks together, still laughing as they both took a sip. The alcohol hit Megan's bloodstream and sent warmth moving all through her limbs. Her skin felt extrasensitive as she shifted in her seat and the wool of her dress moved over her skin.

Gabe's eyes on her only added to the heat. It had been a very long time since she hadn't felt like a mother or a CPA.

Beneath his hungry blue eyes, with another couple of sips of her incredibly strong drink in her, she couldn't help but feel like a woman. It didn't help that she remembered only too clearly the feel of his strong arms around her, the press of his lips when his mouth came down over hers as he claimed the kisses she had been so desperate to give to him.

And yet, before she knew it, they were eating and laughing as he ended up telling her some of those stories about growing up as one of six brothers who acted first and thought later. Maybe she should have pretended she was okay with the way their evening was going, but she'd never been good at pretending. Had never understood the hows or whys of being someone she wasn't.

"I shouldn't be having this good a time with you."

"I've heard I'm irresistible," he teased.

Damn him for the way he always made her smile.

Of course, if smiles had been all there was between them, everything would have been perfectly fine.

Knowing there was no point in arguing with his too-true statement, she said instead, "That must be why you don't have a girlfriend or wife, right? So many women, so little time."

She expected him to laugh at that, but instead his expression tightened down. "I'm no saint, Megan, but I'm not the devil, either."

"I didn't mean anything by it," she quickly backtracked, "just that I can see why a guy like you would have fun playing the field."

"A guy like me?" His eyebrows were raised in question and he put down his silverware to sit back in his seat and watch her as he waited for her to explain.

She tried to keep her voice light as she said, "Like you said, there's a certain irresistibility about you and—"

"You're bound and determined to resist me, aren't you?"

His statement stopped her in her tracks. "You're bound and determined to resist me, too," she reminded him. "And I certainly can't remember anyone ever telling me I'm irresistible, so we both know who has the short end of the stick here." She pointed her index finger at her chest. "Me."

She was so caught up in her speech that it took a few seconds for her to realize she'd just made a complete idiot of herself. Thankfully, just then the alarm on her phone went off.

She shoved her chair back. "The sleigh ride coordinator will be bringing Summer to meet me here. I should go stand by the entrance so she sees me."

Gabe stood, too, and grabbed her hand before she could run away through the restaurant and catch her breath.

As he pulled her into him, she could almost taste his mouth, knew she was going to give in to his kiss. But when they were only a breath apart, instead of taking her mouth with his, he simply said, "I'm the one who's trying like hell to resist you, Megan."

Just another half an inch and he could be hers. She could blame the alcohol, could claim that it had all been out of her control. But just as she was teetering on the edge of letting her walls come down to take what she so desperately wanted, she heard Summer call out.

"Mommy! Gabe!"

She stepped away from Gabe so quickly, she bumped into another table.

"Sorry!" she said to the couple without even looking at them, and then she was turning to Summer and the sleigh ride guide. After thanking the women for bringing her daughter back safely, she turned to Summer and said, "Hey, honey, how was it?"

"Awesome!" Their waiter immediately brought a third chair over for Summer and, when Summer declared that she was starved, took her order.

After thirty mind-blowingly awkward minutes where both of them tried to ignore their mutual attraction while Summer chattered about the kids she'd met on the sleigh ride, a couple of whom were from her soccer team, and all the fun things they'd done during the past two hours, they all finally left the restaurant. Megan felt like a wet dishrag that had just been wrung out. Hard.

They were almost away from the biggest—and most dangerous—temptation she'd ever faced in her life when Summer turned to Gabe and asked, "What time should we meet you tomorrow morning for snowboarding?"

"How about 10:00 a.m.?"

"Awesome!"

As Summer went running off to look for their room number and the elevator door closed on Gabe's gorgeous face, a half dozen words on the opposite spectrum from *awesome* were running on repeat through Megan's mind. Because if dinner with Gabe had nearly done her in, how was she going to make it through a whole day with him, in beautiful Lake Tahoe, in one piece?

The views of Lake Tahoe were jaw-dropping. Not only was the lake a perfect sparkling blue, but the pine trees were coated in new snowfall from the night before. The entire mountain looked like a winter wonderland.

However, by the time Megan had fallen over for the hundredth time the next afternoon, she simply didn't have the energy left to appreciate the incredible natural beauty all around her.

All she could do was lie in the snow and laugh at herself. "If I had a white flag, I'd raise it right now."

Gabe had dropped to his knees to help her up, and as he lifted his goggles she found herself looking into his smiling eyes.

"You've almost got it."

"You're a terrible liar." She was too exhausted and surely bruised all over to do more than nod in the general direction of Summer, who was working on tricks at the far end of a ramp the ski resort had set up for snowboarders to play around on. "I'm afraid Summer is going to be the only snowboarder in our family." She shot a nasty look at the board attached to the big boots she'd rented for the day. "I hope my skis will forgive me for cheating on them."

He helped her up into a sitting position. Together they watched Summer go from trick to trick, a tiny whirl of energy on a snowboard that looked way too big for her.

"That kid of yours is a natural."

"I know. She's a natural at everything."

Gabe shot her a look. "You don't sound entirely happy about it."

She bit her lip, knowing she'd already given too much away. And yet, for all the falling and cursing she'd done into face-fulls of snow today, she'd truly enjoyed being with Gabe. Fortunately, it had been easier to ignore all the things her body was aching to do with him when they were bundled up in snowboarding gear and hats and goggles. She'd simply been able to let herself enjoy being with him. He'd been patient with her and Summer, had known just when to push Summer to the next step...and when to let Megan quit while she could still hobble off the mountain in one banged-up piece.

"She can be such a daredevil, always reaching for the thrill without thinking about the ramifications of her actions." She couldn't stop herself from adding, "She's the picture of her father. She got way more than her blond hair from him."

"That's funny," he said softly, "because when I look at her, all I can see is you."

She met his clear blue gaze on a surprised breath. "When she was born, she looked so much like him that I can remember wondering if anyone would believe I had anything to do with the little miracle in my arms. And then as she grew older and was always trying to climb a little higher and jump a little farther and go a little faster…well, I worry about her sometimes. Worry that she'll end up pushing too far or too fast one time. Like her father did when his plane—"

The rest of the sentence was swallowed by her gasp as she watched Summer make a particularly bold move with her snowboard.

Landing triumphantly, Summer looked over at where they were sitting and waved. On a choked laugh, Megan gave her daughter the required thumbs-up.

Gabe reached for her hand then. And even though they were both wearing thick gloves, she swore she could feel his heat through the layers of fabric and insulation.

"There's a difference between risking smart and risking dumb. You raised her smart, Megan." She couldn't help but get lost in his eyes as he said, "And not all risk is bad."

His words ran from her brain to the parts of her body that were suddenly screaming out for his touch. She knew he was talking about Summer, about her fears as a mother...but what if that wasn't all he was saying?

What if he was saying he'd changed his mind? What if he was trying to tell her he wanted to take a risk? With her. And that he wanted her to take it, too?

With him.

"Mom, look who's here! I told Karen we'd probably be out here today and to come find me."

Megan yanked her hand out of Gabe's so quickly her glove almost came off in his hand. One of the girls from Megan's soccer team lifted her goggles.

"Hi, Ms. Harris."

The girl's mother was a few seconds behind on her skis, and after Gabe had helped her up, Megan quickly made the introductions. Fortunately, she knew Julie was happily married, so the appreciative gleam in her eyes when she looked at Gabe wasn't anything more than how a normal female would react.

Damn him. Megan had to admit he really was irresistible, looking just as good in snowboarding gear as he did in jeans or his fire gear.

She couldn't bear to think how good he'd look without anything on at all.

"Karen hasn't been able to stop talking about a sleepover with Summer all day."

Megan's brain stuttered away from the imagined picture of a naked Gabe to what Julie had just said. "A sleepover?"

"Sorry," the other woman said, "I should have asked, is there any chance I could steal your daughter for a night of staying up too late and eating too much junk food at our cabin? I know the girls would just love it."

Normally, Megan wouldn't have blinked at the offer. Summer and Karen got along great, and while she didn't know Julie that well, she wasn't at all worried about leaving Summer with her for the night.

What she was worried about, however, was the thought of being alone again tonight. And not just for a few hours. All night long, just her and her lonely bedroom, with Gabe one floor away, all alone in his bedroom.

It was a recipe for disaster.

"That's really sweet, but—"

Summer and Karen had boarded over by then and the combined "Please!" and "Pretty please!" from the two girls wasn't something Megan could selfishly ignore just because she didn't trust herself not to do something reckless with the gorgeous man beside her.

"You know what, I'm not going to be able to do much more than soak in the bathtub tonight, anyway," she said, gesturing to the snowboard at her feet. "I'm sure the girls will have a lot of fun."

After they arranged for Julie and Karen to pick up Summer at five, and Summer followed them down the mountain, Megan was working to prepare herself for one final run down the hill when Gabe said, "So you've got a big night in the bathtub planned, huh?"

She couldn't miss the husky note in his voice, especially when he pulled off his glove and reached out to slide away a lock of hair that had blown in front of her mouth.

And when she trembled at his touch, Megan made a quick calculation and decided it was far safer to hurtle down the hill on the snowboard than it could ever be to risk letting him touch her like that again.

Or worse, beg him for more.

Eleven

Gabe let Megan turn down his invitation to dinner that night, knowing she was right. One night alone together had been barely manageable. One more just might push them over the edge.

Especially since he couldn't push the fantasy image of her in the bathtub, the warm water and soap suds sliding over her naked curves, out of his head.

Nine o'clock found him sitting in the bar with a couple of guys from the firehouse having a burger and drinking a beer, listening to them talking about the girls they'd been hitting on out on the slopes that afternoon.

"Hey," one of them said after they'd all gotten another refill from the well-endowed waitress that one of his buddies was clearly hoping to get it on with later. "Did you know your brother Zach is doing house calls now?" At Gabe's frown, Dick explained, "I dropped by to have my tires rotated, and while we were shooting the shit, he was talking about some girl he'd met the night before at your mom's party who had the same tires. She got a flat so he went by her place to fix it for her."

Gabe stopped with the beer halfway to his mouth. He'd forgotten all about his brother's offer to fix Megan's tire.

"Man," their other friend John said, "she must be really, really hot for Zach to head over to her house to personally change her tire."

Gabe slammed the beer down so hard on the table it sloshed out onto his hand. Zach was a great brother, and definitely knew his way around a car, but Gabe knew him better than nearly anyone else. And he was very much afraid the only reason Zach had offered to change Megan's tire was as some kind of screwed-up foreplay.

In a matter of seconds, Gabe was shooting out of the bar, heading down the hall and knocking on Megan's hotel room door. He couldn't think straight, couldn't see anything but a vision of his brother pulling Megan into his arms and seducing her.

Oh, hell, no.

She was his.

He slammed his fist into the dark brown wood again, and when she finally opened the door, he stepped inside, caught the edge of the door in his hand and pushed it shut behind him.

"Gabe?"

She was standing in front of him wearing nothing but a towel, her hair wet, her shoulders and arms still covered in droplets of water.

"You can't date my brother," he growled. "Not any of my brothers."

"What are you talking about?"

He advanced on her even as she backed up to get away from him. "Zach. He went to your house on Sunday, didn't he?"

"He fixed my flat tire."

"I'll bet that's not all he wants to fix." He had her almost pinned against the wall by then. "He's going to ask you out. The answer is no."

Surprise turned to outrage in a flash of her green eyes. Instead of continuing to retreat, she was the one advancing on him this time.

"I'll say yes if I want to."

"Like hell you will."

She moved a step closer. "Just because you saved my life doesn't mean you can tell me how to live it."

Everything went still for Gabe. "Do you want to say yes? Do you want to date my brother?"

Megan stopped, too, right where she was, her eyes wide, her breath coming in short pants against the towel she was gripping closed at her throat.

"No."

The breath he hadn't let himself take came rushing through him in a flood of relief. "I swear," he said, hearing the pure raw need in his voice and knowing he couldn't do a damn thing to stop it, "I tried to have self-control."

Megan's lips were wet where her tongue had just come out to lick at them. "Me, too," she admitted in a whisper.

As he reached for her hips and took a handful of the towel in each hand to pull her body into his, Gabe admitted to himself that jealousy over Zach changing her tire was just the final excuse he'd needed to take what he wanted all along.

Megan.

He wanted Megan.

And tonight he was finally going to have her.

Megan stood in the circle of Gabe's arms, knowing everything she wanted was just a breath away—and that, at the same time, it could all be gone just as fast. He'd kissed her before and still left.

Right or wrong, she knew that if that happened tonight, she'd be left needing, wanting, without him.

She'd never been a woman to trade on her looks for anything in her life. Just as she'd never deliberately acted against what she knew she should do. She shouldn't seduce Gabe into staying. Not when she knew better. Not when a whole lot more than just one hot night could end up on the line.

But there was a first time for everything, she was starting to realize…even listening to that wily and seductive little voice in her head that told her everything would be all right, that it wouldn't hurt anyone or anything for her to take this one night and enjoy every single second in his strong arms until the sun rose again in the sky.

Maybe if that sensual woman buried so deep inside her hadn't been lured out little by little over the past few days by this beautiful man, she might have been able to ignore the voice. The need.

But, for one night, desire insisted on getting its due.

She lifted her gaze from Gabe's mouth to his eyes just as she loosened her grip on the towel. She felt him still against her as he realized what she was doing. And then, he was shifting his grip on her hips to give her the room to let go of the towel completely.

White cotton fell away from her damp skin and landed in a heap on the ground…leaving her completely naked before Gabe.

"Sweet Lord, you're beautiful."

His reverent whisper ran over her, through her, caressing the nerve endings at the peaks of her breasts, the throbbing heat between her thighs, all the way into that spot in her heart she'd vowed to keep safe from a man like Gabe.

She waited to feel his hands come back around her hips, naked skin against naked skin. She knew what would happen now, that in a matter of moments she'd be beneath him on the bed and they'd be going at each other without any preliminaries necessary.

But a moment later, as his hands slid gently into her wet hair, she realized her mistake. Gabe Sullivan wasn't like other men, who would have gone straight for the ultimate prize.

On the contrary, he was surprising her with—*oh,*

my!—a sweeter kiss than any other man had ever given her.

His mouth covered hers, molding her lips with his so softly she almost couldn't feel anything at all. Just warmth. And so much pleasure as he deepened the kiss, finding the curves of her lower lip with his tongue and slowly sliding across it, that she couldn't hold back a whimper.

"Gabe, please."

She didn't realize that she was begging—already, with nothing more than just a soft kiss—until he said against her mouth, "Slow, baby. That's how we're going to do this tonight."

"I don't know if I can do slow," she said, her body reinforcing her words by moving closer to him so that her bare breasts were pressed into his chest.

The rough gauge of his long-sleeved wool shirt rubbed so deliciously against her nipples that she gasped at the incredible sensation of rubbing her naked body up against his fully clothed one. There was something so deliciously naughty about it all. Megan hadn't ever been naughty. She had only ever let herself get that close to danger, and the adrenaline that came with it, in her private fantasies.

But something about Gabe made her suddenly want to see all those dangerously seductive fantasies come to life.

"Megan."

He groaned her name, sounding like a man lost, just as lost as she knew she already was to him. His hips ground against hers, backing her up against the wall, her thighs opening to let him in. And, oh, how she loved the way the thick bulge behind the zipper of his jeans pressed into just the right spot.

She shouldn't be this close to the edge, shouldn't be only the barest touch, the slightest caress, away from coming apart for him. But the truth was that every moment they'd spent together not touching, not kissing, trying to keep their distance from each other, had been foreplay.

Some of the most intense foreplay of her life.

"I could take you now, could be inside you in seconds." His voice was rough at her ear, his words blunt and oh-so-sexy, making her heart race with wanting what he was describing. "Just like this, up against the wall, your legs wrapped around my hips, with you coming around me as I take you hard and fast."

Yes! That was what she wanted. What she needed.

Only, instead of doing any of those things, he stilled his hips against hers and lifted his face from that spot beside her ear where he was filling her head with naughty visions. His blue eyes seared her with heat.

"But that's not how we're going to do this tonight, Megan."

Her eyes widened at the confident statement. "But what if that's what I want?" came from between her lips, barely above a whisper.

"You'll want this more," he said, and then he was bending his head to lick into the hollow of her shoulder.

She arched her neck into his sweetly sensual kiss, her skin trembling beneath the tender onslaught.

No man had ever talked to her like this, told her what to anticipate, promised her ecstasy if only she'd follow where he led. She was just pragmatic enough, had taken care of herself for long enough, to think that she shouldn't like whispered promises from a man who clearly knew exactly how to drive a woman wild with wanting. And yet as his mouth traveled up her neck, alternating soft little bites with the warm press of his tongue, she knew the truth for what it was.

She loved it.

He pulled back and slid his hands from her hair, down her arms to take her hands, and that slow glide of the calloused skin on his palms across the inside of her elbow, her wrist, was just about as good as any orgasm any other man had given her.

Gabe threaded his fingers intimately through hers and even though she was already naked, even though she'd been all but begging him to take her up against the wall moments before, the feel of being held like that—like more than just a lover for the night—rocked all the way past her skin and bones, heading straight to the core of her heart. And, amazingly, even though he'd shifted away enough to easily take in her nudity, he never looked away from her eyes for a single second.

It was crazy for tears of emotion to rush at her and she tried to blink them away before he noticed, but maybe it was the hitch in her breathing that gave her away.

"You and me, we're going to talk to each other tonight. You're going to tell me when I make you feel good...or if I don't."

She licked her lips, knew he was right. They weren't kids taking a tumble together. "It's good so far," she said in a soft voice. "Really good."

"But?"

Any other man would have pushed past her obvious emotions, but Gabe was doing just the opposite.

"I expected hot." She slid her thumbs against his palms. "I was ready for hot."

His eyebrow quirked up at that. "Really?"

She shook her head slightly. "Well," she admitted, "maybe not exactly *ready* for it, but I'm not surprised."

"Me, either," he said, and then, "Tell me what's surprising."

She didn't know how to put words to it, other than to say, "Everything else."

His eyes darkened, his fingers tightening on hers. "I wish I were surprised," he said in a low voice, raw with need and something else she was afraid to dissect. He lifted her hands to his mouth and managed to kiss them both at the same time.

Oh, God, what this man was going to do to her... how would she ever recover from this night? she wondered helplessly as he slowly brought her hands back down and began to move them apart. If it were just hot sex, that would be one thing. But what if he were looking to seduce more than just her body?

What if he was going for her heart, too?

His eyes moved slowly from her face down to her

breasts, and held. The seconds ticked by, one after the other, as he took in every inch of her skin. She couldn't stop herself from following his hot gaze to her breasts, and both of them watched as her nipples puckered up hard, pulling her full breasts up higher on her chest.

"Touch me," she begged, desperate to feel his hands, his mouth, on her. "I need you to touch me."

Gabe gave no indication of having heard her, nothing but the way he took their joined hands and placed hers on either side of his jean-clad hips. He didn't rush as he slid his fingers from hers, and those painfully drawn-out moments of waiting only added to her need.

And then—*finally!*—he was reaching for her, his fingertips feathering out across her stomach and then up her rib cage. She sucked in a hard breath at the intense pleasure of Gabe's touch. He hadn't even come close to her breasts yet, but already she felt insanely good.

She bit her lip as he continued his sinfully slow path of sensual destruction up her body.

"So soft," he murmured, just at the lower swell of her breasts. "So pretty." His palms shifted that final inch to cup the full flesh. "So perfect."

There was no holding back another moan as his thumbs both moved across her nipples at the same time, not a chance of keeping her back from arching her chest farther into his big hands.

But when he lowered his head and blew across one of her nipples, she nearly came right then and

there. His eyes met hers, full of approval and un-
abashed pleasure at her reaction. "You're sensitive,
aren't you?"

He rubbed his thumbs over both nipples again,
which completely forestalled her being able to answer him, as it was taking every ounce of her concentration just to keep breathing.

"Megan?"

His low voice urged her to answer him, just as he
bent slightly to blow a hot patch of air against her
other breast.

"Yes," she gasped out as he followed up the breath
with the sweet pinch of his thumb and forefinger over
her tightly aroused flesh.

And then, before she realized what was happening, he was lifting her into his arms and carrying
her over to the bed.

"I don't want your legs to give out when you come
for me," he explained in a matter-of-fact voice that
didn't take away from the sensual promise even one
little bit.

She had already pulled back the covers before he'd
arrived, and he laid her down on the clean sheets. She
wouldn't let her hold around his neck go, wouldn't
give him any choice but to move onto the bed with
her. Who knew how he'd tease her otherwise? Maybe
he'd make her touch herself while he watched and
that was when she'd come so hard, with his eyes on
her, all the while knowing his hands, his mouth, his
shaft, would be there soon....

She forcibly stopped her imaginings on a shudder, but Gabe had already caught it all, her breasts peaking against his chest harder than ever as the naughty vision continued to assault her already lust-addled brain.

"Tell me what just got you so worked up."

"You."

And it was true—Gabe was all she could think about, all she could feel, all that existed for the night. But he was quicker than that, could clearly sense her evasion.

"What else?"

His gentle but firm question, that small upturn of his beautiful lips as he watched her expression carefully, had her answering, "I was wondering what you were going to do to me to—" She swallowed hard, not having ever had any practice at talking dirty in bed. And yet, even though it was another thing she shouldn't want, that sensual woman deep inside made her say, "To make me come so hard."

He shifted over her and she had to close her eyes at the wonderful press of his muscles into her, the feel of roughened fabric over her sensitive skin.

He lowered his head to the other side of her neck from where he'd licked before and pressed circles of pleasure against her skin with his tongue. Only this time, he didn't stop there, thank God. Instead, he moved lower, the slow slide of wet heat over the upper swell of both breasts taking her breath away in a rush of sensation. Closer and closer he came to her nipples, licking shockingly soft circles over the soft flesh, heading in toward the peaks like a bull's-eye.

And then—*oh, God, please!*—she felt him just brush up against the edge of her tightly puckered areola, and her hips were bucking hard into the taut muscles of his thigh as she tried to take herself over the edge he seemed so determined to keep just out of reach, when he lifted his head.

"What did you come up with?"

No! He couldn't do this to her now. Couldn't stop when she was so close.

"I can't—" She panted. "I need—"

But as her vision cleared, she could see that he wasn't going to give her what she needed until she gave him his first.

"Tell me what you were thinking I would make you do."

Desperate for even a small orgasm to take the edge off this crazy need coursing through her, she blurted, "You made me touch myself."

His eyes lit with even more arousal at her surprising statement.

"And?"

"And—" She wasn't really going to say this, was she? She couldn't possibly give away such deeply held fantasies to a man who could never be anything more to her than just one perfect night, could she? Nonetheless, the words spilled from her lips. "And after you made me come for you, you made me come even better with your hands, and mouth, on me."

She was rewarded with Gabe's lips over the tip of one breast. For all his talk about slow, there was nothing easy about the way he suckled her, and she didn't want there to be.

Megan threaded her hands into his dark hair and held him to her, loving the sweet suction of his lips and tongue and teeth over her shockingly aroused flesh. Nothing had ever felt this good. This right. And when he shifted his attention to her other nipple, even though she should have known how to prepare herself for the pleasure of his mouth, she couldn't even come close. Not when the pleasure of being with Gabe continued to shock her from moment to moment.

His hands cupped and caressed her even as his mouth stole her every lucid thought away. It wasn't just foreplay, wasn't just sex…what he was doing to her was worship, pure and simple.

And through it all, she rocked and thrust herself against his thigh, her arousal growing to a fever pitch with every pull of his tongue against her, with every stroke of his fingers over desperately aroused skin, until she was right there, right on the edge of that orgasm he promised her she'd have.

The shock of cool air rushing over her skin hit her hard enough to have her eyes flying open as Gabe lifted himself away from her and off the bed. Before she could get her brain to cooperate, he was lowering himself into the chair in the corner.

"Show me, Megan," he said in a husky voice. "Show me how you like to be touched."

But she was already shaking her head, getting

onto her knees to come after him and pull him back onto the bed with her.

"You already know." And it would be so much easier, so much safer, if he just touched her instead.

But he wasn't coming back toward her outstretched hand. "Let me watch this first time. Let me see you come apart with your hands on yourself."

This was crazy. She shouldn't even be considering doing this, should never have told him about her fantasy. Heck, she shouldn't have had the fantasy at all!

But how long had she pushed away her own reckless urges? How many years had she forced herself to turn from adrenaline, to focus on always being safe, always taking the sure but slightly boring path before her. She wished she didn't know the answer, wished she didn't have to admit that even before she'd lost her husband, she'd been playing it way too safe.

For one night, could all rules be off?

For a handful of hours, could the sky be the limit?

And could she trust not only Gabe but herself enough to take off the reins and run free for just a little while?

The answers came from somewhere deep inside— three *yes*es that actually seemed to come with more relief than fear—and she found herself moving back onto the bed while Gabe watched her from across the small room.

"You still have all your clothes on" ended up being her only remaining protest as she settled back against the pillows.

"You belong naked," he told her.

"You do, too," she said in a hoarse voice, knowing without having to guess just how beautiful he was going to be without his clothes on.

His mouth moved up into a smile at her words, but the smile couldn't do a thing to extinguish the fire in his eyes.

She tried to be comfortable with her nudity, tried to act as if lying there on the bed before him with one hand over the curve of her breast and the other on her stomach was a normal thing for her to be doing.

But it wasn't. Not at all.

Utterly unable to hold anything back from Gabe until now, she found this moment was no different. "I don't know how to do this."

"Yes, you do," he said in that low voice that never failed to send shivers through her. "You were fantasizing about it just a few minutes ago. Go back to that fantasy and let yourself live it. Give us both the pleasure of you touching yourself, Megan."

He was right. She'd had plenty of practice masturbating in the past few years. Not with toys that she would have been afraid one particular curious little mind would find in her drawer, but with her own hands, her own fingers.

Just like Gabe wanted her to do right now.

While he watched.

What they were doing was so forbidden—so far outside the realm of the "normal" sex she'd ever permitted herself to have—that despite her nerves, she could feel herself growing even more aroused.

Maybe if she closed her eyes, maybe if she pretended she was alone, then she could—

"Megan."

She opened her eyes and looked at him, only to find him shaking his head.

"Watch me watch you."

Another flood of arousal poured through her at his softly spoken command and the force of her desire was actually strong enough in that moment for one of her hands to find its way between her legs, the other to cup her own breast, just as he'd done precious minutes ago.

She was so turned on that even though she would have sworn before a judge and jury she could never climax like this, in pure exhibition, in front of a man—any man—she knew it wouldn't take more than a few well-placed presses of her fingers against herself for her to fall over the edge.

But when she noted Gabe's intense concentration as he watched her through half-lowered lids, as a muscle jumped in his jaw and the bulge in his jeans threatened to break the zipper in two, suddenly she didn't want to rush it.

She slid two fingers between her lower lips and found her own wetness. She purposefully teased herself. But she couldn't stop her hips from rocking into her hand, didn't have any control over the hand on her breast, either, as she pulled at her nipple and brought the delicious sensations to a fever pitch within herself. Feeling lost to reality, as if she was floating apart from the world she'd lived in for twenty-seven years, she began to buck up into her fingers.

"Megan." Gabe's groan came from across the room. "God, this is hot. So incredibly hot. But I can't keep doing this. Not this time."

A split second later, the bed was dipping and his big hands were on her thighs, holding her open for his mouth to take over where her right hand had been playing across her body.

The pleasure of his fingertips moving across her slick, aroused flesh—and then, oh, Lord, his tongue, those lips, the slightest scratch of his teeth—shoved her over the edge before she was ready for it to happen.

Her hips took on a life of their own as she pressed herself into him, as she gasped out his name over and over again. She was never going to survive this orgasm, knew that she couldn't handle this kind of pleasure, only to find herself being driven higher as he slid two fingers inside, sucked her clitoris in between his lips and sent her reeling all over again.

Fireworks across her line of vision gave way to a split second of darkness as the pleasure peaked again, then finally began to let her out of its grip. And yet, even though she'd just had two senselessly great orgasms, one after the other, Gabe's tongue was still softly stroking over her. She should have been too sensitive for the intimate caress, but she was amazed to find he knew just how to touch her, just where to lick to make her feel good.

And to start her thinking—*already!*—about doing it all over again.

Exhausted from the combination of extreme pleasure and her day on the mountain, she found herself relaxed enough on the bed with Gabe to lie back and let him continue to taste her, his mouth intermittently roving across the tender skin at the inside of her thighs, but always coming back to her core, a slow postclimax seduction clearly intended to ratchet up her arousal, minute by minute.

In the end, it took all the energy she could muster to push herself up and reach for his hands. She tugged at him and even though she could never be strong enough to pull him over her, he understood what she wanted and came willingly.

And yet, even as he made his way up her body, he continued to keep his promise not to rush a thing. He kissed every inch of her hips, her stomach, her ribs, her breasts, her shoulders, on the way to finding her mouth again.

He kissed her long and slow, and if she hadn't already given over herself to him for the night, she would have lost herself in the sweet persuasion of his mouth, the seductive glide of his tongue across hers, the heat and strength of his muscles over her.

She couldn't stand it another second, because for all the delicious naughtiness of being naked while he wasn't, she was desperate to feel the heat of his skin, to know what awaited her beneath all that wool and cotton and denim.

Pulling even more strength from deep inside, she pushed him onto his back and climbed over him.

Twelve

Gabe had always loved women. Their smooth skin, their sweet scent, the sound of their laughter. He'd lost his virginity in high school and hadn't had much of a break since then. Sex was a regular part of his life, right up there with food and sleep.

But for all the women he'd shared a bed with, sex with Megan felt completely different. Almost as if he was discovering the thrill of making love for the first time. He could have spent all night tasting her, bringing her over the edge again and again, just to hear her cries of pleasure, just to feel her slick flesh clench and pull at his fingers, his tongue, one more time.

And now she was sitting up over him, her beautiful naked skin flushed from the orgasms he could still taste on his lips, and she was concentrating on the small buttons of his long-sleeved shirt. Her tongue moved to lick at the corner of her mouth as she slipped the first button free.

Instead of moving to the next one, she gave him

a quick, naughty little smile, and bent down to press her mouth against the patch of skin on his chest that she'd just revealed. Her hair was soft against the underside of his chin and her lips were warm. She didn't just stop at a kiss, her tongue moving over him next, followed by the slight graze of her teeth.

He knew he'd brought this sensual torture on himself, that by forcing her to let him go slow while he'd been loving her, he'd given her every reason to toy with him like this.

He could have her on her back again in seconds, could be unzipped and inside her before she could take her next breath. Lord knew the light flick of her tongue against his collarbone had him on the verge of doing just that.

She lifted her head and he saw the desire glittering in her eyes as she said, "You're right," in a husky voice. "Slow can be good, too."

The pleasure on her face at that discovery was the only thing that could have stopped him from rolling her over and taking her in one hard thrust just then, the only reason he had a chance in hell at continuing to lie still to let her have her naughty way with him.

Megan's hands shook as she moved to remove his next button, fumbling altogether when he wrapped his hands around her hips and pulled her harder over his erection. Her eyes closed and she braced herself with her hands splayed out over his chest as her body instinctively rocked into his.

Hadn't he known all along that she'd be pure sensuality? And yet being with her like this, experiencing lovemaking with the most innately, sweetly sexual woman he'd ever known, was like nothing he could have ever imagined.

"That's it, sweetheart," he said in a low voice as he moved his hands around to her breasts and she rode the zipper of his jeans. "Come again for me, just like this."

Her eyes fluttered open then, full of surprise, and he knew she hadn't realized what she was doing.

"But it's your turn now," she protested in a breathy voice that made him even harder behind his zipper, if that was possible.

"Watching you *is* my turn."

Her eyes widened at the thought that he could get as much pleasure from her climax as she did. He thought she was going to try to argue again, but since he could almost taste her next orgasm, he knew she wouldn't be able to go forward without it.

Megan's breasts were so sensitive he knew it wasn't playing fair to gently roll both of her nipples between his thumbs and forefingers, but he didn't care about being fair. All he cared about was her pleasure, watching her eyes darken as she came above him, her skin flushing all over again with heat and pleasure.

Her eyes widened on a gasp as his caress ricocheted through her and she threw her head back and pressed her breasts harder into his hands, her hips moving hard and fast against his. And then her mouth opened on a moan of such satisfaction that his cock twitched hard in his jeans.

"Gabe!"

His name fell from her beautiful mouth as she rode him to the edge and all the way over. Every muscle in her body tensed, shook, then broke apart as she cried out.

God, how he loved the way she came with every cell, every bit of herself.

She didn't hold anything back. She wasn't trying to seduce him, wasn't working at creating a fantasy so that he'd want her.

She was simply giving in to ecstasy, letting it take her over completely.

Megan came back to him slowly, her body continuing to shudder with aftershocks for several long moments. Finally, her eyes opened and she looked down at him, her hair tousled and wild, her mouth plump and red from where she'd bit it as she came apart over him.

"I was supposed to be concentrating on you," she said softly, and he had to pull her down for a kiss to let her know, yet again, that he considered what had just happened to be *concentrating on him.*

"No," she said, sitting up suddenly. Still straddling his hips with her naked thighs, she gave him a look filled with determination. "No more distractions."

He couldn't tell if she was talking to him or herself, but he supposed it didn't really matter. Not when she was reaching for the next button on his shirt, her pretty green eyes narrowed with concentration.

It popped open, and as she went to work on the

next, he had to put his hand over hers and say, "Aren't you forgetting something?" At her cute little frown, he grinned and said, "One button, one orgasm, right?"

She shoved his hands away, but he could tell she wanted to smile as she replied, "I told you, no more distractions. This is going to be all about you."

And as she undid the next button, then slid down his body so that she could torture his chest with her mouth again, Gabe was caught between laughing and losing it.

This was what life with Megan would be like. Full of joy and sexy arguments over who could make who feel better.

He didn't catch his thought about the future— a future he shouldn't even be contemplating with her—until it was almost passed him. But there was no chance to try to figure out where it had come from, or how to shut it down, when he felt her teeth scrape over his nipple.

Gabe was fully at Megan's mercy as she lifted her head and gave him a triumphantly seductive look while her fingers went to finish off the buttons of his shirt. When she was done, she pushed it open and her eyes went wide.

"Oh." She licked her lips. "Wow."

He didn't say anything, just moved her hands to the snap of his jeans.

"I'll get there," she promised, not taking her eyes off his bare chest. "Give a girl time to look first, fireman."

Reaching out, she slowly ran her fingers over his abdominal muscles, tracing the crevices between them. His skin jumped beneath her fingertips, and he couldn't hold back his sound of pleasure at her sweet caresses. And then she was moving her hands up over his pecs, lightly teasing his nipples.

"You're incredible," she murmured, and he knew exactly how she felt, looking up at the goddess above him. "I knew you would be," she admitted softly.

"I knew you would be, too, Megan."

Her eyes rose to meet his again and that was when he felt it: a deep moment of connection that neither of them had wanted to acknowledge…but now could no longer deny.

Sex was easier, so much easier, than losing control of their emotions, so when she yanked her gaze away and turned her focus back to removing his clothes, he didn't stop her.

Still, in the back of his brain he had to wonder how either of them was going to be able to hide from what was happening here tonight. From what had been happening long before clothes had started coming off. Before their day on the mountain. Before their dinner together. Even before the holiday party and that first kiss.

But figuring it all out, deciding what to do with something that was so much bigger than just one night of incredibly hot sex, that was more than just a handful of orgasms, was too much thinking for a stolen night together.

He watched Megan take a deep breath as if steadying herself before pulling his zipper down. His shaft immediately sprang free from the denim, tenting his boxers. Lifting his hips from the bed, he helped her pull his pants off.

Her lower lip moved between her teeth and he was utterly mesmerized by her wide-eyed expression as she lifted the cotton fabric from his erection and slid it off.

What, he wondered wildly, was she going to do now? Every muscle in his body was tight with anticipation as he watched her take him in, her eyes big and so aroused he nearly lost it without another damn touch.

He watched her reach for him as if in slow motion and then her slender fingers were wrapping around him so gently that he couldn't control the urge to push harder into her fist. She tightened her grip, and Gabe knew that if this was as far as they got tonight, it was already the best sex of his life.

He couldn't pull his gaze away from the sight of her hand around his erection, the way she almost reverently worked him, the slow sweep of her thumb over the broad head. Jesus, he already knew the image of this would be forever imprinted in his brain, that it wouldn't take more than just this memory to send him over the edge again and again.

He was so mesmerized by what Megan was doing with her hand that he was a full step behind as she slowly lowered her head down over him. It wasn't until the tips of her soft hair brushed across his thighs that he realized what she was about to do.

Her warm breath found him first, so soft, so seductive, and then—*sweet Jesus, he was never going to make it through this night in one piece*—she was moving her tongue over him, just where her thumb had been.

It shouldn't have been possible for things to get even hotter than her tongue on him, but the soft little sound of appreciation she made took him there in a millisecond. He felt himself begin to lose it against her tongue and—*oh, Lord*—she was right there, covering him, taking him deep into the hot depths of her mouth.

He didn't want to come like this, not their first time together, but he soon realized as his hands found her hair and his hips thrust up into the perfect warmth that surrounded him, he was just about at the end of his control. If he didn't pull out now, he'd have no choice but to give in to the most incredible blow job he'd ever experienced.

On a desperate groan, he pulled from her mouth, the suction of her lips sounding in a little *pop* in the small hotel room.

She looked up at him in surprise as he shifted them on the bed, a sensual goddess, her full lips red from his kisses and the pleasure she'd been giving him.

She lay back and watched him move off the bed to where they'd thrown his pants. "Gabe?"

He answered her by pulling a condom from the back pocket of his jeans. She reached out her hand and said, "Let me," but he was only one touch away from going off, so he quickly ripped open the package and rolled the condom on.

As he came back onto the bed, she automatically spread her legs for him to move between her thighs. He wanted—needed—to be in her, but first he had to kiss her again.

Her arms went around his neck and she kissed him back with so much passion he got lost there, with his mouth against hers, until she shifted her hips and the head of his shaft was seared by the slick heat between her thighs.

He had to pull away then, had to lever up onto his arms to watch their bodies come together. "You're so gorgeous, Megan" was all he could say as he took in her soft curves, her skin damp with sweat from their intense lovemaking.

She moved her hands down over his chest, his abdomen and then behind his hips. "Take me, Gabe." Her eyes fluttered shut as their bodies began to slide into place. "Please love me."

"Watch with me," he urged her in an unsteady voice, and somehow managed to wait until she'd opened her eyes again and turned her gaze to the shockingly beautiful sight of their bodies coming together.

He rewarded her by pushing in another inch and then sliding out before doing it again and again until he was nearly all the way inside her, one slick thrust at a time.

"Oh, God."

In the end it was the sexy sound of those two little words, along with the feel of her heat clasping around him, that had him finally losing his last grasp on control.

His hands moved from the bed to cradle her head, and with his weight on his elbows and forearms, sliding in so deep, so hard, they both groaned at the intense pleasure of it, Gabe made Megan his.

But even as he made love to her, Gabe knew it was the other way around. Megan had already made him hers with her legs wrapped around his waist, her body opening up to his, taking everything he had to give and giving back even more.

Their mouths met again, along with tongues and teeth, as their bodies gave in to what neither of them could keep from happening another second. He wished he could have loved her like this for hours, that he could let this feeling of being so perfectly, so intimately, joined with Megan go on forever, but he'd wanted her too much, for much too long.

Still, for all his loss of control, he wouldn't go over the edge without her.

From the sounds she was making and the rhythmic clasp of her inner muscles around him, he knew she was close. It was pure instinct to slide one hand between their bodies and lift his mouth from hers.

"Come with me, sweetheart."

She held on to him as her green eyes went dark with pleasure. And then her eyelids were falling shut and she was arching up off the bed as her climax hit them both with so much force that it was all Gabe could do just to hold on tight as he exploded inside her.

He forgot to leash his power, forgot how small she was, forgot that he wanted their first time to be slow and gentle. And Megan was right there with him, tugging his head down, bringing his mouth back over hers and kissing him with all the rough passion he was unleashing on her body.

Perfect.

She was perfect.

On the other side of the storm, they panted in each other's arms and he licked across her sweat-dampened shoulder. Rolling over with her in his arms, she laid her head in the crook of his shoulder, wrapped her arms around him, and, almost instantly, he felt her muscles go lax as she fell asleep.

Thirteen

Morning had always been Megan's favorite time of day. When she used to go into an office, rather than working from home, she had been the annoyingly cheerful person on Monday morning. But waking up in bed with a warm male body wrapped around her was a whole different kind of good morning.

Last night when she'd given in to her desire, she'd known that they could only have one wild night. But even though the first rays of light were starting to peek in through the curtains, it was still dark enough in the room that she could let herself pretend they were still in the midst of their forbidden night together. So when Gabe stirred against her, his erection hot and hard against her bottom, she refused to let herself come fully awake.

Megan had never been a vixen, had never been the kind of woman who would wake a man up in the middle of the night to have him one more time… but nothing that had happened with Gabe so far had fallen under the "normal" category. And until the day really and truly began, weren't all rules still off? Including the ones that said she shouldn't slowly turn in his arms and press a kiss to his chin?

Her heart was beating hard enough that she was certain if he were awake, he would feel it beating through from her skin to his.

When Gabe didn't stir at her soft kiss, she wondered if she'd imagined him pulling her closer into his hips a few seconds earlier. Had he just been moving in his sleep? And, if so, was she bold enough to make the first move like this? To take what she wanted, what she needed, one more time before shutting down those desires forever?

She pressed her mouth a little lower, just below his chin, against the dark bristle of stubble right where his pulse throbbed against his skin. She tasted that pulse with the tip of her tongue, then had to follow that up with several more little licks at his collarbone and then over the shoulder that was raised up off the bed where his arm was curving over her.

Each soft kiss, each stroke of her tongue against his warmth, made her bolder.

Last night there'd been too many sensations to hold on to. The sheer shock of being intimate with Gabe had been more than enough for her to deal with and she hadn't been able to explore him nearly enough. Now, she took that chance, and as she slid her hand up to press against the muscles of his chest, she shifted away just enough to see how small her splayed fingers looked across his broad chest.

She'd often heard woman giggle about firefighters, dreaming about what they wanted to do with them. But Megan had gotten married so young she hadn't really ever had time to build up those kinds of fantasies. And then after David had died, she hadn't let herself think about firefighters or cops or SEALs like that.

Oh, but if she had, she thought with a small smile of pleasure that she didn't bother to contain while Gabe still slept, she would have been dreaming of a man just like this. Big and beautiful and utterly committed to wringing every ounce of pleasure from her.

Pleasure that was only growing with every moment she stole in his arms as her hands roved gently lower.

Megan was so lost to the glory of her explorations of Gabe's body that she was caught utterly unaware as he suddenly shifted and rolled her onto her back. She lost her breath as he came over her, one of his strong thighs between hers, his eyes clear and perfectly awake as he stared down at her.

"You were awake the whole time," she accused when she could get her voice back.

"I am now," he said, and then his mouth was over her breasts and he was using his big hands to push them together so he could lave both nipples at once.

She could feel his erection hard and throbbing against her thigh, knew he had to feel how wet, how ready, she was. She'd never woken up like this, ravished before breakfast by a man who completely stole not only her breath away but also every rational thought she'd ever had. All that remained between them was the slow move of skin against skin, the caress of each other's hands against sensitive flesh and the press of their mouths against whatever they could reach, whatever they could taste.

Megan wanted this final lovemaking to go on forever. She wanted to make sure that she could remember every touch, every moan of desire, every gasp of pleasure for later, when she was alone again. But everything they'd done in the dark, the slow seduction, the naughty risk of doing what he'd asked her to do, only fueled her need for more. As if they were of like mind, in unison, they shifted so that both of her thighs were around his. But then, just when she thought he was going to take her, brand her as his, he was moving them both so that he was on the bottom.

Moments later, she was sitting up on top of him, high enough out of the covers that she could see the sunlight streaming in earnest, the night before nothing but a distant memory.

She shut her eyes tight, not wanting the real world to intrude on her fantasy come to life. Just a few more minutes. That's all she was asking for.

Fortunately, she didn't need her eyes to be open to shift into place over Gabe's erection, which was the only possible thing she could wrap her brain around at present.

She was almost there, could almost feel his heat coming into her so perfectly, when she heard, "Megan."

Very reluctantly, she opened her eyes and looked down at him.

His blue eyes were intense, full of arousal, and something else she couldn't quite figure out. Or maybe it was that she didn't want to figure it out.

Not when she was still trying to pretend.

"Are you protected?"

Her brain couldn't quite process his question at first, it had been so long since she'd thought about things like protection against sexually transmitted diseases.

Or pregnancy.

When the words finally pierced the haze of lust fogging up her brain, she would have shot up off his lap, but his hands were firm around her waist, keeping her right where she was.

"No." The one word sounded overly loud in the hotel room.

What was she doing?

But before she could answer that question, Gabe was reaching over to the side table and picking up a condom she hadn't seen him put there the night before.

She knew, now, that she should stop him from putting it on. And that last night was an aberration they definitely shouldn't repeat.

Of course, she also knew that if he opened up that condom wrapper and slid it over his erection, she wouldn't have a prayer of stopping herself from continuing what they'd started. What *she'd* started.

Because she'd been unable to help herself.

And yet, the tearing of the wrapper never came. Because Gabe was holding it out for her. As if he wanted her to make the choice about making love again.

Her words from the night before came back at her then.

Please love me.

Megan closed her eyes at her weakness, at the way she'd begged Gabe for something so much bigger than just physical pleasure. That was how dangerous being with him was. It was long past time to steel herself to do what she'd told herself she would do come morning, and get out of the bed. But her heart felt like it was being torn in two as she tried to climb off his lap.

The hotel was almost perfectly silent in the early morning, but she swore she could hear the clinking of the prison bars, one after the other, settling into place around her heart, first, and then her body.

Boom!

Megan knew she was being crazy, that she had to be overtired from too much exercise—and sex!— and not enough sleep.

Boom!

Her heart was already trapped, but as another thick bar came down—*Boom!*—instead of letting them continue to fall around her, she took crazy to a whole other place…and lunged back at Gabe.

She grabbed the condom from his hand and ripped it open so fast the latex circle fell onto the bed as she held the two pieces of wrapper in each of her hands.

Boom!

She dived for the condom and scrambled back up

over him, her hands shaking as she lifted the condom over his shaft. But just when she thought nothing could break her panic, his hands covered hers.

Warm. He was so warm.

She lifted her eyes to his and realized she was panting.

"Megan?"

She suddenly saw herself through his eyes, the way one night of incredible sex had turned her completely inside out. He should have been running away from her as fast as he could.

But, for some reason she couldn't understand, he wasn't doing that.

And somehow, when she was looking into his eyes and she could feel him warm and solid beneath her, those bars stopped slamming down around her. As if he could read her mind and knew exactly what she wanted, but was unable to ask for, he slid his hands all the way up her arms, past her shoulders, to cup her face in his palms.

"Come here, sweetheart."

She leaned down over him then, and as their mouths met so gently she felt something shatter inside her chest. Those bars around her heart were all knocking into one another as she gave in one last time to something so sweet she couldn't stop herself from going back for more, couldn't keep her hips from sliding up, then up some more until she was levered over him, her hips directly over his.

Megan took Gabe inside her on a gasp of pure joy. And there was no denying that making love with him again felt incredible, no way to stop her arms from going around his neck to pull him closer, or her legs from wrapping around his hips as they rolled back over so that his wonderfully heavy weight was pushing her back into the bed.

But even as her body hurtled toward an inevitable climax, even as she lifted her hips up to be closer to his, even as his mouth came down over the tip of one breast and she arched into the heat of his tongue—and especially as she tried to keep what was happening in a "just hot sex" box—there was no way on earth that Megan could deny that being with him this morning was different.

Bigger.

And so much scarier.

Too scary to go there alone.

"Please," she gasped out.

Gabe lifted his eyes to hers as he stilled. "Anything," he told her, his voice as raw as hers.

But he couldn't give her *anything*. He couldn't become a man who went to a safe office every day and promised to come home in one piece every night.

And she could never ask him for that.

All she could ask for was this moment, this pleasure.

"Gabe." She lifted one hand to his cheek, cradled him there as her whole world came down to this man, this one moment, this desire that demanded to be sated. They wouldn't get any more moments like this. All they had was now, these final moments of sweet perfection. "I need you here with me."

"I need to be there, too."

His words were as good as a caress, enough to push her to the precipice of pleasure so intense she couldn't even imagine what was on the other side.

For the first—and last—time, Megan opened herself up completely to Gabe, pushed down every wall, shoved apart every prison bar and let him in, so deep that as he slowly slid into her, as he filled all of the empty places she hadn't even realized were there, she could have sworn he touched her soul.

Again and again he rocked over her, around her, inside her, his arms strong, his heartbeat steady, his kisses sweet and demanding all at the same time as they climaxed together.

No one has ever loved me like this, was her last thought before the prison bars started falling back into place, crashing down in a circle all around her heart.

Fourteen

Plain and simple, Megan blew Gabe's mind. To the point where, even though he knew he must be crushing her, he couldn't manage to move a muscle from where he lay, sprawled over her, breathing heavily into the damp crook of her neck.

She was breathing just as hard, and he wasn't surprised, given that their lovemaking had been at least as physical as anything he'd done even as a firefighter.

Gabe thrived on putting out fires. His job was his calling, and every day he went to work with a deep level of satisfaction over the life he'd chosen. But no triumph over fire had ever left him feeling this elated.

Which was why, no matter how many times he'd tried to hold on to the idea of one night—and only one night—with Megan, his brain hadn't been able to pull it off.

He hadn't forgotten what they'd agreed on in her

apartment, but that didn't mean he could discount what had just happened here between them, either.

Slowly lifting himself up off her sweet, soft curves, he looked down into her eyes, still fuzzy from the aftereffects of her climax. He smiled at her, the beautiful woman he couldn't get enough of, and said, "Good morning."

Two short words were all the time it took for Megan to go from pliable and loose and warm to rigid and tense and cold.

The caveman inside him wanted to keep her pinned there beneath him on the bed. Instead, he forced himself to let her scoot away from him.

She reached for the first piece of clothing she could find. He wasn't sure she realized that she'd grabbed his shirt, that she was wrapping herself up in him. The only thing he was sure of was the fact that Megan was desperate to get away from him.

In the decade that Gabe had been taking women to bed, they had only ever tried to get closer to him. They'd tried to find ways to spend more time with him. They'd worked to seduce him. A couple had even hoped for a ring.

But none had ever tried to get away from him.

Until now.

When Megan had made it to the far corner of the room, her back up against the wall, clutching his shirt tightly closed around her, she finally stopped and stared at him with big, alarmed eyes.

"That can never happen again." She shook her head, the hair he'd had his fingers buried in just seconds ago falling over her shoulders like crumpled silk. *"Never."*

Gabe got off the bed and pulled on his boxers to give himself time to think before replying. Back in her apartment their discussion about staying away from each other made sense. Perfect sense.

But now...well, there sure as hell wasn't anything *perfect* about keeping their distance anymore.

After his jeans were back on, he turned to the beautiful woman watching him so warily and said, *"Never*'s an awfully long time. Especially after—" He gestured to the bed. "Seems to me instead of saying *never* we should be discussing things."

The shock on her face was better than that wary fear. "What's there to discuss, Gabe?"

He wasn't at all pleased to note that his name on her lips was no longer the almost-prayer it had been when she was coming beneath him. "Seems like there's plenty, Megan."

She all but flinched at the way he said her name, still a caress, as if they were still in bed together, rather than standing at opposite ends of the room throwing the word *never* around.

"No," she said, her hands clutching even tighter at his shirt, "just because we—" This time she was the one looking at the bed. "Nothing has changed."

"Everything has changed." He didn't want to have to push her like this, but he sure as hell didn't like the way she was pushing him.

"Yes. Okay. Fine." Each of the words was clipped

as they fell from her kiss-swollen lips. "We had sex. And it was great, but—"

"More than great."

"You win," she replied in a hard voice, as if they were on opposite sides of a war, rather than in this together trying to figure out where to go from here. "It was more than great, but it doesn't change anything. You're still you and I'm still me. Which means that it can never, ever happen again."

All she wanted was for him to agree. He could see that. And he'd promised her *anything,* just minutes ago when they were making love.

But how the hell could he agree to *never?*

"Tell me about her," she suddenly asked. "About the victim you saved. The one you dated that it didn't work out with. What was her name? What did she do for a living? What color was her hair?"

His knew what she was doing: she was forcibly trying to remind him of his reasons to walk away from her. Probably before she reminded him of hers—of the husband who'd died in his dangerous job and left her and her daughter all alone.

"Kate. Teacher. Dark."

Gabe watched her carefully as he answered her questions. For all that she was saying she wanted him out of her life, there was no doubt in his mind that she hated putting together a mental picture of his ex. Just as much as he hated to think of her in Summer's father's arms, more stupidly jealous of a dead man than ever now that he knew just how much warmth, how much passion, how much sweetness, Megan had to give.

"What happened? How did you save her?"

"It was an apartment fire."

"Like mine?"

He shook his head. "No. Not nearly as bad as yours." But Kate had been crying, shaking, so scared that he'd pulled her into his arms and hadn't let go of her until the ambulance arrived.

"How did you start dating?"

He didn't want to tell her the truth. But his mother hadn't raised him to be a liar. "She came by the station. To thank me."

Megan flushed. "Of course she did. I should have guessed."

"She was nothing like you."

"Right," she said in that same clipped voice, so at odds with its husky warmth when she was pleading with him to make love to her. "Strange how similar it all seems, though." Her eyes were overly bright as she looked back at him. "Did she have a child, too?"

"No. She was young. Only twenty. Still in college."

"Was she pretty?" She held up her hand. "No. Don't answer that. Of course she was pretty." She took a deep breath. "So, what happened?"

"We broke up."

Just like that, the strong woman moved back to the forefront. "You told me, and I quote, 'It never works out.' Why not?"

"She was young. We both were."

"Sure," she said, "I believe that. But I'm pretty sure this whole firefighter–victim thing is bigger than just you and Kate and how young you were." She looked like she'd tasted something rotten as she said his ex's name. "Tell me exactly why being with someone you've saved is such a bad situation. I want to hear why it never works out."

Damn it, this was the problem with smart women. They knew how to box a guy into a corner.

"Do you know why I'm a firefighter?"

"I'm sure it's because you love to help people." She paused a beat, then lifted her chin in a clear challenge. "And you love the thrill of danger, too."

"Most people, once they learn what I do for a living, that's all they see. The firefighter." Damn it, he didn't want to tell her this, not when he knew exactly what she was planning to do with the information. "When that moment where their life is on the line is the first time you meet someone—"

"It's all they ever see."

He wasn't at all surprised that she understood. "Right. But no one can be a hero 24/7."

"Of course you can't."

He should have known she'd see too much, that she'd hear all the things he wasn't saying. Because even though she wanted him to just go away, she was watching him carefully as they spoke about his ex.

"There's more to the story, isn't there?"

Shit. He didn't want to tell her this, didn't ever like to talk about it. Even his family didn't know how bad things had gotten with Kate. Only his brother Zach, who had been with him when they'd found her.

"She didn't take the breakup well."

Megan's eyes widened and for a moment he thought she was going to come over to him. Instead, she simply asked, "What happened, Gabe?"

He swallowed, those horrible minutes when he'd found Kate bleeding in his house coming back to him as if five minutes instead of five years had passed.

"She said she couldn't live without me. That I was the only reason she was still alive. I found her in my apartment just in time. She had cut herself. Her wrists. She was bleeding." He swallowed hard, seeing it all over again. "It wasn't pretty...and I wish every day that it hadn't come to that for her, that somehow I would have known what she was thinking of doing and been able to stop her." The breath he took shook through him. "Fortunately, she got help after that, but I still wish I could rewind time so that we never went on that first date, and she never thought I felt more for her than I did."

"Gabe." Megan's voice was hollow around his name. "My God, how could she have done that to you?"

How, Gabe had to wonder, had he ever compared this strong, magnificent woman standing before him to the girl he'd stupidly dated half a decade ago?

"You're nothing like her, Megan," he told her, believing it more every time he said it. "You're strong. She wasn't. You're not looking for anyone to take care of you. I think—" he paused, weighing his words carefully before saying them "—that was all she ever wanted from me."

"I'm sorry, Gabe, so sorry you had to go through that." She shook her head. "No wonder you've got that rule about fire victims. It makes perfect sense." She blinked at him. "I'd have the same rule. And I wouldn't break it. Not for anyone."

"Megan," he began, even though he wasn't sure exactly what he was going to say to her. All he knew was that she had to stop painting everything so black and white.

She moved one hand from his shirt to hold it up in a classic stop position.

"The fact remains that you saved my life. And my daughter's. I'll never be able to forget what you did for us. You're right that I would never do anything like that to you, but how am I supposed to stop seeing you as a hero for what you did?" He hadn't made a move toward her, so she dropped her hand. "You'll always be the larger-than-life firefighter who risked his life for me, Gabe."

Damn it. Everything she said was making sense, but all those moments when they hadn't been talking had made sense, too. So much sense that he still couldn't quite wrap his brain around the magnitude of the fireworks that had lit and exploded between them.

"You deserve to be with a woman who sees you for everything you are." She swallowed hard. "And I deserve a long life with a man who isn't bound and tied to chasing danger. I can't go through what

I went through with David. I just can't. Please," she said softly, "don't make this harder on both of us than it needs to be. We shared one incredible night." She looked out toward the window. "Part of a morning, too, and that's going to have to be enough." She turned back to him. "I need to check out of my room and go pick up Summer soon."

"You're leaving this morning?"

"Yes. As soon as I get Summer."

"Do I get to say goodbye?"

"Goodbye," she said, purposely misunderstanding him.

Gabe had heard the word *heartbroken* many times, but he'd never understood it until today.

Thinking of the rest of the week in Lake Tahoe without Megan and Summer made his chest feel as if it was cracking open, right down the center.

"Summer will wonder what happened."

"You're bigger than that," she told him in a soft voice. "Please don't use my daughter to try to get me to change my mind about us."

Was he really bigger than that?

What rules would he break for the chance to be with this woman?

His?

Hers?

All of them?

Suddenly, she seemed to realize that she was wearing his shirt. A small sound of dismay came from her lips as she pulled it tighter around her. "You need your shirt."

Gabe knew he should tell her he didn't need the shirt to make his way back to his room. Barring that, he should turn and let her strip it off in private.

But for all the times he'd been called a hero, right now he was just a man.

And if he was being kicked out of her life, if *never* was all that he had to look forward to, he wanted one last look at her. One final chance to imprint the most beautiful woman he'd ever known into his memory.

"Yes, if I'm leaving, I guess I do."

She blinked at him, a doe caught in the headlights. "I didn't realize I'd grabbed it." She was biting her lip and flushing at the thought of being naked in front of him again. As if she didn't want him to think she'd purposely put on his shirt because she wanted a part of him around her, she added, "It was the closest thing to the bed."

A half dozen thoughts shot through his brain at once.

He wanted to pull her into him, take her back to bed and remind her how good they were together.

He wanted to tell her he didn't have any of this figured out, either, that it didn't make any more sense to him than it made to her, but he didn't care.

He wanted to bring her dead husband back, wanted to erase the ghost from her life so that he could at least be on a level playing field with the man.

He even wished he could become someone who liked suits and cubicles and computers for her.

But, as Megan started to come toward him, he couldn't do any of those things. All he could do was watch her, drink her in, memorize every line and contour on her beautiful face. Her eyes were too bright, but her shoulders were back and her chin was still up as she moved out of the corner.

From the first moment he'd seen her, he'd known how brave she was. Nothing had changed between then and now, nothing but the knowledge of how soft, how giving, how sweet, she was, in addition to all that bravery. All that strength.

She opened the shirt and let it fall from her shoulders. Her mouth was open slightly, her eyes big, her skin flushed.

Sparks jumped between them and he knew all the *nevers* in the world couldn't make their perfect chemistry any less.

Completely naked again, she gathered up his shirt in one hand and held it out to him. "Here."

He took the shirt from her, their fingertips touching as they made the transfer. He waited for her to turn, to gather up her clothes from the floor, to cover herself with something, anything.

Instead, she stood there naked before him.

"Never," he said softly, needing to reclaim that word and turn it around. "I've never seen anyone as beautiful as you."

She put both of her hands over her heart as if she were trying to hold it inside. "Please."

One word had never held so many potential meanings, but Gabe knew the room was in danger of backdraft if he stayed to try to figure out which *please* this was—the one that was begging him to stay...or begging him to go.

He'd learned early on in his firefighting career when to go deeper into the flames, and when to retreat to reassess.

Now, Gabe forced himself to put his shirt on, walk to the door, open it and leave the room.

But he refused to say goodbye.

She had done the right thing.

The smart thing.

The only thing she could do in good conscience as the mother of a little girl who had already lost one man who was important to her.

But none of those truths made watching Gabe leave hurt any less.

Especially since she also knew she'd done the stupidest possible thing by sleeping with him in the first place...by becoming just like all those other firehouse girls who lived for the chance to share a bed with a firefighter.

Megan didn't know how long she stood in the middle of her hotel room, naked, lost.

Empty.

The sound of a shower going on in the room upstairs jarred her back to life.

Her fantasy night was over. Fantasies, she told herself, were like dessert. Delicious, but you couldn't eat chocolate and whipped cream for every single meal without getting really sick.

Finally, she lifted her hands from her chest and

ran them through her hair. It was time to get back to her real life, a life she loved, with a seven-year-old who kept her on her toes. As she stepped into the shower, Megan told herself that everything would go back to normal now and she'd be fine.

More important, now that she'd made the very difficult decision to stay away from Gabe, her heart—and Summer's, too—would remain safe from harm.

An hour later she was standing at Julie's cabin, ringing the doorbell, shivering in the cold.

"Megan, good morning! Perfect timing. Come on in and have breakfast with us."

She pasted a smile on her lips. "Thank you." She wouldn't be able to eat a single bite, she already knew that. She stepped inside the warm cabin, but even though she was no longer standing in the snow, she still felt ice-cold.

It wasn't until she found Summer hanging from the ladder that went up to the loft like a little monkey—"Hey, Mommy! I had the best time ever last night!"—that Megan's heart finally expanded back to the right size.

This time it was a little easier to tell herself that she'd done the right thing…and that the two of them were going to be just fine.

Without Gabe Sullivan in their lives.

Fifteen

Gabe's days passed one after the other in a snowy blur as he drove his body to the limits of its endurance. Even the miniblizzard that had had everyone tucked warm and dry into the lodge at the base of the mountain hadn't stopped him from going out. But no matter how hard he pushed himself, he hadn't been able to stop thinking about how unwavering Megan had been about the two of them not seeing each other again.

The women he slept with always wanted to talk about things, always wanted to try to prolong their relationship.

Not Megan.

Sure, at first he'd been committed to steering clear of her. Yes, he'd thought dating her was the path to the dark side. But that was before he got to know her, before he realized she was nothing like Kate...and before he tasted Megan's sweet lips as their bodies came together in a long, sweet burst of the purest pleasure he'd ever known.

Only, somehow, in the morning he'd been the only one rethinking their "agreement."

All Megan could say was *never* and *no*.

Gabe had rarely heard the word *no* in his life. Especially not from women. Didn't she realize what throwing down a gauntlet like that did to a guy like him? That she might as well have issued him a direct challenge?

"How's the powder been?"

For the first time in two days, the sky was clear blue and the sun was shining. Zach had decided to come up to his ski condo and the two of them had agreed on some ice fishing for the afternoon.

"Good."

They didn't say anything more during the short drive to the iced-over pond. It was one of the nice things about hanging out with his brothers: they didn't always need to talk. Plus, when one of them was feeling grouchy, the other usually knew just how hard to poke...and when to back off before he got a fist to the jaw.

Each grabbing a folding chair, pole and tackle box out of the truck bed, they headed out onto the ice. They cut open two holes in the ice and sat down in front of them, their lines hanging in the freezing water.

For the first time in days, Gabe stopped to appreciate the silence. He'd always liked the mountains during winter, even navigating the sometimes rough conditions. Although, he couldn't stop himself from thinking, he'd much rather be here with a seven-year-old who couldn't stop talking…and her gorgeous mommy.

"How is she?"

When had self-obsessed Zach turned into a mind reader?

Gabe hadn't forgotten the way Zach had flirted with Megan at the holiday party or that he'd gone over to her house to change her tire.

"None of your goddamned business."

Zach looked amused as he sat back deeper in his cloth chair as only a brother would when knowing he was getting under his sibling's skin. "You don't know, do you?" Shaking his head, his brother said, "Never even got into her pants, did you, before she kicked you to the curb?"

Gabe sprang from his seat so fast, he had surprise in his corner as he knocked Zach off his chair and onto the ice. The sound of his brother's skull hitting the ice was the best thing he'd experienced in days.

"Talk about her like that again and I'm going to tear you apart," he promised in a menacing voice.

Zach was in great shape, but Gabe's career meant he had twenty pounds of muscle on him.

"Uncle."

When Gabe climbed off him and got back into his chair, Zach groaned and said, "You're all losing your minds. First Chase got engaged. And then Marcus got serious with Nicola and is practically living on the road with her while she's touring. I should have figured you'd be next."

"Stay away from Megan," Gabe warned. "She is off-limits."

Zach slowly sat up and grinned. "I knew it," he said, "as soon as I saw the two of you at Mom's party. And I can't blame you. She's one seriously hot mama."

Gabe knew his brother had started with one broken-down old car and turned Sullivan Autos into a megabucks business, but continuing to talk about Megan made him the dumbest person on the planet.

"I warned you." Gabe cracked his knuckles menacingly and pretended to prepare to mess up Zach's face.

His brother held up his hands again. "A joke! It was a joke." Zach shot him a serious look. "Swear to God, I didn't think you'd go there again with a fire victim. Not after what happened with what's-her-name."

Here he'd thought Megan's dead husband was the only ghost between them. Now, suddenly, he realized Kate's was, too, just as much.

Zach kept talking, saying, "When Marcus was going through all of his crap with Nicola a few months ago, I thought the rest of us agreed on the score. That it's better to keep things easy. Casual. Fun. Especially you, after what happened that time with that girl who tried to kill herself in your house."

Zach looked as earnest as he got and Gabe knew he believed what he was spouting wholeheartedly. And he was also right that a few weeks ago Gabe would have been right there with him.

Now, Gabe told his brother, "Megan's different."

"Another one bites the dust." Looking disgusted, Zach made the sound of a plane falling from the sky and crashing hard.

Gabe stared at his brother, but he didn't see him.

Was that how Megan's husband had died? Who had told her? When? How?

And how had she told Summer? Gabe needed to know more about her. Not just about her husband's death, but what she ate for breakfast. Did she like to hike or was she more of a biker? Did she have any siblings? Where did her parents live, and did she have a good relationship with them?

Yes, Megan had kicked him out of her room that morning, but he was equally to blame for their breakdown of communication. Because just as he'd barely been able to see her through the haze of thick smoke when he'd found her in her apartment two months ago, even though he'd been with her several times since, he hadn't wanted to let himself see her for who she really was. Instead, he'd told himself it was smarter to force himself to look at her through the thick haze of smoke created by his ex's crazy behavior.

He hadn't been able to forget what Megan had said when they'd been making love in her hotel bed. *Please love me.* Were they simply heat-of-the-moment words…or were they strong enough words, from a deep enough place, to finally start cutting through the dark, heavy smoke that lingered from his past?

And hers, too.

Gabe closed up his chair, grabbed his pole and tackle box and headed back to his truck. "Time to go."

"But we just got here! Why are we leaving already?"

Gabe revved the engine and Zach had to scramble after him to throw himself and his fishing gear into the truck right before it skidded out across the snowy terrain.

As his brother muttered beside him about love making people crazy, Gabe went through what he knew so far. Megan had drawn her line in the ice and she didn't plan on budging. And he'd understood where she was coming from—had been right there with her, in fact.

But that was when Gabe hadn't planned on skating over the line he had drawn, too.

Not until he'd just realized—with some help from a brother who turned out to be a hell of a lot more perceptive than he looked—that the ice was always shifting.

No one had ever told Gabe to just go away like she had. And sure, his pride was involved. So yes, he couldn't deny that getting Megan to come around was a challenge. But although he thrived on challenges, lived for facing down untenable situations that other people would go out of their way to avoid, Megan was far more than a challenge.

She was a flesh-and-blood woman that he not

only desired, but also that he admired…and liked a great deal.

More than he'd ever liked anyone before.

Liked her so much, in fact, that Zach was probably right on the money and *like* might already be starting to head toward something a whole lot bigger than that.

They skidded around an icy corner so fast his brother cursed loudly as he grabbed on to the door to keep from slamming his head into the window.

Feeling alive again for the first time since he'd walked out of Megan's hotel room four days ago, Gabe just grinned.

He already knew with utter certainty that Megan wasn't even close to being like Kate.

Now all he had to do was find a way to convince her that he wasn't at all like her ghost husband.

It was time to fight fire with fire.

His grin widened at the firefighting cliché as he slammed on the brakes in front of Zach's cabin and all but shoved his brother out into the snow.

Gabe already missed Megan and Summer like crazy…which meant that it was long past time to put his brand-new plan into action.

Sixteen

Megan was beyond glad Gabe hadn't called her. For a while there in her hotel room, when he was saying they should "discuss" things, she'd actually thought he wanted more than just one night of sex with her. That he'd wanted a relationship.

He must have come to his senses after the memories of the hot sex had worn off.

A guy like him was probably used to tons of hot sex, she figured. Unlike her. Because even though she had been smart and put a stop to ever doing that—or *him*—again, she couldn't stop replaying their lovemaking in her head. Over and over. Not just at night when she was safely under her covers, either, but throughout the day her mind kept drifting to Gabe and his mouth and his hands and his—

"Mommy, are you listening to me?"

She looked into her daughter's big green eyes, which were filled with irritation at the lack of attention she was getting. "Sorry, honey. Do you need help choosing what else to pack? Do you have enough jeans and long sleeves just in case it's cold in L.A.?"

Just as they did every New Year's, her parents were taking Summer to Disneyland for a few days. Megan would have gone with them—roller coasters were just about the only scary thing she let herself do anymore because she knew they were regularly safety tested by on-staff engineers—but she was still behind with a couple of her clients after dealing with the fire and moving and resettling into their new apartment. A few days to herself where she could work every minute that she wasn't sleeping was precisely what she needed to get back on track so that she could start the new year on steady footing.

Yet again, she gave silent thanks that Gabe hadn't come after her. A clean slate was exactly what she needed with her job and her love life.

Not, of course, that love had anything to do with what had happened between them. It had just been hot sex, she reminded herself sternly.

"I was wondering about Daddy."

Megan's careering thoughts all centered back down on her daughter again. She smiled and pulled her little girl onto her lap on the bed.

"What do you want to know?" When Summer didn't answer right away, Megan said, "He loved to blow kisses right here on your tummy."

She grabbed Summer and kissed her before she could squirm away, laughing.

"I know that," Summer said, "but was he big and strong?"

Megan stopped and blinked at her. "You know what he looked like. Yes, he was big and strong." They often went through old photo albums together, so this wasn't news.

"Do you think he'd have taught me to snowboard, like Gabe did?"

Megan had to work like crazy to keep her expression normal. She wasn't the only one comparing Gabe to David.

"Of course he would have. And he would have been just as proud of how quickly you picked it up as we were." She caught her slip too late, realized she shouldn't have said *we,* that she should simply have said how proud *she* was of Summer.

She watched her daughter chew on that information for a few seconds. "Do you think Grams and Gramps will let me ride Tower of Terror this year?"

Megan should have been used to the way seven-year-old brains jumped from one subject to another, but it took her a beat longer than it should have to respond. "I'm sure you'll find a way to convince them." She got up off her daughter's bed and murmured, "I'm going to go make sure their plane is on time." Megan needed a little alone time to process the strength of the relationship that had already formed between her daughter and the firefighter she'd shoved all the way out of their lives just a few days earlier.

Before she'd even left the room, Summer was back in her small closet, pulling out clothes and shoving them into her already overstuffed suitcase.

* * *

They met her parents at San Francisco International Airport an hour later, and as she hugged her mother and father, she suddenly wished she had decided to chuck in her work for a few more days so that she could lose herself in the magic of Disney with her family.

But, yet again, she was too busy being smart to let herself have any fun, wasn't she?

"You look lovely, honey." Her mother held her at arm's length and studied her carefully before they started to walk over to the on-site Italian restaurant where they had planned to have lunch before the three of them got on their plane to Los Angeles. "Have you met someone?"

She could read the hope in her mother's eyes, knew that while she hadn't been happy about how young Megan had married, she'd also thought her daughter was far too young to be living alone. Her mother wanted another husband for her, a father for Summer, and more grandchildren. Preferably back in their Minneapolis suburb, where she could watch over them all.

"No."

She felt her mother's eyes on her, too shrewd, and braced herself for more questions, but Summer jumped in first.

"Did Mommy tell you we learned to snowboard last weekend? It was awesome!"

Megan forced herself to smile. "Well, it was awesome for Summer, at least. I'm going to be sticking with skis from here on out."

"Gabe said you just needed to practice some more," Summer said, before dragging her grandfather off to show him a stuffed animal she was coveting in one of the airport stores.

Her mother raised an eyebrow. "Who's Gabe?"

Megan answered the question as directly as she could. "He's the firefighter who got me and Summer out of the building."

Her mother's other eyebrow moved up to join the first and then she grabbed Megan's hands and closed her eyes for a moment as if she were reliving the terror of finding out she'd almost lost them both. When her mother opened them again, they were glassy with unshed tears. "I love that firefighter. With all my heart."

"Mom! You don't even know him."

At her outburst, a dozen strangers turned to look at them.

"I know everything that matters. He saved my babies."

God, this was just what he'd been talking about, the way people only saw him as a firefighter…and not as the man he was outside of his job.

Wonderful. Charming. Caring. Funny. Not to mention the best lover who ever lived.

Her mother knocked into her musings with, "So you went snowboarding with him?"

"No," she said first, before admitting, "Yes, but it was an accident." Summer's laughter had her looking over at her daughter. "Summer did a little bit of scheming to make it happen."

Her mother smiled. "That's my smart little grand-daughter."

"I'm not—" She paused, changed it to, "We're not seeing him anymore."

That eyebrow went back up. "Why not? Is he unattractive?"

Megan could feel herself flushing. "No."

"Mean?"

She frowned. "No. Of course not."

"Ah, so he doesn't like children?"

"Are you kidding? He loves them." She only realized what she'd said after the words were already out. "Look," she said to her mother, "it's complicated. We're just not right for each other."

Her mother studied her carefully, again. "Honey, I know we haven't always seen eye to eye on everything, but can I just give you one piece of advice?"

Megan tried not to groan. "Go ahead."

"I know it was hard to lose David, especially so suddenly, but you were more than strong enough to deal with that. Strong enough to repeatedly ignore my urgings to come back home."

Megan was about to open her mouth to tell her—yet again—that San Francisco was her home.

"I know, honey. You are home." Her mother gave her a sad smile that said while she wasn't happy about that fact, she'd at least finally accepted it. "I've never seen you look like this. Not even when you were with David."

Guilt washed through Megan and her mother must have seen it because she grabbed her arm.

"Summer's father was a nice man, but he wasn't the only nice man out there. He's gone, Megan. Don't you think it's time to move on? Don't you think it's time to let yourself risk falling in love again?"

Megan looked up into her mother's serious face. What could she say to her?

Oh, well, Mom, thanks for the heartfelt advice, but after Gabe and I had crazy monkey sex in Lake Tahoe, I told him not to contact me and Summer again.

Thankfully, just then Megan's father returned with Summer showing off her new pink stuffed poodle in its carrying case, and then they were all heading into the restaurant and eating spaghetti and listening to Summer talk.

Seventeen

Timing is everything.

—*Firefighting 101*

Gabe Sullivan would never be a wine connoisseur like Marcus. He'd never be able to take the perfect picture like Chase or throw a baseball one hundred miles an hour like Ryan. And he would never make a movie studio a hundred million dollars over a weekend like Smith regularly did.

But he did know one thing better than almost anyone.

Firefighting.

It was long past time to take those rules he lived and breathed by as a firefighter and apply them to the rest of his life.

Specifically, the woman he hadn't been able to stop thinking about for the past week.

It was December 31. The last day of the year. It had been a good one.

But he was planning for the next year to be a whole heck of a lot better.

Skill—and staying smart—had always been the main tenets of Gabe's success as a firefighter.

But he'd never been stupid enough to discount luck, and that feeling deep in his gut that told him when to keep going—and when to run like hell.

He pulled up outside Megan and Summer's apartment. The sky was clear blue above him, perfect for a night of New Year's Eve fireworks…and for him to deploy the first stage of his plan. He hadn't called ahead to make sure they'd be here, but he had a good feeling about this.

No doubt Megan would try to fight their attraction. He expected that and was prepared to work harder than he ever had at anything to convince her to come around. Gabe knew it wasn't going to be a quick turnaround.

But, he thought with another slow grin as he remembered their oh-so-sweet lovemaking in Lake Tahoe, a little anticipation wasn't necessarily a bad thing.

He took the steps two at a time up to the door into her apartment building, his long strides quickly putting him in front of her place. He was just about to ring her doorbell when the door opened.

Jesus, he thought, just as stunned as he'd been that day she'd come to see him in the hospital, *she's beautiful.*

"Gabe?" She put her hand over her chest as if to try to still her heartbeat. He could see her pulse moving in the gorgeous curve of her neck. "What are you doing here?"

Instead of answering her question, he looked down at the basket of clothes in her hands. "Laundry."

"You need to do laundry?" she asked in a confused voice, and he liked the way he'd stunned her into losing the thread of what she was doing.

As he smiled down at her, thinking how adorable she looked with her ponytail, sweater and jeans, she flushed. "Oh. You mean me? Yes. I need to do laundry."

That was right when she looked down at the basket. When her face flamed even hotter, Gabe followed her gaze to the scrap of pink lace lying on top. She quickly shoved a T-shirt over her panties, but not before Gabe added another goal to his list: to take Megan to bed while she was wearing those pink panties.

She looked back up at him and he had to shove his hands deep into his jeans pockets to keep from pulling her against him and kissing her beautifully soft lips.

"I came to see you and Summer."

She licked her lips, clearly nervous about his unexpected appearance. He loved how strong she was... but he also liked that he could make her nervous.

It was why he'd wanted to surprise her, so that he could gauge her genuine reaction to seeing him again, rather than letting her prepare for the meeting and get all those walls she was so fond of built up.

As he'd learned at the firefighter academy, timing was everything.

"Summer isn't here. She's at Disneyland with her grandparents."

Gabe had planned on including Summer in their plans for the evening, and he would miss the little girl, but he couldn't deny his pleasure at this chance to be alone with Megan again.

"She must be having a great time."

Megan pulled the basket of clothes closer to her, as if they could protect her from whatever his intentions were. "She is. I just got off the phone with her. She met Mickey and Goofy at breakfast this morning. I usually go with them, but I had to work so I couldn't."

Gabe continued to grin at her as the pulse in her neck continued to rock and roll. "You're nervous about seeing me again."

She shook her head too fast. Too hard. "I'm surprised." But she didn't meet his eyes as she said it.

"Surprise."

Her eyes flew to his and he could have sworn she shivered at the husky tone of his voice. But then, a moment later, he watched her still herself and pull her shoulders back.

"We talked about this. In Lake Tahoe."

"No," he reminded her. "We didn't *discuss* anything at all."

"Fine," she said in a short voice. "We can discuss it now. And then you can go."

He was surprised—but not in a bad way—when

she stepped fully into the hall, slammed her door shut behind her and stalked to the stairs. He followed her down to the basement, admiring the angry sway of her hips as she shoved her shoulder against the laundry room door and let it swing back in his face.

It was tempting to laugh, but he was afraid she'd take it the wrong way. He appreciated her spark, knowing he would never be happy with a submissive partner. He'd take her facing off against him a hundred times over having her shrink into his arms as if he alone were responsible for the sun shining.

She yanked open the washing machine, shoved the clothes in, poured what looked like half a bottle of detergent over them, then pushed in her quarters. When the machine started to—loudly—crank to life, she turned to him, her arms crossed over her chest.

"Go ahead. Discuss away."

"You're beautiful, Megan."

Her eyes widened with pleasure at his compliment for a split second before she tamped it down. "I've got work to do."

She went to move past him and Gabe decided he had no choice but to reach for her. He grabbed her hand and pulled her against him. "Give me a chance."

She was stiff against him, but she didn't pull away. "I can't. And you know why."

"No," he told her softly, "I don't." Before she could protest, he said, "You know about my past. I want to know more about yours, Megan."

He could see by the stubborn set of her mouth that

she wasn't happy about being cornered like this, that she didn't think he was playing fair.

But if there was one thing Gabe knew for sure, it was that playing fair never got a firefighter where he wanted to be. But while he wasn't asking her to welcome him in with open arms—not yet, at least—erasing *never* would be a good start.

She yanked her hand away from his. "Fine. I'll tell you what you're clearly dying to know. But not in the laundry room." She took a step back. "After you."

He grinned, knowing she must have figured out how good the view had been on their trip downstairs. Little did she know that her sassy attitude turned him on just as much.

He waited for her to let them into her apartment. Just as he had the first time he'd been there, Gabe immediately felt comfortable in her space.

After all but slamming the door, she sat down hard on the nearest seat. "What do you want to know?"

"How was your week?"

"Fine." A core of politeness she couldn't curb was clearly what made her ask, "Yours?"

"The snow wasn't the same without you and Summer."

Her mouth softened before she could stop it. A moment later, she was sitting back against the seat and rubbing a hand across her eyes. For a split second, Gabe felt guilty about having barged back into her life like this. She looked tired, as if she hadn't been sleeping well.

Neither had he…not since the night she'd slept in his arms.

"Tell me how your husband died, Megan."

"I already have. His plane crashed."

But just as she'd sensed there was more to his story than he'd been telling her, he knew in his gut that she was holding something back. She got up off the couch, her strong shoulders sloping inward. In that moment, even though he'd promised himself he'd go slow, Gabe couldn't stop himself from moving to her, from wrapping his arms around her and tucking her head beneath his chin.

"It's okay, Megan."

She whispered something against his biceps, and as his insides went up in smoke at the feel of her mouth against his skin, he couldn't make out her words for the life of him.

Slowly, he spun her around in his arms and he was surprised by the anger in her eyes.

"No, it isn't okay. He wasn't fighting for our country. He wasn't training for a mission. He was screwing around at the local airfield, taking out a private plane for a joyride in the middle of the night."

Her body was rigid against him and it was pure instinct to rub his hand down her spine.

"They told me his instruments failed and it was too dark for him to land." Her eyes were dark, and still angry, as she said, "Everyone thought he was such a hero and I was just so damn angry at him for being so stupid."

Not stopping the slow stroke of his hand over her

back, her skin vibrating beneath his palm, he agreed, "It was stupid."

His words seemed to bring her back to him, to the realization that she was standing in his arms. She worked to move away from him and he made himself let her go.

"I've never told anyone that."

"Thank you for telling me."

She looked momentarily lost for words…like all the anger had been wrung out of her. "Is that what you wanted to know?"

"Some of it."

She looked confused. "What else?"

"What do you eat for breakfast?"

Her frown was one of surprise, this time, rather than frustration. "Raisin bread. Toasted."

Gabe filed that data away for one day down the road when, hopefully, he'd get the chance to feed her breakfast. "Do you like to hike?"

"Yes. But not hills."

He grinned at the San Francisco girl who didn't like hills. "What about biking?"

"Not much. I'd rather be on foot, or in a boat."

"Do you have siblings?"

Her frown had been replaced by a bemused expression. "No."

"Where did you grow up?"

"A little town just outside Minneapolis. My parents still live there. They're always trying to get me to move back."

Everything in Gabe rebelled against the idea of

losing Megan to a Midwestern town. "You belong here."

She looked faintly irritated at his tone, but she agreed. "That's what I'm always telling them."

"Do you get along with your folks?"

"Yes." She scrunched up her nose. "Except when I don't."

He had to laugh at her honest response. No woman had ever pleased him this much, both in and out of bed.

Her mouth twitched at the corners and he watched her war with herself for a moment before shaking her head as if she were disappointed with her actions. "Are you thirsty? Hungry?"

Something inside Gabe's chest unclenched at her offer. She hadn't agreed to anything yet, but she wasn't kicking him out, either.

"Always," he replied.

The twitching turned into a full-on smile. "Why am I not surprised?"

Did she realize she was flirting with him? He hoped not. Otherwise, she was bound to make herself stop.

"Without Summer here I haven't bothered to go shopping, so there isn't much."

She was just opening the fridge when he asked, "How about I go move your clothes into the dryer while you rustle up something to eat?"

"No," she said quickly, her flush giving away the train of her thoughts, making both of them think about those pink panties again. "I'll run and do it. You just sit tight and I'll be right back."

All of the guys at the station took a meal shift when they were on duty, so although Gabe might not have been the neatest guy in the kitchen, he knew his way around a decent repertoire of meals.

A short while later, he had the makings of a pretty great omelet on the counter. He was just pouring the eggs into the hot skillet when Megan came back inside.

"Gabe?" She looked stunned to see him behind the stove. "You didn't have to cook."

He slid the glass of juice he'd poured over to her. "I enjoy it. Sit." He looked over at her desk in the corner of her small living room, covered with papers and a couple of big, fancy calculators. "Looks like you've been working hard."

She nodded, looking tired again. "Still playing catch-up with a couple of my clients. Fortunately, I'm just about there."

"Good," he said, holding back the rest of what he'd come here to say.

Timing was everything.

He slid the omelet from the skillet onto a plate, buttered the raisin bread that had just popped up from the toaster, grabbed two forks from the top drawer and moved over to the tiny breakfast bar to join her.

"Thank you," she said softly. "I can't remember the last time someone besides Summer cooked for me."

"Her muffins are great."

"They are," she agreed, "but now I'm wondering if I should teach her how to make omelets instead." She looked up at him with an even bigger smile. "The raisin bread is great, too."

Somehow he managed to stop staring at the beautiful woman next to him and push his fork into the eggs. She followed suit, and just as he was finishing his first bite, she made one of those soft little sounds that made him immediately hard.

"Ohmygod," she moaned in one long syllable, "this is so good."

Amazingly, praise from her over something as small as eggs and toast made him feel as good as if he'd single-handedly put out a five-alarm fire.

"I'm glad you think so," he said, and then while he held her captive with his cooking prowess, he decided the timing was finally right. "Got any plans for New Year's Eve tonight?"

She seemed startled for a moment. "Wow, how'd it get to be December 31 already?"

Smiling at her, he said, "I'll take that as a no."

"Yes," she said, and then, "No. I haven't made any plans." Her eyes widened as she realized where he was going with his question. "You're not suggesting that you—" she pointed at him "—and I—" and then at herself "—spend it together?"

"Hey, that's a great idea."

"No, it's a terrible idea."

"Do you like fireworks?"

"That's irrelevant."

"You do, don't you?" he said with a grin. "I'll bet

you love them—the bigger, the better." The way her skin flushed in response was answer enough. "Watch them with me tonight on my roof."

He could feel how tempted she was by his suggestion, but then she said, "I shouldn't."

But both of them knew *shouldn't* was a hell of a long way from *couldn't*.

"But you want to, don't you?"

That gorgeous exasperated look reappeared on her face. "Of course I want to!"

He didn't bother to hold back his grin at that admission. "What if I promise not to kiss you until next year?"

The heat between them flared into full-on flames.

"Nice try," she said. "Next year is only a few hours away."

"I'd have to break my promise if it were anything longer than that." He reached for a tendril of hair that had fallen across her cheek. "And I don't ever want to break a promise to you, Megan."

Eighteen

Megan knew what the right answer was. Just two letters. *N* and *O*. Those were all she needed to string together and then he'd leave.

But after only two lovely days in Lake Tahoe with Gabe—and one truly incredible night—she'd missed him so much.

She'd missed his smile. His warmth. His humor.

She'd even missed that delicious hint of danger that faintly pulsed from him.

And now, like the most wonderful gift in the world, he'd appeared on her doorstep. She'd tried to scare him away by being snippy and unpredictable, but he'd simply grinned his way through it…and then held her while she raged about old hurts.

It had been only fair to tell him the truth about David after he'd told her about Kate. The thing was, she could have just told him the facts and left off the part about how angry she'd been—and, she was surprised to realize, still was—about it. But when he'd put his arms around her, he'd been so solid, so warm, so *there,* that she hadn't been able to stop it all from spilling out.

Just as she hadn't been able to stop herself from making love with him in Lake Tahoe.

So how, she had to wonder as she looked up and found him staring at her, was she going to be able to stop herself from saying, "Yes, I'll go watch fireworks from your roof."

His gorgeous mouth curved up into the biggest smile yet. And, oh, how she loved it when he smiled at her like that.

As though she was the only thing that mattered.

No one but Summer had ever looked at her like that, but as her daughter moved further from those baby years with every passing day, Megan got that look less and less.

They finished the delicious omelet without saying anything more and she was surprised yet again when he took the plate to the sink and washed it clean.

"I could get used to this kind of service," she said without thinking. Which seemed to be her usual M.O. around him.

Gabe's eyes were full of heat as he looked back at her. "Could you?"

She pressed her lips together and tried not to follow suit with her thighs beneath the counter, even though she was feeling *really* hot and bothered. There was no way he could see what she was doing. So then why did it seem like he had as he said, "In some countries it's already a new year, you know."

The rumble of his low voice was almost as much of a caress as his hands would have been across her skin. Worse, she wanted that kiss just as much as he did.

Which was why she pushed off the stool and said, "I'd better go see if the wash is dry."

He put the dish towel back on its hook. "I'll help fold."

So much for her escape.

There was nothing even remotely sexy about the laundry room. And yet, as they headed back into the small basement, sex was the only thing she could think about as she reached into the humid dryer and pulled out the clothes. Blushing at the thought of Gabe folding her underwear, she looked closely for it, but she didn't see it anywhere.

"Need some help in there?"

She could hear the amusement in his voice as she remained with her head stuck in the dryer. Lord only knew what it was doing to her hair, which had been known to scare small children—and grown men—when humidity caught hold of it.

"Nope," she said in an overly bright voice. "I'm just looking for something."

"This?"

Megan finally lifted her head from the dryer and found Gabe standing behind her with pink lace dangling from one finger. As she watched him stroke the lace between his thumb and forefinger, she felt scalded from more than the heat still pouring out of the open dryer door.

"Where did you find it?"

"Stuck to a towel." He pointed to the stack he'd already folded and put in her laundry basket.

"The lace does that sometimes."

She knew she was standing there like a frizzy-haired idiot, babbling about absolutely nothing of importance. Why couldn't she act normal around him? Cool and composed.

But she knew why.

All she could think about was kissing him.

Or rather, the pain and suffering of having to wait to kiss him until 12:01 a.m. so that he could keep his promise to her.

She was never going to make it. Not if she wanted to hold on to her sanity, anyway.

"I was thinking," she said as she tried to non-chalantly fold one of Summer's dresses, "the whole New Year's thing is kind of overrated. People always make such a big deal about it, but it's just like any other day."

She could feel his eyes on her, even though he was folding another towel.

"And you're right," she continued in what she hoped was a light voice, "there are plenty of places in the world where it's already past midnight. Like Paris. They've already had their fireworks there."

She held her breath as she waited for him to grab her and pull her against him and take the kiss she was begging for. But all he did was take the crumpled mess she was making of Summer's dress from her hands. Sixty seconds later he had not only the dress but the rest of the clean clothes folded.

He cooked, he cleaned, he did laundry…and he knew exactly how to kiss her, where to touch her, how to take her to the edge and then back over it again before she had a chance to recover from her first hit of pleasure.

"Let's drop this off upstairs." He picked up the blue basket as if she hadn't been hinting with everything she had for that kiss. "And then we can head over to my place."

Megan was a breath away from knocking the laundry basket from his hands and launching herself at him. But it was one thing if Gabe seduced her into letting him steal a kiss after midnight to celebrate the start of another year. It was another thing entirely if she was the one begging for his kisses.

Especially when nothing had changed. She still couldn't let herself fall in love with him. And she certainly couldn't let Summer get attached to him.

Loving a man like Gabe and then losing him… well, she didn't think she'd ever be able to recover from that. No matter how strong her mother—and everyone else—always said she was.

Fortunately, the roof of his building was sure to be crowded with all the other residents out watching the fireworks. Because despite knowing better, Megan simply couldn't trust herself to be strong when she was alone with Gabe.

They'd watch the bright lights in the sky, they'd

press their lips together once in a crowd of revelers
and then she'd go home. To her own bed.

Alone, thank you very much.

Nineteen

Don't psych yourself out.

—*Firefighting 101*

Thirty minutes later, Megan stepped out of the elevator into Gabe's penthouse apartment in Potrero Hill and her mouth fell open. He slipped her coat from her shoulders, but she was so busy taking in the views from every window that she barely noticed.

"These views are incredible." She turned to him. "How do you ever do anything but stare out the windows?"

"I thought you might like it," he said as he moved across the room to stand beside her. "It's usually clear like this in the winter, but in the summer—"

"—it must be like floating on a cloud of fog."

He'd wanted to kiss her at least a hundred times since she'd opened her front door, and now, as she stood staring dreamily out his living room window, Gabe was working like hell to stick to his plan and keep his promise.

It was just that she looked so good in his house. So right. Despite the great bones of the building, the views and location, he'd always felt like something was missing.

Now he knew exactly what it was.

How different would it be if Megan and Summer lived here with him? If all that color from their small apartment were in here? If their clothes hung in the closets and Summer's drawings were up on his fridge?

Knowing he was getting ahead of himself, that nothing past tonight's fireworks was even settled, Gabe forced himself to take a step away from the only woman who had ever ripped his control to shreds.

"That omelet barely took the edge off," he told her. "How does Thai food sound for dinner? There's a great place around the corner that delivers."

Her face lit up. "I love Thai."

Jesus, he wasn't just jealous of a dead man—now his envy extended to Thai food, too.

"Make yourself comfortable while I order one of everything."

She laughed and said, "Sounds great," but she never left the window the entire time he was on the phone. Gabe knew without a doubt just how much she must miss being up high enough to see out over the city as she had in the apartment that had burned down.

He hung up the phone and she was still so mesmerized by the lights of the city that she didn't notice him put a couple of glasses of red wine on a nearby bookshelf.

A minute later he said, "Excuse me."

Megan was clearly shocked to see him holding a large overstuffed chair over his head. "What are you doing with that?"

"Hoping to make you more comfortable," he said as he slowly lowered it to the floor. And also, maybe showing off a bit, he had to admit to himself as her eyes traveled across his biceps, which were now bulging from lifting the heavy chair.

He reached for her hand. "Sit with me."

"The chair isn't big enough for both of us," she protested, but he already had her half on his lap and his arm around her waist.

"Feels like just the right size to me."

God, he loved the way she smelled, like a field of blooming flowers topped off with a hint of sweet female arousal.

"Gabe, we shouldn't—"

"Don't worry," he murmured against her ear, "I'm not going to break my promise."

Did she know just how disappointed she looked as she turned her face away from his to look out the window once more? Gabe made sure to hide his grin from her as he reached over to the bookshelf for the wine and handed her a glass.

"Sullivan Winery's finest."

She took it from him and inhaled with pleasure. "In the interest of full disclosure, I feel that I should tell you I was already a fan of Marcus's wines before we met."

"It's good stuff," he agreed.

She nodded, then said, "And I know I haven't met him, but your other brother Smith—" She stopped suddenly, as if she'd just realized she shouldn't say any more. "Never mind." She took a sip of cabernet. "This is yummy."

"What about Smith? You also want me to know how much you love his movies?"

She licked her lips and shrugged. "You've got to admit they're all pretty good." She stopped again, took another sip of her wine. "Just like this wine." She pointed out the window. "Hey, isn't that the baseball stadium over there?"

He narrowed his eyes. "You're a baseball fan, too, aren't you?"

"Blame Summer," she said, giving him her most innocent look. "Her father used to take her to games when she was a baby and she's loved it ever since. She was really thrilled about meeting Ryan at your mother's party. He's her favorite pitcher."

Why did he have to have so many brothers? The stem of his wineglass almost snapped beneath his irritated grip.

Megan's eyes were dancing as she pointed to the huge picture of an African sunrise on the wall. "I have to ask—did Chase take that?"

"Yes." The word came out more clipped than he intended it to.

That was when he caught her smiling over the rim of her glass and realized that any illusion he'd ever had of being in charge of their evening was just that—an illusion.

Because in a matter of sentences, Megan had him right where she wanted him: acting like a jealous idiot.

Again.

Wanting a little retribution, he pulled her closer to him, her back pressed into his chest. "I'm glad you're here, Megan."

She was stiff against him for a few seconds and he thought she might actually push away from him. But then, he felt her settle against him, the top of her head against his chin.

"I am, too."

Gabe could have sat there with her all night in perfect silence and watched the lights turn off and on all across the city. Because even though he was holding on to his control by a very thin thread with her soft curves pressing into his hips, Gabe had never been so comfortable with another person. Not even his family.

Too bad the Thai delivery person wouldn't stop ringing the damn doorbell.

Megan didn't look any happier about it than he did. "I guess one of us should get that."

He didn't kiss her, but he did bury his face in her hair for a split second before putting his hands on her waist and lifting her off his lap. "You get the door. I'll grab some plates."

God, she was gorgeous as she moved across the room and chatted with the young man—who also couldn't take his eyes off her. Gabe had been with plenty of women who knew exactly what they were doing around men, women who "worked it."

Megan was pure sensuality from head to toe without doing a darn thing other than breathing.

He was so caught up in her spell that she had reached into her purse for a tip before he could take care of it. The teenager was so busy staring at her, he would have forgotten to take the money if Gabe hadn't cleared his throat and snapped the kid out of it.

Megan closed the door and carried over the bags of food. "This smells amazing."

"Poor guy could barely string two words together in front of you."

She gave him a look like he was crazy. "What are you talking about?"

"You, Megan. And how beautiful you are."

She looked so stunned that he quickly took the bags from her before they dropped, and put them on the table.

Stunned turned to shy. And disbelieving. "You keep saying that."

"Because I can't stop thinking it, every time I look at you. Every time I think about you."

She stared at him, her eyes searching his. "I've never met anyone like you, Gabe." She dropped her gaze to her hands, before she lifted them again to his face. "I'm glad you were the one who found me and Summer." She took a deep breath. "And I'm glad she insisted on bringing you muffins." She bit her lip. "I'm even glad she tricked you into teaching us to snowboard."

If he went to her now, he knew he wouldn't just break his promise by kissing her, he'd take her right there, on the rug in the middle of the living room floor.

He pulled out a chair for her at the table. "Come. Eat."

He was hoping—praying—she'd need her strength later.

Her cell phone rang as she sat down, playing "You Are My Sunshine," and he moved to his own seat as she pulled it out of her pocket. "Hey, honey, how's Mickey?"

He loved watching the way her whole face lit up as she talked with Summer. His mother had always been there for him and his siblings, and as a kid he'd assumed that was how everyone's mothers were. As an adult, he realized just how lucky he'd been.

And how lucky Summer was, too.

"Wow, that sounds like an amazing light-and-fireworks show. I can't wait to hear more about how they made the water all those colors when you get back home."

He served them pad thai and cucumber salad as she laughed at whatever Summer was saying. But then she abruptly stopped laughing.

"What am I doing tonight?" She picked up her glass and took a gulp of her wine. "Just like you, sweetie, watching the fireworks in a little bit."

Gabe stopped plating their food. He wanted to hear what Megan told her daughter. Would she admit to being with him?

Megan listened carefully to the voice on the other end. "No, honey, not by myself. With a friend."

Gabe didn't like the way she wasn't looking at him and he had to remind himself to have patience. The night was going well, better than he'd hoped. The problem was, where Megan was concerned, he wanted more than he ever had from another woman.

And he wanted it *now*.

Finally, Megan lifted her eyes to meet his over the plates and containers of food. "I'm going to watch them with Gabe."

He could hear Summer's happy squeal over the phone.

"I don't know if he can come to the phone right—" She stopped partway through her sentence as he held out his hand for her phone. "Actually, here he is."

He couldn't decipher Megan's expression as he said, "Hey, pretty girl. Been on any scary rides today?" He listened, chuckling at her descriptions of the rides. "Your mom hasn't even been on that one?" He lifted an eyebrow in Megan's direction. "Wow. You're some pretty brave stuff, aren't you? Here's your mom again." He was still laughing when he handed the phone back to Megan.

"Yes, we wish you were here." She turned away slightly, letting her hair fall over her face. "I really miss you, sweetie. I'm so glad you've been having fun with Grams and Gramps. Can't wait to see you tomorrow. I love you." She put her phone on the table, but she didn't take her hand off it.

He wanted to ask her why she hadn't wanted to tell Summer they were together. But he already knew the answer to that, didn't he? And he didn't want to remind her of those reasons. Plus, he didn't like how sad she looked after saying goodbye to her daughter.

So he picked up his fork and worked to get her laughing about the time he and Ryan had decided to hide out on Tom Sawyer Island past dark and had almost been locked in for the night.

"You should have seen Ryan," he said. "Like a little baby, crying for his mommy."

She grinned at that. "Somehow he doesn't quite seem like the crying-for-his-mommy type."

"Ever seen him get nailed on the pitcher's mound?" He looked down at his lap to make sure she got his point about where the ball had landed.

"Has that actually happened?"

This time he was the one grinning. "More than once. And while his ex-girlfriends cheered, you'd better believe he was crying."

Gabe had been attracted to Megan from that first moment she'd walked into his hospital room. But, as much as he was counting down the minutes until he could kiss her without breaking his promise, it felt so good to hear her laugh that he knew, without a doubt, that their connection was so much more than skin-deep.

So deep that her laughter didn't stop at his heart... but landed smack-dab in the middle of his soul.

Twenty

At 11:45 p.m. they headed up the stairs to the roof. Megan stopped at the threshold of the completely empty roof, clutching the bundle of blankets Gabe had given her. "Where's everyone else?"

He shot her a strange look. "You thought there were going to be other people up here with us?"

"It's a big building."

He nodded. "It is. But I own the top floor. And the roof is mine alone."

"Oh."

She was such an idiot, coming up here with him. Even in a crowd, she wouldn't have been safe from the way she wanted him. She understood that, now, after several more hours in his wonderful company.

But alone?

She was doomed.

"I've had a great night with you so far, Megan." He watched her carefully. Probably expecting her to turn and run like the coward—the practical, heart-protecting coward—she was.

"I have, too," she agreed, forcing herself to creep forward onto the roof.

That was when she noticed the pretty string of lights, and the large outdoor blanket covered with colorful cushions. There was a bottle of champagne, two flutes and a tray of chocolate-covered strawberries. But that wasn't all. He'd also put out a bottle of sparkling apple juice and a kid-appropriate plastic wineglass with painted butterflies on it.

Her heart turned to goo.

"You did all this?" She pointed at her chest. "For me and Summer?"

"I couldn't think of anyone else I'd rather spend New Year's Eve with."

He took the blankets from her arms and she felt almost naked without them to hold over her heart. As if that soft shield would keep it from falling head over heels for this beautiful, kind—and shockingly sexy—man standing in front of her.

"This is—" She gestured to the pretty scene before them. "It's magical."

His grin was playful, pleased...and sensual. All at the same time. "Come look at the view from up here. It's even better than the window downstairs."

She took his hand, but as he moved them so that she was standing at the rail and his body was keeping her warm—and safe—she didn't look out at the view. Instead, she turned her head so that she could look at him. "You're not playing fair, Gabe, are you?"

She could almost taste his kiss just then. But all he did was pull her tighter into him. "Thank you for coming here tonight. And staying."

His mouth brushed against the top of her head then, and maybe that was breaking his promise, but, oh, how she wanted him to do just that, so badly that she was almost vibrating from the need to feel his lips on hers, his hands on her skin.

Megan stood in Gabe's arms, her eyes closed, and let herself just enjoy being with him, shivering at the pleasure of his warmth, his strength, the way he looked at her.

"You're cold."

She didn't have a chance to tell him it wasn't the air that was making her shiver before he was taking her over to the pile of oversize pillows and pulling her down with him. He covered them both with blankets before picking up the bottle of bubbly.

Megan snuggled down under the covers, Gabe's thigh brushing against hers as he popped open the cork and poured. "Are you trying to get me drunk?" she teased.

She loved his smile, how easily it came. He made her smiles come easier, too, she suddenly realized. Only Summer had ever made her feel this carefree, this happy. Only Summer could make her forget about all the work she needed to get done, the bills that needed to be paid, the fridge that needed to be filled.

Until Gabe.

Maybe it was his close physical proximity under

the blanket on the romantic city rooftop that made it hard for her to hold on to a single thought that wasn't about how much she wanted him—and that kiss!

Maybe it was the way he always made plans for three, rather than trying to pretend she didn't have a daughter.

Maybe there was still some of that hero worship he was so worried about going on because he'd saved her life.

Or maybe it was simply the daredevil inside her that was dying to break out and do something crazy like have sex outside, where there was a teeny-tiny chance that someone might look out a faraway window and see them.

Whatever it was, at this point, after several hours of what felt like prolonged foreplay, Megan simply didn't care anymore about the reasons for what she was feeling.

All she knew was that the five-minute countdown to New Year's was *way* too long.

His answer to her teasing question finally came as he handed her the glass. "Do I need to get you drunk?"

Feeling herself flush as she shook her head, she pushed the rim to her lips and tilted her head back, her nerves causing her to pour more of the delicious champagne down her neck than into her mouth.

There wasn't any chance to feel embarrassed about making a mess with the drink, though, because Gabe's thumb was there, brushing over the liquid that had spilled. He was about to bring it to his own lips when she grabbed his wrist. "Wait. That was my drink."

His eyes flared with such intense heat that she almost had to kick off the blanket.

Hardly able to believe what she was doing—but knowing she would die if she didn't get to taste some part of him in the next five seconds—she brought his thumb to her mouth.

And sucked it in between her lips.

She didn't know who groaned first, herself or him, as she swirled her tongue over the pad of his thumb, tasting the champagne, but mostly that unique, slightly smoky taste of his skin.

A flavor she hadn't been able to forget since Lake Tahoe.

"I'm keeping my promise." His voice was husky as he lowered his head to her neck, where he'd brushed away the liquid. "No kisses yet" was the last thing she heard him say before she felt the slow sweet press of his tongue over her pulse point.

She arched herself against his mouth even as her teeth came down lightly over the flesh on the tip of his thumb.

He lifted his gaze back to hers and just the look in his eyes was nearly enough for her to come apart right there. He slowly pulled his thumb from her mouth and moved his hand to the curve of her hips, pulling her onto his lap.

She was straddling his erection, already rocking into him, as he said, "God, you're sweet."

A moment later, the first blast of color shot out

in the sky above them, joined by the crowds of people cheering from the streets, but all Megan knew was that it was—*finally*—time for Gabe to kiss her.

Only, she never gave him the chance, because her hands were already in his hair and she was attacking him, kissing him with more passion than she'd ever realized she possessed. His mouth claimed hers right back, his tongue tangling with hers, their combined gasps of long-awaited pleasure joining right in with the explosions from the fireworks and the sounds of happy strangers in the distance.

"Now." She pulled her mouth away from his. "I need you right now."

She reached for the hem of her sweater and yanked it up over her head, taking her long-sleeved T-shirt with it. She reached for the button of her jeans next, her hands trembling not with cold but with pure desperation to be naked with this man.

She'd never been this kind of woman, never needed to have sex so badly that she was practically ripping her clothes apart in her hurry to get them off. But then, she'd never been with anyone like Gabe before, had she?

Besides, how could a girl's mind not be warped by all those muscles? All that barely leashed power when he was holding her? Kissing her? Loving her senseless?

"Hurry," she said, and then he was yanking off his clothes, too, his shirt joining hers across the roof where she'd tossed it.

Of course, she'd forgotten that he had more practice getting clothes off and on quickly in the fire-house than she did, and she was still getting shoes and socks off by the time he'd stripped down to...

Nothing.

"Wow." Her hands stilled as she took in his gloriously naked body. "Women would pay really good money to see that."

"I'll keep that in mind if I'm ever looking for a new career."

Realizing her crazy thoughts must have just spilled out of her mouth, her hands became even more useless, but then Gabe was there, kneeling in front of her, slipping off her shoes and socks and tossing her jeans to the side.

She reached for the waistband of her panties just as he undid the clasp of her bra and then, a moment later, she was naked, too, and he was the one staring.

"Mine." He was crawling up over her now, pressing her against the pillows. "You're mine, Megan."

She could barely gasp out the word, "Yes," before his mouth was back over hers and he was kissing her.

She was his.

Twenty-One

Play well with others.

—Firefighting 101

When Gabe had made his initial plan, he'd decided that if things went well and he ended up being lucky enough to get naked with Megan again at some point in the future, he'd go slow. He'd savor every inch of her beautiful body and focus on bringing her right to the edge of ecstasy and then over so many times that she wouldn't be able to keep denying their connection.

But he hadn't counted on their combined desperation to be with each other.

Gabe picked up the condom wrapper he'd dropped on the blanket, and before he could rip it open, Megan was leaning up to grab it in her teeth and pull it open. She caught it before it fell onto her chest and then she was reaching down to his throbbing erection and sliding it over him, the arousing touch of her slender fingers causing him to grit his teeth to keep from exploding right then and there.

And then her hands were in his hair and she was pulling his mouth down to hers at the exact moment that she wrapped her legs around his waist and took him inside. He swallowed her gasp of pleasure and gripped her hips in his hands to drive deeper, harder.

A big man, Gabe had always been careful to make sure he didn't hurt his lovers. But as her inner muscles clenched against his shaft, the pleasure of being with her again was so intense he couldn't hold on to a single thought, couldn't do anything but give in to the intensity of his desire for the woman writhing and crying out beneath him.

She arched into him and he leaned down to capture one of her nipples between his lips, sucking hard, loving the sweet taste of her skin against his tongue. The fireworks were still going on above them as she came apart beneath him, her pelvis grinding against his as she rode out her orgasm, her hands in his hair holding him over her breasts.

He didn't have a chance of holding back a single second longer, not when her strong muscles were gripping him for everything he was worth. Lifting his head from her breasts, he shifted his weight to his knees, grabbed her ankles and lifted them up to his shoulders.

He had to get deeper, had to touch every part of her.

Her hands went to his forearms so that she could hold tight as he drove higher, harder, into her.

"Oh, God," she whispered as her eyes fluttered closed. "That feels so good. So, so good." Her head was falling back, her hands moving to her own breasts as she took everything he was giving her and begged, "More, Gabe. Please."

He hadn't thought anything could drive him higher, but the sound of her sweet voice begging him like that, watching her touch herself while he loved her, did crazy things to his insides.

"Sweetheart," he groaned as the fierce physicality of their lovemaking gave way to emotions just as fierce inside him. "Don't make me go here alone."

But even as her eyes opened and held his, even as her mouth opened on a silent scream of pleasure as she shattered again, even as his own body followed her down that path of perfect destruction, Gabe knew he hadn't just been asking her to come with him.

No, what he was asking for was so much bigger than just sex, more than just the best orgasm he'd ever had.

Gabe didn't want to claim Megan's body alone. He wanted her heart, wanted to know—to *love*—every part of her.

Because with every moment they spent together, he was realizing more and more just what a daredevil she really was. She loved heights, and hadn't blinked twice at having wild monkey sex out in the open on his roof.

How long had his beautiful thrill seeker been pushing away the truth of who she really was? Since her husband's death?

Or even before that?

* * *

Megan couldn't do anything more than cling to Gabe and bury her face against his broad shoulder. She could barely breathe, so how could she possibly pull her thoughts together to examine what had just happened between them?

He was holding her just as tightly as he shifted them so that his body, instead of the pillows, was cushioning her. She loved feeling him all around her, inside her, knew she'd never get enough of him, even if she lived to be a hundred.

The shock of that thought—of the future she'd sworn she wouldn't have with him—had her blinking her eyes open, trying to clear the fog of temporarily sated lust from them.

Oh, my God, she'd just had sex on the roof.

The roof!

She hadn't wanted to think too long and hard about just how risky what they were doing was. Not if that thinking would have gotten in the way of Gabe's kiss. But now, as she looked around at the buildings that surrounded his, she knew the probability was fairly high that someone might have seen them.

She yanked the blanket over her naked body even as something inside her buzzed a teensy bit in an exhibitionist thrill.

Gabe ran his hand over the curve of her bottom beneath the blanket. "Do you think we made anyone's New Year's?"

She wanted to be shocked by him, by the cavalier way that he was acknowledging they might have been spotted. "I hope not!"

But even as she spoke in her primmest voice, Megan couldn't deny the tingle down low in her belly from thinking of another couple setting out to watch the fireworks…and seeing them making love instead. Those were the kinds of thoughts she only ever let herself have in the secrecy of her most private, kinky fantasies.

Worse still, she couldn't even blame him for what had happened. Not when she was the one who had ripped off her clothes in plain sight of the other buildings and rooftops and then begged him to hurry and take his off, too.

His chuckle was warm, full of the heat that hadn't dissipated between them. "I'm just teasing you, sweetheart. The nearest building taller than this is far enough away that someone would have needed a great pair of binoculars to see us up here." He tipped his finger beneath her chin. "You say Summer is the only risk taker in the family, but that isn't true."

Making love with Gabe was incredibly intimate. But the way he was talking to her, as if he knew the secrets of her soul, felt even deeper. She felt like he was seeing in too deeply, past all the walls she'd worked so hard to build to keep herself—and her precious daughter—safe.

She shivered and he immediately picked her up, blanket and all.

"Time to get you warm again."

Megan knew she should just say thank you for the

fireworks—even though the only ones she'd been able to pay any attention to tonight were the ones that combusted between them—and tell him she had to go home, but she'd already broken her latest vow to stay away from him. And she'd been working really hard since Summer had left. She was so tired.

But most of all, it felt so good to let him hold her like this, just for a few more seconds.

Gabe ran kisses over her hair, across her forehead, over her cheek, and she had to turn in for one on her lips. When they were halfway down the stairs to his apartment, he stopped and concentrated on kissing the remaining oxygen from her lungs.

"Happy New Year."

She had to run her tongue across his gorgeous lower lip before saying, "Happy New Year."

Megan expected him to carry her into his bedroom, but he didn't stop at the huge king bed covered in a beautiful blue-and-brown quilt. Instead, he moved into the bathroom.

"How about a bath to start off the new year?"

The sinfully delicious thought of being naked, slipping and sliding against Gabe in his whirlpool tub, was almost enough to make her consider it. Still, she hadn't been able to get in a bathtub since the fire. "Why don't we shower instead?"

She turned her head up to kiss him, but smart man, even though he indulged her, it was clear that he saw right through her distraction. "I want to take a bath with you, Megan."

Oh, my. She took a deep breath to try to steady herself. "I guess I can try."

He brushed a lock of hair from her eyes, once again seeing more deeply than she wanted him to. "Is it because that's where I found you? In the bathtub?"

If she had been stronger, if she had felt less safe cradled in Gabe's strong arms, if he were anyone else, she might have tried to deny it.

But how could she lie to this man?

"I thought we were going to die in there. In the bathtub."

"I never would have let that happen."

She couldn't stop herself from asking the one question that had played over and over in her head for the past two months. "But what if you hadn't come in time?"

"No what-ifs." He took one of her hands and laid it over his heart. "Not tonight." He leaned forward and pressed a soft kiss to her lips. "Don't let the fire take any more from you than it already has, sweetheart."

But didn't he see that she felt caught in an endless loop of what-ifs? Not just about the fire, but about the two of them, about Summer and her future, and—

She scrunched her eyes up tight, hating those what-ifs, every last one of them. "You know what?"

"Tell me, Megan."

She took a deep breath and opened her eyes. "It's a new year. Time for a new start. To wash the past clean."

She was old enough, wise enough, to know she couldn't change who she was, the way her brain and heart were wired, in one short night. But she could take a baby step toward pushing the weight of all those fears off her shoulders.

Especially if the step involved getting into the bathtub with a man whose eyes were promising her such incredible pleasure.

"Run the bath, Gabe."

He continued to hold tightly to her with one hand while he reached for the taps with the other. While the tub was filling with warm water, Megan turned to stare in wonder at the man holding her on his lap and had to reach up to run her fingertips over the slightly raised scar on his forehead.

"I wish you hadn't been hurt." His eyes closed for a moment as she feathered her fingers over his forehead.

"That day in the hospital—" He looked at her, the depth of emotion in his eyes shaking her, all the way through to her core. "I'm sorry I was such a jerk." He reached for her hand, pulled it to his lips and pressed a soft kiss into her palm. "That moment when you walked in and I saw you without all the smoke, without the flames, I knew you were special."

"You nearly died saving us," she said in a voice that was barely above a whisper. "You had the right to behave however you wanted."

He shook his head. "I was stunned by how strong my feelings for you were already. But that was no excuse for my behavior."

Megan had warmed up in his house, but now that he was talking about feelings and fear, she felt herself go cold again, shivering at all the things she didn't want to face. Not yet, anyway.

Knowing he must be able to see how uncomfortable their conversation was making her, she could feel Gabe shift gears as he lifted her palm to his mouth again and nipped gently at the sensitive flesh. "I didn't take the time to undress you properly on the roof," he said as he began to peel back the blanket.

"I'd say you did just fine," she murmured as she leaned forward to press a kiss to the top of his sinfully gorgeous chest. She was half relieved at the way he was letting her stay out of the deep end of emotion, but, strangely, half disappointed, too.

"Only fine?" His voice was husky as he curved his palm around her breast and skimmed over the tip of one nipple with his thumb. The same thumb she'd been sucking and biting up on the roof.

"Mmm" was all she could manage by way of a response, and then he was pushing the blanket all the way off and stepping into the tub with her in his arms.

Nothing had ever felt so romantic, so sexy, as this shared bath. They'd done exciting and risky outside beneath the fireworks, but as she sank into the warm water and rested her back and head against Gabe's chest, she sighed at the pleasure of getting to fulfill all the sides of her desires in one sweet night.

He cupped his hands so they filled with water and poured them over her skin, wetting every inch of her body, even her hair. It felt so luxurious to be pampered like this, felt like more than just sex, more than just need.

He'd just had her, and had to know he didn't need to do all this to have her again. But he was doing it, anyway.

She had to nuzzle into his biceps, had to press a kiss against them as he moved to pick up the soap.

"Trying to distract me?"

"No," she replied honestly. "I just had to kiss you."

Using her hair wrapped around his fist, he gently but firmly turned her face to his and captured her lips in a shockingly sweet kiss.

It was a long while before he let her up for air.

"Same here."

The soap had slipped from his fingers during the kiss and he had to search for it under the water, his hands moving along the outside of her hips.

"It's not here." He moved his feet at the bottom of the tub searching for the soap. "Not here, either."

"I think I know where it is."

His eyes were on her mouth as he asked, "Where?"

She picked up one of his hands and put it on her stomach. "You're getting closer." He slid down only a little bit, teasing her. "Almost there."

She held her breath as he shifted his hand over her curls, and then he was cupping her sex, his broad palm covering every inch of her slick heat, and her breath was coming out in a rush of pleasure as she tilted her head back against his shoulder.

There was no stopping her hips from pushing into his fingers, and thank God, she knew he was done teasing her when two thick fingers spread her aroused flesh and his other hand moved to concentrate on her clitoris.

His tongue and then his teeth found her earlobe and despite the warm water, despite the heat of his body behind her, she was racked with shivers.

"You're so beautiful, sweetheart. So damn beautiful." His tongue licked out just at that sensitive spot beneath her earlobe a split second before he urged her, "Come for me. I need to see it. Need to feel it."

But she was already there, already panting and bucking into his hands as the tremors inside her belly turned into a full-fledged, unstoppable earthquake.

"Gabe!"

He helped her ride out her climax, never letting up for one single second with both his hands, and when she finally came back to earth in the bathtub, she realized just how big, how hard, he was against her lower back.

Fortunately, he was well prepared as she spotted a condom wrapper on top of the blanket. Not caring at all that he'd known what a sure thing she was going to be tonight, she leaned over the tub to pick it up. She ripped it open—with her hands this time, instead of her teeth, although that had been fun and more than a little crazy—and he silently lifted her hips up out of the water so that she could slide it onto his gloriously erect shaft.

"I know we agreed no what-ifs tonight, but I can't help but wonder, what if—" she paused, licked her lips "—you helped me live out a fantasy?"

She suddenly wanted a chance to reclaim not just the bathtub but also her hope for the future, rather than always going forward holding on to fear.

His hands moved over her thighs, her kneecaps, in the water. "What kind of fantasy?" The raw tenor of his words nearly had her giving up the fantasy and climbing onto his lap instead.

"I've never taken a bath with a man before tonight."

"Good."

She had to smile at his jealous pleasure over being her first. She was glad, too, glad that she could experience these fantasies for the first time with Gabe.

"But sometimes when I'm alone and I'm—" She paused on the words she wasn't used to speaking aloud.

"Touching yourself?"

She nodded. "Sometimes I like to think about being in a tub like this and—"

She bit her lip again and he growled, "If you don't stop doing that, I'm not sure we're going to get to your fantasy."

Her eyes wide, she let her lip go. "Oh." She almost bit her lip again and caught herself at the last second. "Okay."

"Megan." She heard the sensual warning in his voice, which was quickly backed up when he said, "What's your fantasy?"

But she'd already figured out she'd never be able to put voice to it. Instead, she'd have to show him.

With as much grace as she could manage considering how aroused she was, and how nervous at the same time, she moved her limbs beneath the water so that she wasn't facing Gabe anymore. Looking at him over her shoulder, she slowly lifted up onto her hands and knees.

"This," she said in a whisper that was almost swallowed up by the sound of water moving in the tub. "This is my fantasy."

His groan ricocheted off the tiled walls, and then, thank God, he was moving, too, and cupping her bottom in his big hands. But even though she was playing it as risky as she ever had with a lover, she was shocked when he leaned forward and pressed a kiss to first one cheek and then the other. Slowly, he moved his mouth up from her lower back to what felt like each vertebra along her spine, until he was biting at the curve of her shoulder.

"Is this it, Megan? Is this your fantasy?"

She couldn't speak, could only nod and hold on tight to the edge of the tub as she pushed her bottom into the curve of his hips. Water splashed all around them as he thrust into her from behind, and this time when she lost hold of her sanity, he was right there with her, pounding into her so hard, so deep as he came, that she didn't know where he left off and she began.

With one of his big hands on her breasts, the other between her legs and his teeth and tongue on her neck, Megan completely shattered in Gabe's arms.

Twenty-Two

Figure out how to handle the inevitable highs
and lows.

—Firefighting 101

Gabe loved watching Megan sleep so peacefully, a
small smile on her lips as she curled in closer to him.
He felt content, and happy being with her like this,
as sunlight streamed in on a new year.

But while his sisters had called him clueless at
least a thousand times over the years, Gabe knew that
even though Megan had talked about new beginnings
and washing the past clean, odds were pretty darn
high that she'd be just as upset about ending up in bed
with him as she'd been the first time in Lake Tahoe.

Just because he'd made up his mind about what
he wanted didn't mean she had.

She stirred again and slowly opened her eyes.

"Good morning, beautiful."

He was damn glad to see that her eyes didn't go

wide with horror this time. Instead, she reached up to slide one hand through his hair. "Hi."

But before he could get his hopes up too high, she was moving from the bed.

"Summer's coming home today and I need to get a few things ready for her."

Gabe wanted to pull her back down onto the bed with him, but he knew he should take this as a step forward from what had happened in the hotel room. She wasn't running to the farthest corner. Wasn't throwing around the word *never.*

As it was, it had been a stroke of sheer luck that he hadn't been called into the station overnight. His official shift started in a few hours, enough time to make love to her again, to run his tongue over every sweet inch of her skin—

Stick to the plan, hotshot.

Deciding to heed that voice in his head that had been right so far, he said, "Why don't you take a shower and I'll go upstairs and get your clothes."

She looked more than a little surprised by how quickly he agreed to her plan to get on with the day. Away from each other.

"Okay." She paused, smiled a slightly wobbly smile. "Thanks."

He grinned at her back as she walked, gorgeously naked, into the bathroom and closed the door behind her with a soft click. Hopefully, she'd have a hell of a time taking a shower without remembering every little thing that had happened in the nearby bathtub just hours before.

He pulled on a pair of faded jeans, went upstairs to get her clothes and left them for her on his bed before going out to the kitchen to make breakfast.

A few minutes later, she walked toward him, her hair wet around her shoulders, her expression slightly shy. "I could smell the bacon from the bathroom."

Gabe didn't want to push his luck, but some things were unstoppable, like pulling her into his arms and kissing her. When they were both breathing hard, he pulled back an inch.

"I like waking up with you in my bed." He took her hand and pulled her over to her seat at his dining table. "I like watching you eat, too."

But before either of them could take a bite, his cell buzzed. He quickly looked at the code on it.

Megan was frowning at him when he looked back at her. "Do you need to go?"

"No, not yet. In a couple of hours I'll start my shift. It was just a reminder from one of the guys about taking over his shift, too."

"How long is your shift?"

"I'm usually on for forty-eight hours. But this one will be seventy-two."

She looked shocked by the hours. "Will you sleep at the station?"

"If I can."

She looked as serious as he'd ever seen her. "I wish things were different, Gabe, but they aren't. Last night was great, but…" She took a deep breath, looked him straight in the eye. "Nothing has changed."

Her words settled like cement in the bottom of his gut and it wasn't easy to keep his voice relaxed. "You're having breakfast with me. That's a change." A huge one, for the better.

She pushed away from the table, shoving her phone into her pocket and grabbing her purse from his couch as she headed for the door. "I need to go."

Gabe wanted to beg her to stay, wanted to force her to confront their feelings for each other, wanted to make her admit those feelings weren't going to go away just because she was scared about her past repeating itself with him.

Instead, he took her plate into the kitchen, pulled off a sheet of tin foil and moved her food into the foil. He grabbed the keys to his truck. "I'll take you home."

"I'd like to walk."

He could tell from the stubborn tilt of her chin that she was set on getting out of there—and away from him—as soon as possible. And, for all his male cluelessness, he knew better than to do anything that would push that stubbornness up a notch.

"Thank you for sharing New Year's with me, Megan."

She blinked up at him, looking almost surprised that he hadn't insisted on taking her, anyway. Or, he thought as her expression shifted again, had she been expecting him to kiss her again to try to get her to stay for breakfast? Was she disappointed that he hadn't? And didn't she realize he wouldn't force her to do anything? That he didn't want her to resent him for pushing her too hard, too fast?

Finally, she said, so quietly he would have missed it if he hadn't been so attuned to her every breath, "I had fun."

She turned to go, but then, at the last second, she moved back toward him. This time, he was the one who was surprised as she took the warm foil packet from him, said, "Thanks for breakfast," and went up on her tippy toes to press a quick kiss to his cheek.

Nothing made sense anymore. Megan was old enough to know right from wrong, to know when she was setting herself up for a huge fall. So then what was she doing, falling back into bed with Gabe whenever there was one nearby?

She could accept that there wasn't a woman alive strong enough to resist his charm. She couldn't imagine anyone not liking him. Only, liking someone, appreciating someone for his good qualities, laughing with him, enjoying a meal together—all of that was very different from begging him for a kiss.

Worse, she'd taken it further than begging. Much further. She'd actually ripped her clothes off and then shredded his, too. And, okay, maybe making love on his rooftop had been unavoidable given a long week of wanting him, of thinking of him whenever her brain wasn't otherwise occupied with work or Summer.

But what had happened in the bath…she lost

her breath just thinking about it, remembering how boldly she'd asked to live out a secret fantasy with him.

And how wonderfully he'd complied.

Megan was walking up a steep hill, but in the stark light of a new day—of a new year—she simply couldn't keep lying to herself. She wasn't breathless because of the hill.

She was breathless because she was thinking about Gabe.

But that wasn't the only thing she couldn't lie to herself about.

She was falling for him, couldn't seem to help falling deeper and deeper beneath the beautiful spell he was weaving around her body…and her heart.

Megan tightened her grip on the foil-wrapped breakfast he'd made for her as she climbed to the top of the hill. The view from this neighborhood never failed to take her breath away, and as she stood to catch her breath for a few moments, she wished she could share her wonder at the sunlight sparkling on the blue water in the bay with someone.

With Gabe.

A fire truck drove by just then and she looked more carefully at the firefighters inside than she ever had before. Did they have wives? Children? Siblings? How did all those people who loved them deal with the danger, with the possibility of losing them to smoke and flames and falling beams?

When she was twenty and dating David, the big shock had been finding herself pregnant. She hadn't known to fear the dangers inherent in his job as a fighter pilot. She'd been too scared thinking about her pregnancy, about giving birth, about having a little baby who depended on her. And, of course, she'd had to deal with the idea that she and David were going to be married. She'd assumed, like all twenty-year-old girls, that she'd have time to find her knight in shining armor, that she'd keep dating different men until she found him.

Nothing had turned out as she planned. She hadn't expected to lose that unexpected husband. She hadn't expected to find such joy in being a young mother.

And she'd never thought to find her knight in shining armor during the scariest moment of her life, huddled in the bathtub with Summer while flames raged around them, the last possible place she would ever have expected to find love.

Love.

Oh, God. The foil breakfast packet fell from her fingers and landed on the sidewalk with a thud.

She'd known she was head over heels for the way Gabe laughed, the way he kissed her, the way his hands moved over her skin.

But love…

No, she thought as she bent down to pick up the food from the pavement. She didn't want to lie to herself. She truly wanted to start the year with a fresh, clean slate of truth. Only, she now knew something else, something she could never have understood as an innocent twenty-year-old who'd been getting ready to grab life by the horns.

Sometimes, when things were too difficult to face, the best thing to do was to stuff them away.

Because sometimes, pretending was the only way to keep moving forward.

Twenty-Three

It was one thing to pretend when she was alone. It was another thing entirely to keep it up around Summer. Especially when her daughter's favorite question seemed to be, "When can we see Gabe again?"

Fortunately, she knew he was busy with his multi-day shift. Each day, when Summer asked for a trip to the fire station, Megan held firm. "If he isn't working, he's probably sleeping. We can't bother him."

Summer was back in school when Sophie called Megan to meet for lunch. Of course she wanted to see her friend. But she was worried that the pretending that had been difficult with Summer might just prove to be impossible with Gabe's sister.

Fortunately, Sophie's wide smile of greeting outside the little bistro was all it took for Megan's nerves to disappear.

"You look great."

"You do, too."

Yet again, Megan wished she could pull off Sophie's simple chic. Instead of wearing jeans and a sweater like everyone else in the bistro, her friend had on a long wool skirt that swished around her ankles as they walked over to their table. She thought back to their conversation in the potting shed when Sophie had been upset over someone. A man.

Well, whoever he was, Megan thought, he had to be blind not to notice her sweet, pretty friend.

As soon as they ordered, Sophie asked, "Did you do anything fun during Summer's winter break from school?"

Megan barely kept her eyes from widening in alarm. She couldn't possibly lie to her friend, but at the same time, she didn't know what she could say about Gabe to his sister. Not when her feelings were currently twisted up in a tight knot.

"We spent some time in the snow for a few days and then came back home and did a few hikes, some craft projects, and memorized most of the *iCarly* episodes on cable. And of course she got way too many presents from her grandparents. What about you? How were your past couple of weeks?"

Sophie pulled a booklet out of her purse. "I finished putting this together. It's the proof copy before they send the final order to the printer."

Megan read the title aloud. "*The Greatest Love Stories of All Time: An Annotated Bibliography.* Now available at your local library. Compiled and edited by Sophie Sullivan.'" She grinned at her friend. "This is fantastic. Congratulations."

"Thanks." Sophie made an unexpected face. "I'm

really pleased with it, although I feel like the title is a little misleading."

"Why?"

"Not all of these stories have a happy ending. Of course, it doesn't make them any less compelling."

"Just more real," Megan said softly.

Sophie slipped the book back into her bag. "You must miss him."

This time, Megan couldn't stop her eyes from going big. Oh, God, Sophie knew about Gabe! She opened her mouth to say something, to try to get Sophie to understand that she wasn't trying to hurt her brother, but before she could find any words that made sense, her friend was saying, "I wish I had gotten to meet your husband."

Relief knocked through Megan so quickly she actually slumped back in her seat.

But Sophie misread her reaction. "I'm sorry. I should know better than to bring him up. After all, my mother never loved anyone but my father."

Megan frowned. "Didn't your father pass away when you were a child?"

Sophie nodded. "I was two."

Megan quickly did the math. More than two decades. That was a long time to be alone. Too long, especially since the last of Mary Sullivan's kids had grown up and moved out a good five years ago.

"Surely your mother has dated, right?"

"No," Sophie said with a small frown. "Not as far as I know."

"Why do you think that is? Would your father not have wanted her to find love again?"

"I don't know," Sophie said softly. "But from the way Marcus and Smith talk about him, I don't think he was that kind of man." Her friend looked up at her with an expression so similar to Gabe's that Megan almost dropped her fork. "Maybe," Sophie said in a considering voice, "she's been afraid to love and lose again."

"But she seems so fearless with all of you. Even with Gabe, whose job is so dangerous." But even as she said it, Megan understood why Mary Sullivan let her children live the lives they chose. "I used to watch Summer on the playground and cringe as she'd shimmy up a pole to the top of the play structure and fling herself onto the roof. She was so much smaller than the other kids, but she had no fear. She still doesn't—and every day I prepare myself a little more for when she tells me she wants to be a sharpshooter or a race car driver."

Sophie laughed at that, and while Megan knew she was at risk for showing her hand regarding her growing feelings for Gabe, she needed to know. "How do you deal with the thought that Gabe might not come home from a fire one day?"

Her friend thought about it for a moment. "Marcus could probably grow apples instead of grapes. Chase could paint instead of taking pictures." Sophie shook her head. "But when we were kids, all Gabe ever wanted to be for Halloween was a firefighter."

Megan raised an eyebrow at that. "Seriously? Every single year?"

Sophie grinned. "He's nothing if not focused."

Megan felt herself blush. She knew firsthand just how focused he could be. And how wonderful it was to be the woman he was focusing on.

She looked up to see Sophie giving her a rueful little smile. "And, honestly, this might sound bad, but I try to remind myself that, statistically, he's more likely to get hit by a car than die on the job. And we all get into cars knowing the danger, right?"

"I suppose so."

All of Sophie's arguments made sense. Still, there remained a disconnect between what Megan's mind understood…and what her heart believed.

Sophie's eyes hadn't left her face. "Can I ask you something this time?"

Megan tried not to tense. "Of course."

"Have you seen Gabe again? Since the party, I mean."

"Yes," she said honestly.

Sophie smiled. "Good."

Megan braced for her friend to ask more questions, to try to get the whens and hows out of her. Instead, Sophie simply said, "Want to split a piece of chocolate cake?"

"Of course I do."

The two women grinned at each other, and as soon as Sophie raised her hand in the waiter's direction, he sprinted over to see what the prettiest woman in the restaurant needed. And yet, Megan had the sense that Sophie was totally clueless as to the amount of attention the men around them were giving her.

For a few moments she debated keeping out of her friend's love life. But then, what kind of girlfriend would she be? Besides, Sophie had already waded into things with her and Gabe, hadn't she?

The cake came quickly, and as they both picked up their forks to dig into opposite sides, Megan asked, "Any luck with whatever sent you into the potting shed a couple of weeks ago?"

Sophie looked up at Megan in surprise. "The potting shed?" A moment later, her cheeks flamed. She shook her head. "No. I don't think luck is ever going to be in the cards on that front."

Megan frowned. "Are you dating anyone?"

Again, Sophie shook her head. "Not really. A couple of guys keep calling, but I'm not really interested."

Obviously, her friend was saving herself for someone. Again, Megan knew the easier thing was to back away from this discussion. It would be safer to talk about the weather or their plans for the weekend.

But Megan was tired of having acquaintances. She wanted real friends, women she could share tears and laughter with, women she could confide in.

Maybe it was time to step out on a limb.

"Is the guy you're interested in worth it, Sophie?"

Her friend covered her eyes with her free hand and made a sound that was a cross between a laugh and a sob.

She looked at Megan with such sad eyes that her stomach clenched. "Sometimes I'm sure that he is, but then other times...well, I have to wonder if I'm just fooling myself because I don't want to see who he really is."

Megan was heartbroken for Sophie for having fallen into what seemed to be unrequited love with a man who might not deserve it.

But even as she pushed the slice of cake a little closer to Sophie, and the two of them fed their careening emotional states with chocolate and carbs, she couldn't help but think about Gabe.

And the fact that he definitely *was* worth it.

Summer was bouncing on the playground as she waited for Megan to come pick her up from school.

"Glad to be back at school, huh?" she said as she ruffled the top of her daughter's blond hair.

"Guess where we went today for a field trip?"

Megan tried to remember what it had said on the permission slip she'd filled out a few months ago. But before she had a chance to guess, Summer opened her backpack and pulled out a plastic firefighter's hat.

"Oh," Megan said, her mouth suddenly dry. "Wow, how exciting."

"Gabe was there and he was so awesome showing us everything. We got to slide down the pole from the top bunks and hang out in the ambulance and sit in the seats at the back of the truck."

During the short walk back to their apartment,

Summer regaled Megan with firehouse stories. And as she started slicing cheese and apples for their afternoon snack, she couldn't stop thinking about one word.

Fate.

She'd never been a big believer in things like that, had always believed that solid decisions and hard work were what paid off. And they had.

But, really, it was getting to the point where it felt like the universe was screaming at her to *pay attention!*

"And, Mommy, he asked if you like roller coasters as much as I do."

Megan surfaced from her strange thoughts as she realized what Summer had just said. "What did you tell him?"

"I said of course you do. That you aren't afraid of anything."

Megan put down the paring knife and went to put her arms around her daughter. "Thank you, honey."

As Summer hugged her back, so hard that her little arms shook with the force of it, she lifted her green eyes and said, "What for?"

"Just for being you."

And for believing in me when I sometimes forget to believe in myself.

A few minutes later, while Summer was eating her snack and coloring at the kitchen table, Megan picked up the wireless phone and walked into her bedroom, closing the door.

She forced herself not to hang up when his voice

mail kicked in. "Hi, Gabe. It's Megan. I know you're still at the station working, but when you're back home and rested, I'd—"

She had to stop, had to take a breath, had to remember Summer saying, *You aren't afraid of anything.*

"I'd love to see you again. Maybe we could meet for lunch sometime during the week?" She added, "Sometime soon, I hope," before hanging up.

Twenty-Four

The next day when he knew Summer would be at school for the next few hours, Gabe knocked on Megan's door. He'd been on a medical call when she'd left her message. As soon as he got back to the station and made it through his paperwork, he'd quickly started planning a surprise for her. One he hoped she'd love.

He'd missed her like crazy these past few days, had wanted to call her a hundred times. But he knew he couldn't push her, couldn't risk having her run, possibly for good this time. As he waited for her to contact him, he kept reminding himself that she hadn't said goodbye.

Instead, she'd told him she'd had fun…and she'd kissed him on the cheek.

Still, it had been a seriously sweet moment of relief when he'd heard her voice on his phone. But when she opened the door, gorgeous as always in a pair of jeans and a sweater, what he felt went so far past relief, past lust, into uncharted territory, that he finally knew for sure.

He was in love with her.

Overwhelmed by the depth of emotions he felt for this beautiful woman standing in front of him, he probably would have just stood and stared at her for hours were it not for Megan reaching for his shirt, taking a handful of the material in her fist and pulling him toward her.

He finally reacted, dragging her body against his just as she made a play for his mouth. They kissed as though it had been three years since they'd last seen each other rather than three days, clothes flying off all around them just as they had up on his roof.

Sex had never been this desperate a need before, had never been as vital as breathing, as necessary as food and water. But it wasn't just the quest for an orgasm that drove them stumbling over to her couch, that had him ripping off her bra, yanking her panties down her legs and dropping to his knees between her thighs.

It wasn't just that he wanted to give Megan pleasure, that he wanted to hear those sexy little gasps and moans as he licked through her already wet folds and slid two fingers inside her clenching heat.

It was more than the contact high he got from her shuddering climax as he circled her clit with his tongue, then sucked it in between his lips and took her over the edge.

Even that moment, when he reared up over her, a condom already on, gripping her hips hard to pull her even closer and driving into her, it wasn't what his need was all about.

No, it went deeper than just the physical pleasure of being with the woman he loved.

Because, for the first time in his life, as Megan's head fell back against the couch, as her back arched and she wrapped her legs tightly around him, covering his hands with her own right before they both came apart in each other's arms, Gabe knew what it must have been like to be Adam.

And to need to claim Eve as *his*.

Gabe looked with pleasure at Megan sitting beside him in his truck. He wanted her again even though barely fifteen minutes had passed since they'd made love. It had been tempting to take her to bed and stay there all afternoon, but he knew she'd love his surprise. And he hoped there'd be many more days—and nights—of lovemaking in their future.

"I'm glad you called," he told her, not pausing before reaching for her hand. He was pleased when she slid her fingers between his.

"I am, too." She looked out the window. "Although I believe I'm the one who asked you to lunch, and here you are taking me off to some secret place."

He could tell from the excitement in her voice that she enjoyed being surprised. How, he had to wonder, would she like it if he took control of their lovemaking the next time? If he didn't tell her what he was going to do to her, if he made her guess how he was going to make her come next?

They pulled into a dirt parking lot and he came around to help her out of the truck, his hand around her waist, enjoying the feel of her curves as he stood a little too close and made sure she slid down the length of his body.

Just as he hadn't stopped himself from holding her hand while they were driving, he didn't stop himself from kissing her now. Her mouth met his just as hungrily, her arms wrapping around his neck, her hands threading into his hair.

They'd kissed dozens of times before this, but this kiss was different. He'd always known she wanted him, had always felt the strength of her desire for him. But now it was as if a lock had sprung open. Where it had almost been as if she was powerless to resist kissing him, now he got the strangest sense that she was kissing him for no other reason than because she *wanted* to.

When they finally came apart for air, she was smiling up at him. "I love kissing you, Gabe."

His mouth was back on hers a second later and they were off onto round two. Only the loud sound of a horn caused them to remember that they were in the middle of a public parking lot near a huge white tent.

"Where are we?" she asked.

He grinned and held her hand tighter. "You'll know soon."

A few seconds later, her eyes grew big with pleasure. "I saw an ad for this circus last month, but I thought it was gone already."

"It's the last day. I was hoping you'd like my surprise."

"Are you kidding?" She looked like Summer when she was excited. "I love the circus! Summer actually makes fun of me, says I'm more excited than the little kids are about the acrobats and animal tricks and flying trapeze. When I was little, I used to dream about running away with the circus. I was going to be the girl who amazed everyone by dancing on the elephant's back."

He had already bought two VIP tickets and they headed inside to their center ring seats, right in front of the action. He loved this side of Megan, when she forgot to hold back from him to protect herself, when she gave him a window into who she really was. Not just the great mother, not just the intelligent CPA… but a woman who thrived on thrills, on adrenaline, on excitement.

Just as much as he did.

When he bought them popcorn and cotton candy and caramel-coated peanuts, she said, "If Summer finds out we ate this stuff, she's going to read me the riot act."

Gabe grinned. "Isn't it supposed to be the other way around? Aren't you supposed to be the one telling her to stay away from junk food?"

"They're learning about nutrition in second grade. If you're wondering, this—" she held up a big wad of pink cotton candy "—is not growing food."

He laughed. "I loved seeing Summer at the station." He didn't want to pressure Megan, knew she still needed time to work things out about them, but she had to know. "I've missed her."

Megan's eyes softened. "She missed you, too. Actually, Gabe, I've been thinking—"

Before she could say anything more, the crowd lights went black and the stage lights went on. He wanted to pull Megan out of the tent to hear what she'd been about to tell him.

What was she thinking?

That she wanted to be together?

Or that she didn't?

She was immediately caught up in the circus show, but Gabe couldn't concentrate on anything but her.

Megan loved every second of the circus. She could hardly look as nimble acrobats tossed themselves around the ring. She held her breath when the tiger trainer got in the ring with ten deadly animals. She laughed until her stomach hurt at the antics of the clowns.

And still, for all that her senses should have been filled to the brim, she couldn't forget for one single second the man sitting beside her. No one she'd dated had ever thought to take her to the circus. It was always the same white tablecloths and hushed voices, stilted conversation about work and investment portfolios. She'd never let any of those men get close enough to find out her hopes and dreams, what made her laugh or cry.

But even though she'd repeatedly tried to push

Gabe away, even though she'd worked hard to guard her heart from him, he'd figured her out. From the fireworks show way up high on his roof to the innocent, childish fun of the circus, he was filling her soul up, one sweet experience at a time.

Not to mention the wonder of the way he made love to her.

At the end of the show, she jumped to her feet, clapping so hard her palms stung.

"Thank you, Gabe. It was—" she had to search for the right word, finally finding it in Summer's favorite exclamation "—awesome! Totally awesome!"

She quickly bought a few little trinkets to give to Summer. When she glanced back at Gabe, he looked pleased with how much she'd enjoyed herself, but strangely worried, too.

"Didn't you have a good time?"

"I did, although to be honest, just watching you enjoy it made it the best circus I've ever been to."

Megan flushed at the heat in his eyes. It was amazing how being with Gabe made everything around her so much richer, so much brighter. She hadn't realized all the shades, all the contours, she was missing until he had—literally—burst into her life.

She enjoyed holding his hand and snuggling close to him as they walked back to the parking lot. He pressed a kiss to the top of her head and everything felt so right.

"When do you need to pick Summer up?"

She looked at her watch. "In about an hour."

She found herself being tugged in the opposite direction from the truck, out toward the ocean. A few minutes later, they were sitting on a log looking at the Golden Gate Bridge.

He had that serious look on his face again. "Gabe, something's wrong, isn't it? You had that same look back under the big top."

"No, nothing's wrong. At least I hope there isn't." He ran his hand through his hair, leaving it looking sexily rumpled as he explained, "When we were talking about Summer, you started to say that you'd been thinking about things. But you never got a chance to tell me what it was you were thinking."

Her heartbeat kicked up. Back in the circus ring, she'd been so overwhelmed with his lovely surprise date that her mouth had been moving without much editing from her brain.

But now, Megan was nervous. Habit made her want to get up off the log and run away from Gabe as fast and as far as she could.

It was so very difficult to remain right where she was and face not only Gabe but also her own fears.

"I've been thinking a lot about us" was the only way she knew how to begin.

She had to reach for his hand to steady herself. He was just as warm, just as steady, as he'd always been. Nothing about this conversation was going to be easy. But that was no excuse not to have it, no excuse to keep hiding her feelings from Gabe.

"I never intended to let you so far into my life," she made herself say with painful honesty.

"I know, sweetheart."

"You didn't, either," she had to point out, and was surprised when his mouth moved into a small smile. "You tried to fight what's between us just as hard as I did."

"Only until I realized that I didn't need to fight it. That apartment fire just happened to be the way we met. Nothing more."

His words opened something up inside her chest, that part of her that had worried, despite everything, that he still looked at her as the fire victim with stars in her eyes.

"The thing is, Gabe, everything was—is—so great with you. Not just the sex," she said in a soft voice. He lifted his hand to her face, his knuckles brushing against her cheek, making her tremble. "Making love with you is, well…" She licked her lips. "It's amazing, but just talking, laughing, snowboarding… I love every minute we've spent together."

"I do, too."

She needed him to understand. "I wasn't just fighting because of my past. I was fighting because of Summer. I was so afraid I'd fall for you and let her get close to you and you'd become even more of a role model to her than you already were. And that would only break her heart more when you left."

"I'm not going to leave."

His words stopped her in her tracks. "How can you know for sure?"

Before she realized what he was doing, he'd

scooped her up from the log to sit in his lap. He was so big and she loved how feminine she felt in his arms, how safe he always made her feel.

"Here's how I know," he said, pressing his lips to hers a moment before saying, "I love you, Megan."

Her breath caught in her chest. She hadn't seen this coming, hadn't expected Gabe to declare himself like this today.

Unable to believe what he'd just said, she didn't realize she'd said, "You do?" until the words were out.

"I do, sweetheart. You are the bravest person I know. That day in your building, when it was burning, your love for your daughter made you so strong, made the difference between our living or dying. I lost a piece of my heart to you right then and there."

"I always thought I was so strong," she whispered, her voice barely rising above the surf, "but the truth is I've been scared for so long. Even before David died." She didn't want to hide anything from Gabe anymore. Or herself. "We met when I was twenty. I hadn't really dated anyone seriously before. He was older and dating him was exciting. He never pressured me to do anything I wasn't ready for and after a couple of months it made sense to sleep together."

She could feel Gabe tense beneath her. "I'm sorry. I know you don't want to hear me talking about going to bed with another man. Especially after saying you…"

"I love you, Megan," he said again, filling in the blanks for her when she faltered at the word *love*.

"I'm sorry to be telling you this now, but I need

you to understand," she said, squeezing his hand, beyond glad that he was there for her to hold on to. "Being intimate with David didn't even seem like that much of a risk at the time. It was what everyone was doing in college, sleeping with their boyfriends." She paused. "Only, everyone else didn't find out they were pregnant on their twentieth birthday."

This time Gabe was the one squeezing her hands. "I was terrified. Terrified about having a baby. Terrified about marrying a man I wasn't even sure I loved. I think that was the moment I vowed I was going to live a risk-free life, to protect myself from ever feeling that way again. His death only reinforced that vow."

She made herself hold his gaze as she admitted, "Being with you is risky on so many levels, Gabe. Not just for me, but for my daughter, too."

His expression, his voice, was gentle as he said, "I can't even begin to imagine how scary it must have been to find yourself dealing with so much, so young. But when I look at you and Summer—" he stopped, smiled as he thought of her daughter "—I know she's the best thing that's ever happened to you."

The moisture building up behind her eyes threatened to spill. "She is."

"Then aren't you glad you made those risky choices? Because taking those risks gave you Summer."

No one had ever pointed it out to her like that. And he was right, she would go through all those terrifying moments again just for the chance to cuddle with her daughter, to see Summer's face light up when she laughed, to be a part of her daughter's journey from little girl to woman.

"Say it again, Gabe. Please."

His hands moved from hers to her face, so strong and gentle, his thumbs caressing her cheeks. "I love you." His mouth moved to hers and he emphasized his declaration with a kiss that said the exact same thing.

When they pulled apart, despite the butterflies in her stomach, Megan couldn't say those three words. But she could tell him, "I want to try. You. Me and Summer. I want to give us a chance." And there was one way to prove to Gabe that she meant it. "Do you have time to head to her school to pick her up?"

"Yes," he said, his expression telling her he knew exactly what her gesture meant. "I'd love that."

After they drove to her apartment in silence and parked his truck outside the building, Gabe held her hand for five straight blocks. Summer was beside herself with glee at seeing Gabe on the playground, and as the kids rushed around the firefighter and all talked at once, Megan stood back, watching.

She'd been as brave as she could be today. She'd told Gabe things she'd never admitted to another soul, namely that she'd married her husband because she'd been a scared young woman who couldn't imagine going forward any other way, rather than for love.

Only, for all she'd said today, Megan hadn't told Gabe everything.

He'd said the words *I love you* so easily. And, oh, how she'd wanted to say them back. But she couldn't. Not yet. Not until she felt more settled, more sure about the decision she was making.

Gabe and Summer walked over to her, hand in hand. Summer was chattering away a mile a minute, with Gabe somehow taking in every lightning-fast word. The warmth that started in the center of Megan's chest before spreading outward had nothing to do with decisions.

And everything to do with the sweet possibility of a future full of love.

Twenty-Five

"Ooh, Mommy, look! It's Justin Bieber! I need a picture with him."

Summer ran over to the uncannily lifelike wax figure of the young pop star and Megan quickly snapped a couple of great shots with her digital camera. When she turned around, she couldn't see Gabe anywhere in the room, not even over by the Kim Kardashian figure most of the men were drooling over.

Megan, Summer and Gabe had come down to Fisherman's Wharf on a clear, cool Friday night to eat clam chowder in sourdough bread bowls, but had ended up inside the wax museum instead. Amazingly, none of them had ever been there before, thinking it was something for tourists, not locals. Megan couldn't remember laughing so much. Her cheeks actually hurt and she was pretty sure her abdominal muscles would be feeling it, too, the next morning.

Still, she wasn't at all prepared to see Gabe standing next to his brother in the next room. Or, rather, the wax version of Smith Sullivan.

"He never told us he was here," Gabe said with a wicked grin. "Boy, are we all going to have fun with this one. Can you take a couple of shots of us?" He draped one muscular arm around the shoulders of the wax figure and Megan noticed several strangers in the room stopping to stare. Especially when Summer said, "Hey, isn't that your brother, Gabe?"

He grinned at her. "Sure is, sweetie. And it looks like he's got a bad case of ear wax…all over!"

As Summer giggled, Megan mused that while each of the Sullivan brothers was unique, all six of them shared a certain…well, *rugged gorgeousness* was one way of putting it. Even in wax, Smith Sullivan was quite a hunky sight.

Of course, a flesh-and-blood Gabe Sullivan put the figure to shame.

A few minutes later, they saw Nicola's wax figure in the corner at the same time.

"We met her at your mom's party!" Summer exclaimed. Clearly full of pride, she said, "I don't need a picture with her because I totally know her. When do we get to meet Smith, Gabe?"

Gabe ruffled her hair. "Next time he's in town, I'll have him buy you an ice-cream cone."

"Cool!"

As Summer ran off, Megan's chest suddenly tightened. It was just what she'd been afraid of. That Summer would assume these group outings meant her mother and the firefighter were going to be together forever. Long enough, at least, to eat ice cream with *the* Smith Sullivan.

Megan could feel Gabe's eyes on her. His arms were next, wrapping around her waist to pull her lightly against him. "I heard they'll kick you out of the wax museum if they see you frowning."

She buried her face in his neck and breathed in his warm and smoky scent until she was able to stuff away her fears again. All the while, he held on to her, his large hand stroking her back.

"I'm having a great time, Gabe. So is Summer."

"That makes three of us, then."

He took her hand and they joined her daughter by the superhero wax figures, all of her hopes and dreams pooling around his offhand statement.

That makes three of us, then.

Oh, how she longed for that to be true. A husband, a family for her daughter, with no more heartache, no more struggles.

Just love.

But how could that ever be a reality for her and Summer when Gabe was a firefighter? One who wasn't afraid of running into burning buildings if it meant saving someone inside.

Stop it, she told herself in a firm inner voice. She'd promised both of them that she'd try. Which meant putting the brakes on her worries and fears for a little while and just enjoying being with him.

An hour later, Gabe was dropping them off at home on the way to his night shift at the station.

They'd agreed he'd come over for dinner on Sunday night after his shift, but Megan already missed him.

Besides, he'd been holding her hand for hours. Touching her, too, soft little caresses on her face, her back, her hips. She was burning up for him, but with Summer between them, Megan couldn't do anything about her desire.

Desire that she was afraid was going to make her come completely unglued before long.

"Thank you for a lovely evening," she said in a slightly husky voice.

She reached for the doorknob, but before she could open the door, Summer said, "Aren't you guys going to kiss good-night?"

A strangled laugh came from Megan's lips, and when she looked over at Gabe, his eyes were dark with the same barely restrained desire she was grappling with.

"Of course we are," he said.

A moment later, his lips were against hers, warm and delicious. It was just enough of a kiss to whet her appetite for more, and when he pulled back she felt dazed.

Summer smiled at the two of them, clearly pleased to see that her matchmaking had worked out so well. "See you Sunday, Gabe. That was fun."

On Sunday night, the three of them were sitting on the living room carpet, trying to extract a thigh bone in a tightly contested game of Operation.

Well, a tightly contested game between Summer

and Gabe, anyway. Sitting this close to Gabe had Megan's hands so shaky she could hardly play. Again and again, she set off the red buzzer by bonking the tweezers into the sides of the small holes on the game board.

Summer and Gabe were neck and neck with their piles of little bones and organs when Summer pouted. "This isn't fair. You do this kind of stuff for your job. I'm just a kid."

Megan waited to see if he was going to be fooled, but he merely raised an eyebrow. "I'm trained as a paramedic, not a surgeon."

Summer made a face. "It's practically the same thing."

Gabe smiled at her daughter. "Not even close, but nice try, kid."

When Summer cheerfully said, "Your turn," Megan knew she wasn't done rummaging through her bag of tricks to try to make sure she won the game.

Gabe picked up the tweezers and was just about to go for the brain when Summer let out a shriek. "Oh, my gosh, what a huge bug!"

Megan winced as her daughter's piercingly high voice penetrated her skull. "What bug, Summer?"

But her daughter was busy staring at Gabe's hand where it had stilled right over the playing board, rather than bonking into it and giving her the potential win.

Megan couldn't help but laugh. "He's one of eight, sweetie. I think you're going to have to try harder than that to distract him."

A second later, Gabe reached in, grabbed the brain and almost had it all the way out when the tip of the tweezers slid against the board. The red buzzer sounded and Summer grabbed the tweezers from his hand, expertly pulling out the brain.

"I win!"

"Nice work, Summer."

Megan couldn't imagine a single one of the guys she'd dated playing this game with Summer, let alone enjoying it. Not to mention dealing with her antics so well.

"You have school tomorrow. Time for bed," Megan said. "Go brush your teeth and get your jammies on and I'll read you a story."

"Can you read it to me tonight, Gabe?"

Perhaps Megan shouldn't have been shocked by Summer's request, but she was. No one else had ever read her daughter a story, not even her father, who'd always preferred to be outside on the grass playing with her when she was a baby than indoors with her teething and chewing on a book on his lap.

"Megan?"

Rather than answering Summer's question, Gabe's eyes were on hers, and she could read the question on his face: *Is this okay with you?*

Every minute the three of them spent together, she watched Gabe and Summer draw closer. They were two people who genuinely enjoyed each other's company.

Her daughter had fantastic taste in men.

And yet, for some reason this felt like another big

step, after so many other big steps. First, spending a Friday night together at Fisherman's Wharf, acting like a family. Then, kissing Gabe in front of Summer. And now, Gabe telling her a bedtime story.

What if something happened to him? What if Summer got used to Gabe playing games with her and reading bedtime stories and then—

She caught herself a split second before her brain reeled off into panic land.

I need to try. Just keep trying.

"Sounds great to me."

Gabe scanned her face, the smile she'd pasted on it. "Maybe," he said softly, "we could all read it together."

Relief swept through her, love fierce on its heels. She'd never thought she'd meet a man who understood her this well, who could read her secret thoughts without her saying a word.

Thirty minutes later, Summer was tucked into bed and they were headed out to the living room.

"I loved listening to you read *The Magic Tree House* to Summer, the way you did all the characters."

He shrugged as if it were no big deal. "Sophie's pretty good at putting on the pressure to get us in there to read to the kids during story time at the library."

Megan loved the thought of Gabe sitting on a little plastic chair reading to a bunch of kids…and their drooling mothers. She could only imagine the kind of fantasies he must inspire in those women during what had to be the best thirty minutes of their month.

The very same fantasies he inspired in her.

"Ready for your bedtime story?" He pulled her onto his lap on the couch.

"But I'm not tired yet," she said softly.

His beautiful mouth moved up at the corners and she thought he was going to kiss her. Instead, he nuzzled into the curve of her neck, making her shiver with his tongue.

"Once upon a time there was a man."

"Not a prince?"

"No," he said with a soft nip at her chin. "He was a perfectly average, ordinary man. But one day he got lucky and met the prettiest woman in the entire world."

"Are you sure she wasn't average and ordinary, too?"

His teeth found her earlobe, sending thrill bumps over the surface of her skin. "I promise you, she was extraordinary. She was so pretty he couldn't believe she was talking to him."

"Did they kiss?"

His mouth moved closer to hers as he said, "Oh, yes…and those kisses rocked his world."

Finally—*finally!*—he was kissing her mouth and her toes were curling from the passion erupting all through her. But despite how frantic she was to make love with him, she somehow managed to remember that her daughter was sleeping down the hall.

Megan had decided it was okay for Summer to

spend time with Gabe, for outings and game nights, even for bedtime stories. But there was no way she would ever be okay with her daughter seeing a man come out of her mother's bedroom in the morning. Not until things were far more serious, not unless there was going to be a wedding soon.

Considering she couldn't even bring herself to say *I love you,* she knew better than to keep kissing him like this with her daughter only a couple of walls away.

She shifted on his lap. "Thank you for coming over tonight."

"Thank you for inviting me."

Judging by the thick bulge in his pants and the hunger in his eyes, she knew he was just as ready for wall-banging, crazy-monkey sex as she was.

Feeling like the worst kind of tease, she said, "I want you to stay, but—"

One finger covered her lips. "I understand, Megan. I would never want to do anything to hurt Summer, either."

She very reluctantly climbed off his lap and they walked, hand in hand, over to the door. After another long kiss good-night, and another sweet *I love you* from Gabe, he was halfway down the hall when she called out.

"You never told me how the story ends, Gabe." She held her breath, waiting for his response.

His expression held all the love and desire she knew he felt for her.

"It doesn't."

* * *

Megan was blurry from lack of sleep when she walked Summer to school on Monday morning. Her body had been buzzing from Gabe's kisses, but she hadn't bothered trying to take care of it herself. Not when it wasn't the orgasm she needed.

It was the man himself.

She'd never been a woman who chased after men, partly because she'd married so young, but mostly because it just wasn't her personality. But it was pure female instinct that had her heading away from Summer's school in the opposite direction of her house.

Ten minutes later, she rang Gabe's doorbell, her heart pounding from how quickly she'd covered the pavement to get to him. But as she waited, she suddenly realized she had no idea whether he'd be there or not, whether he was out for a run or picking up bagels for breakfast. And when he didn't immediately open the door, she could practically taste her disappointment.

She was just turning to head back home when the door opened.

"Megan?"

Clearly, the universe was doing her a favor, because not only was Gabe home, but he was wearing a towel wrapped low around his hips. She was still busy gaping at his sculpted muscles when he said, "Come in, sweetheart."

His hand was warm on the small of her back. "Is everything okay?"

She finally noticed his concerned look at the way

she'd shown up like this, out of breath and likely wild-eyed in her desperation to see him. To be with him.

"No," she said with complete honesty.

"Is it Summer?"

His instant panic radiated out to her and she quickly put her hand over his racing heart to calm him. "Summer's perfect. I just dropped her off at school."

"Then what?" His hands were in her hair as he pulled her closer to search her face for clues.

"I missed you," she whispered, shyly dropping her eyes at her stark admission. "Friday night. Sunday night." She lifted her eyes to his. "I felt like I was going to go crazy if I didn't see you again." She put her arms around him and reveled in the strength beneath her fingertips.

"I ran zigzags back and forth around this city all morning," he told her in a raw voice as his gaze dropped to her lips and then moved back up to her eyes. "It was either that or use my tools to break into your apartment and climb into your bed with you."

A moment later, he'd picked her up and was carrying her into his bedroom. Megan was thrilled that he was as desperate as she was to pick up where they'd started—and never had a chance to finish—that weekend.

"How long do you have?" he murmured against her earlobe, his tongue flicking against the sensitive flesh just behind it.

"As long as you need," she told him as she pressed

her own kisses against the curve of his neck, one side of his broad shoulders.

His eyes lifted to hers, dark not only with passion, but also with something so much bigger, so much richer, than just physical desire. "Forever, Megan." The two words rumbled from his chest, catching her straight in the middle of hers. "That's how long I'm going to need with you."

Megan gasped at his response to her offhand reply. She'd just been talking about making love this morning, about a few stolen hours in his bed away from the work she needed to do for her clients. But he'd answered her as if she'd meant something entirely different.

Which, if she were being completely honest with herself, she had.

She tried to catch her breath as he lowered her to the bed. She knew he loved her, but for all the times he'd said those three sweet words to her in the past week, he'd never pressured her to return them. He knew she was trying, knew being with him was the biggest risk she'd taken in years. But now, as she lay beneath him on his big bed and he looked at her as no man ever had—as though she were the sun, the stars and everything in between—she wanted so badly to give him back what he so effortlessly had been giving her.

"I—" The words got caught in her throat, jammed by the resurgence of the fears she'd been pushing away, one by one, every time Gabe was with her.

No, not just then. Every time she thought about him. Every time Summer said his name and smiled.

She licked her lips, tried again. "Gabe, I—"

His beautiful mouth covered hers just as she faltered again, his kiss telling her he understood…and that he wasn't going anywhere. She lost herself in the love he poured into the kiss, wrapping her arms and legs tighter around him, needing him to be so much closer.

"I'll wait for you, Megan. As long as I need to wait."

Thankfully, he didn't wait for her to respond, didn't allow for any uncomfortable silences between them. Instead, he reached for the hem of her tank top and pulled it up and over her head.

"Pink is my new favorite color," he murmured when he saw her bra.

Without realizing it, she'd put on the bra that matched the panties he'd seen in her laundry basket that day he'd surprised her by coming to her apartment. But before she could admit to herself that she'd worn them on purpose—hoping for just this response—he was lowering his head to her and running his tongue over the upper swell of first one breast and then the other, just where the lace gave way to sensitive flesh.

She was panting and arching her back into him by the time he lifted his head. "You should know, I've had more than one fantasy about those pink panties."

"Me, too," she whispered.

His hands faltered just as he reached for the button

of her jeans. A moment later, he was unzipping and drawing them down her legs, pulling off her shoes and socks while he was at it.

"Tell me one of them," he said in that low, hungry voice that never failed to send heat and desire all through her, starting deep in her belly and radiating outward.

But she'd already had a chance to act out more than one fantasy with him. This time, she wanted to know his.

With his hands roving across her hips, her stomach, over her rib cage, it was hard to get the request out. "You already know one of my fantasies. I want to hear one of yours."

His smile was so powerfully sensual she almost came right then and there, with nothing more than that look in his eyes and his large hands cupping her still-covered breasts.

"One of my fantasies," he said softly as he lifted himself off her so that he could rake his eyes down her entire body, "involves surprise." He paused. "And trust."

Whatever she'd been expecting him to say, it hadn't been this.

It hadn't been his asking her for *trust.*

Of course she trusted him. She'd let him into her life, into Summer's life. She had wild sex with him and knew that, even though he was so much bigger, she'd never have to be frightened about what he could have done to her.

As if he was giving her time to think about what

he'd just said, he got up from the bed and took off the towel. When he turned back to her, he was gloriously naked and so hard his erection was standing straight up against his hard stomach.

It would have been so easy just to pull him down over her, to brush past whatever surprise, whatever fantasy, he wanted to have come true, and make love without any more talk about trust. But she knew that wouldn't just be cheating him of his fantasy…it would be cheating herself, too.

"Megan?"

The moment of truth had come. He'd given her time to think, to mull, to decide. He hadn't forced the issue on the word *love,* but she could see he wasn't going to back down on *trust.*

Not trusting her voice, she nodded.

His answering smile was as encouraging as it was sexy. And then he turned away and reached into his dresser drawer. A few seconds later, he pulled out a tie.

Her heart raced as he approached her.

"Have you ever been blindfolded?"

She bit her lip, shook her head.

"Have you ever wanted to be?"

She knew a flush covered her cheeks as she nodded. Before, when she'd had this fantasy, it had been a nameless, faceless man blindfolding her. Gabe had starred in every single one of her fantasies since the fire.

He lowered the silk over her eyes and gently lifted

her head from the pillow to tie it. "Can you see any-thing?"

She could see light creeping in along the edges, but that was all. "No."

"Good." Promises of sensual pleasure filled the short word. "If you can promise to stay just where you are, to trust me to make you feel good, we'll save tying you to the bedposts for another one of my fantasies."

She was shocked that she could become even more aroused. Somehow, without her ever giving voice to her hidden desires, he knew them.

His warm hands moved under her to unhook and remove her bra and then they covered her breasts, his fingers rolling over her erect nipples. "You like that plan, don't you?"

Since her body had already answered him, it was fairly easy to say, "Yes." She licked her lips. "I like it very much."

She heard him groan softly, felt the mattress shift beneath his weight as he moved. "My sexy little risk taker."

Her surprise at his words got lost in the sensa-tion of Gabe settling between her thighs, his hands on the sensitive skin between her legs, pushing her open for him.

"If you could only see how wet you are."

His fingers pressed gently against her panties, which she knew had to be soaked by now from the way he was teasing her. Right from the start, she'd loved the way he spoke to her, the supersexy, slightly

dirty talk that she'd never thought to experience…
but had always secretly wondered about.

His heat seared her and she bucked into his hand.
She was so close already that it wouldn't take much
more to push her over the edge. Especially with her
vision taken away, every touch, every scent, every
sound, was so much more potent. So much more
powerful.

And then, suddenly, wet warmth covered her, his
tongue stroking her through the pink lace.

She had to put her hands in his hair, had to buck
her hips up into his mouth. There was no skin-on-
skin contact, but it didn't matter. She didn't need it,
just more of the delicious pressure of—

"Oh, God." The words left her mouth as he pulled
aside her panties and his tongue was there. On her.
Over her. In her.

His fingers were everywhere at once as his tongue
and teeth worked over her most sensitive flesh. One
hand caressed her breasts, pinching her nipples just
perfectly, the other drove inside her, and for the first
time ever, Megan actually screamed as she came, a
ragged sound that she wouldn't have been able to believe belonged to her if she'd been able to think at all.

For long moments, as waves of pleasure continued
to rise, explode, then crest through her, Gabe continued to play between her legs, across her breasts.

She felt limp and exhausted by the time her climax finally receded. But when she felt Gabe slowly
crawling up over her, so close that his rock-hard erec-

tion rubbed over her skin, she was hit with a second wind.

He kissed his way up her body, soft love bites that had her trembling again by the time he reached her face.

"Thank you for trusting me."

He slid the blindfold off at the same moment that he slid into her and she felt herself open up to him in a way she hadn't ever opened up to anyone before. The walls she'd built, those final prison bars around her heart, came crashing down as he held her so gently and kissed her so sweetly.

If ever there was a time in her life to take a risk, it was now. If ever there was a person to risk it all for, it was Gabe. But before she could make her lips form the words, he was saying, "Come over to the other side with me, love," and up, up, up she went as her next climax stole away every last thought, along with any possibility of speech.

All that remained was the love pouring from him to her…and back again as she finally let Gabe all the way into her soul.

Twenty-Six

Megan had her arms tightly wrapped around Gabe and, with her hands spread out over his chest, she could feel his heart beating, hard, steady.

She hadn't come to him this morning for sex, hadn't come simply to scratch the itch that only he could reach.

The truth was that she'd come for this connection.

For more happiness than she'd ever thought was possible.

For love.

"Gabe?"

"Mmm?"

He brushed the damp hair from her forehead and pressed a kiss to her skin. She loved his easy affection, that he wasn't a man who felt he needed to hold anything back to be macho or manly. Not for the first time, she was struck by how well his mother had raised her sons. Yes, many of them were clearly big-time players with the ladies, but she couldn't imagine any one of them purposely hurting a woman.

And, from meeting Chase and Marcus, she could see that once they fell in love, it really was forever. Chloe and Nicola were clearly the center of Gabe's brothers' worlds. She had a hunch about Chloe, one she hoped she was right about. It would be so lovely to be able to hold—and spoil—a little baby in the not-so-distant future.

As she luxuriated in the warm caress of Gabe's eyes on her, the vision of Chloe and Chase's baby morphed into something different. Something that should have frightened her even more...but only sent more joy moving through her instead.

Gabe would be the most incredible father. He was already one of Summer's favorite people on the planet. But Megan was getting ahead of herself.

First he needed to know how she felt about him.

"There's something I've been wanting to tell you."

"I can't wait to hear it, sweetheart."

Megan was silent for a moment as she marveled at being this lucky, that Gabe had been the one to find her and Summer in their burning apartment, that they'd connected afterward and found such amazing sparks, that they'd managed to work through their issues and...

"I tried to make myself stay away from you, to keep you at arm's length, to keep you from getting too close to me and Summer. But I've come to real- ize that even if I succeeded in keeping my distance from you, even if I told you I couldn't be with you anymore, it wouldn't protect me. Not in the least. Because I'd still be scared every time I turned on the news and heard reports of a big fire. And I'd still die inside if anything happened to you." She hated to even think it, let alone say the words, but she knew she needed to. "Pushing you away won't protect anyone's heart. All it guarantees is that I'll miss out on the joy of being with you."

This was it, this was the big moment when she would finally tell him. "I—"

His cell went off just then, a special ring, and although he was clearly frustrated by the interruption, he reached out to grab his phone from the table beside the bed.

"What does that ring mean?"

"It's an urgent fire call." His frown deepened with every word he read.

She sat up in bed, pulling the covers over her naked skin as if that would somehow protect her from what was happening. "It's a bad one, isn't it?"

He nodded, already moving from the bed to put on his clothes. "A truck potentially carrying hazardous materials crashed into several stores in Chinatown."

Oh, God, she thought. *It's a sign.*

It had to be.

All the fears she thought had been loved into submission raised their heads and called out to her, screaming for her to listen, to heed their warnings.

What, they screeched at her, *are you doing? You can still run to safety, before it's too late.*

She'd been lulled into thinking she could be in a serious relationship with him, that she could accept the fear of losing Gabe, but now she realized why. He hadn't been called in to any fires while they'd been together…and she'd purposely kept from asking him about what happened during his shifts because she'd known she couldn't have handled hearing about any dangerous situations.

And here she'd been just about to confess her love to him.

He was fully clothed within seconds and moving back to where she was frozen on the bed. "Megan?"

She shifted in Gabe's arms, moved back toward the headboard, away from him. "Your crew needs you. The people in the burning buildings need you. You need to go." Her words came out harsher than she wanted them to, even as her heart was screaming, *I need you, too.*

But instead of leaving, Gabe put his hands on either side of her face. "I love you, Megan."

He kissed her softly, and when he lifted his mouth from hers, she knew what he was waiting for. It was her turn to say the words, to admit just how much she cared about him. It was what she'd been on the verge of doing a split second before the urgent call came in.

But she still couldn't do it, not when fear for him was eating her up from the inside out.

No matter how much she wanted to, she couldn't stop him from going to the fire. Chaining him to her and Summer, forcing him to live a "safe" life, would kill him inside faster than a fire ever could.

His cell went off again and she hugged him tight, then forced herself to push all the way out of his arms and let him go do his job.

"You need to go," she said again, her brain stuck in an infinite loop of dread, of dark premonition.

Gabe stared at her for a long moment, everything he felt for her in his eyes. "You're right, I need to go now and fight this fire, but I promise I'll come back to you. To Summer."

She shook her head. It was hard to breathe. "How can you make me that promise?"

He moved closer again, took her hands in his, laid them over his heart. "Have I ever broken a promise to you, Megan?"

"No."

"I'm not going to break it now."

With a final kiss, his mouth warm on her suddenly cold one, he was gone.

As Gabe drove to the location of the fire, he knew he had never loved anyone the way he loved Megan. And Summer, too. He wanted them both in his life. He wanted to be a husband to Megan and a father to Summer.

He'd let go of his concerns about dating a fire victim. Megan was so much more than that, and the truth was, he had never really been able to think of her in those terms. She was the antithesis of a victim.

He'd thought Megan was moving past her own concerns, that she was getting used to the idea of his job. But the way she'd just reacted to the fire call... well, she was clearly still fighting those demons her husband had left her with.

Still, hadn't Gabe purposely kept some of the

more extreme fires he'd been to from her? Not because he liked keeping her in the dark, but because
he didn't think it was fair to shove it all down her
throat at once. Judging by her reaction to this fire,
he wanted to tell himself he'd done the right thing
by keeping from her the truth of the danger he faced
on a regular basis.

But, he suddenly realized, he hadn't been fair to
Megan by protecting her from the reality of a future
with him. Didn't she deserve to have all the data at
hand before she agreed to love him back?

His gut twisted at the way she'd told him to go,
at the uncertainty in her previously clear eyes as she
looked at him as if her heart were breaking.

Able to see the smoke from several blocks away,
Gabe drove in as close as he could before grabbing his gear from the bed of his truck, and walking straight toward the fiery mess in the center of
Chinatown.

Gabe could hear gas screaming from the ruptured
pipes of the gas main the truck had slammed into
right before it hit the buildings on the east side of
Grant Street. The crew from Station 5 was already
streaming water to disperse the gas to make sure it
didn't ignite.

Quickly noting the crew had been too busy with
the gas leak and the building's occupants to lay a sup-
ply line around to the narrow alley between buildings, he grabbed the hydrant valve, then the hose
from the nearest engine, and laid in the line.

His captain arrived with Gabe's partner, Eric, just

a step behind him. "Let's see if we can save some of these stores," Eric said.

Gabe grabbed tools and the hose line, put on his face piece and pulled up his hose. He took the nozzle with Eric backing him up and advanced into the building. Turning into the doorway, he opened the nozzle at the ceiling until the flames subsided.

He didn't have any ventilation and the smoke was thick, thick enough that he dropped to his knees to crawl across the room to a window. He got it open but, unfortunately, it didn't make much of a difference.

Slowly, he moved forward into the building, the hose leading the way, Eric at his back.

The situation was bad. Really bad.

But he'd made Megan a promise, damn it.

And he had to keep it.

No matter what.

Twenty-Seven

Megan couldn't do it.

She'd known all along that she wasn't strong enough to be with a man who risked his life every day. It was what she'd told Gabe over and over. Immediately after their first kiss, and then again after their first night together. She'd tried to make him understand how impossible this was for her, had tried to keep her heart safe from falling.

But, oh, how she'd wanted to be with him, how she'd wanted the thrill of his kisses, the warmth of his smile, the special connection he had with Summer. So she'd tried.

She'd really tried.

But the panic that had slammed into her when he'd told her about the fire, about the hazardous materials...no, there was no way she could handle being this terrified on a daily basis.

Even after Gabe left his apartment to head for Chinatown, Megan remained right where she was, in his bed, surrounded by his scent, his things, wanting to feel even that small connection a little longer.

Mere minutes ago, she'd been about to take the biggest risk of her life by telling him she loved him and she'd thought that was so difficult. But now she knew what would be infinitely harder: telling him goodbye.

Forever.

As she finally left his apartment, she was followed by the wonderful memories of being with him. Sitting on his lap looking out at the city lights, watching—and creating—fireworks up on the roof, slipping and sliding together in the bathtub and then curling up with him in his bed. Warm. And safe, so much safer than she'd ever felt before.

No. She couldn't let herself think about any of that.

She needed to go home. Get to work. Stay focused on her client's spreadsheets until it was time to pick Summer up from school. And then, when Gabe came back from the fire—if he came back—she'd steel herself to make the final break with him.

Her steps faltered as she slowly walked along the sidewalk. How much easier would her life have been if she'd never met Gabe? If some other firefighter had saved her and Summer, and she'd simply continued her normal life—meeting with clients, taking care of paying the bills, raising her daughter the best she knew how…and dating perfectly nice men with safe jobs.

No question about it, that safety was what she should have been wishing for.

But now that she'd tasted real joy, utter sweetness, she knew anything else would be bland. Boring.

Oh, God, she was in trouble.

Because even though she was terrified about letting herself love Gabe, wholly and completely, she couldn't seem to save herself—and her daughter—by walking away from him, either.

All the rational arguments, all the spreadsheets and calculations of risk versus reward in the world couldn't stop Megan from turning in the opposite direction...straight toward the dark smoke spiraling up from the busy streets of Chinatown.

It was worse than she could have imagined. So much worse. Not only were several buildings on fire, but there was singed food and clothes from the stores all over the street, rolling down gutters running fast with the water from the fire engines.

As Megan moved through the crowd she caught snippets of conversation about the fire.

"Do they know what the hazardous materials are yet?"

"I heard it was a gas leak that could blow the buildings sky-high."

"I'm scared, Mommy. Are the firefighters going to be okay?"

A line of police officers was holding people back along the street, behind a row of fire engines. She had no idea how they'd managed to get the engines into the narrow street, through the crowds of cars and people.

A moment later a sudden burst of flames shot up out of the roof of one of the stores just to the side of the truck's smashed-in engine.

"We need all of you to back up."

She knew the police officer was right, that she'd be safer farther back. It wasn't fair for her to expect Gabe to be safe if she wasn't doing the same thing.

A few minutes later, when they were almost a full block away from the fire, she saw Gabe's truck double-parked on the corner. Pushing her way through the crowd, she pressed her hand against the cool metal of his door. Realizing he'd left it unlocked, she opened the door and climbed inside.

His truck smelled like him, clean and smoky all at the same time. Her hands were tight on the steering wheel as she stared up at the black smoke spiraling into the air, forming clouds of ash in the previously blue sky.

Her brain was stuck on pause, on a far-too-vivid mental picture of Gabe surrounded by flames, just the way he'd looked the first time she'd seen him in her burning apartment building.

Those visions had started to fade during the past few months, but now she was bombarded with them one after the other. Looking up and seeing him gesturing for her to get out of the tub, to follow him through her apartment to the stairs. How strong, how steady, he'd been as he'd helped her and Summer get to safety.

And yet, even though they all could have been killed and Gabe had ended up in the hospital after the beam fell on him, she knew deep in her core that everything he'd done—everything he'd asked of her that horrible afternoon—had been as safe as it could possibly be.

Gabe hadn't been running around or freaking out. He'd been determined—smart—and his clearheaded approach to firefighting was the reason she and Summer were alive.

The epiphany hit her, so hard and fast she wondered how she could possibly have been so blind all this time, blind even in his apartment when she'd been on the verge of declaring her love to him. She'd still been so caught up in the prospect of danger, in thinking he was going to take unwarranted risks and end up dead.

Of course Megan had known, early on, that Gabe was different from David. Her husband had been an adrenaline junkie. He'd thrived on risk and he'd never thought beyond those thrills, not even after he'd become a husband and father. Yes, while she knew that Gabe thrived on the excitement of his job, she knew he wasn't in it just for the risk, for no other reason than to see how far he could push himself this time.

For Gabe, being a firefighter was about so much more than the thrill of putting out fires. It was about helping people and being an important part of the community.

If anyone could work a dangerous job safely, it

was Gabe. There were no guarantees for any of them about getting sick or being in an accident. But if she'd been able to look past her fears, Megan knew she would have realized all of this long before now— that he loved them too much to ever purposely put himself in the path of foolish danger like David had done so many times.

So many things clicked into place for Megan in that moment. She hadn't wanted Summer to turn what had almost happened to them in the apartment fire into a fear that she'd take forward with her in her life. She wanted her daughter to be fearless, but smart, too. She didn't want Summer to hide her light, didn't want her to shy away from taking intelligent risks.

But even though she understood that kids learned by example, those things were exactly what Megan had done. Until Gabe came along and forced her to face the truth of who she really was.

His love gave her the courage to take risks again.

Now, even though she wasn't close enough to the buildings to see if any of the firefighters coming in and out could be the man she loved, sitting in his truck, she felt better just being this close to him.

It wasn't an easy fire to take down, but several hot, dirty hours later, Gabe was satisfied with his work, with what all of the crews had accomplished in Chinatown. The gas leak hadn't turned into something worse, and while the store owners were going to need to deal with their insurance companies to replace their inventory, the fire had been beaten down before it could demolish everything. A few new front walls and windows would take care of most of the structural work.

He had removed his mask and turnout coat by the time he was halfway down the block. Already, his mind was back to Megan. To what she'd been about to tell him when the call had come in.

And the fear in her eyes when he'd promised to come back safely from the fire and she hadn't let herself believe him.

His truck was right where he'd left it, and he was just about to pull off his turnout pants and throw them, along with the rest of his gear, into the bed, when he got the best surprise of his life.

Within seconds, Megan was out of the driver's seat and jumping straight into his arms, her legs wrapped around his hips, her arms around his neck.

"Thank God you're okay." She kissed him, fast and hard, once, then twice, then three times as if she could hardly believe he was there.

"I'm so much better than okay," he told her when she let him up for air, but he didn't let her go, loving the way she felt in his arms.

She was kissing him on his mouth, on his cheeks, on his nose, his eyelids, everywhere her lips could reach.

He knew how scared she must have been, enough that she'd come to the site of the fire to keep watch over him.

"I'm so sorry I acted like that when you got the

fire call." Her words were falling so fast, he couldn't interrupt. "I'm sorry for the way I acted that first time we made love in the hotel, the way I begged you to love me, then threw you out because I was so torn. For so many years I've been putting up walls and big thick bars around my heart. But even then I knew that trying to control the wild in you would be like trapping you inside that prison with me. So I told myself I needed to let you go for both of us." Tears slid down her cheeks, one after the other. "But I can't let you go."

"You don't have to, sweetheart."

"You told me over and over again how much you love me. How much you love Summer. So many times, I had the chance to say those words back to you, but I didn't take them. And I thought that not saying the words meant I was still safe. But I wasn't, Gabe. Whether or not I was ever brave enough to say it out loud, I still loved you. With all of my heart... and every last piece of my soul." She rested her hands on either side of his face and looked at him with wonder in her eyes. "You shouldn't have to choose between your job and me. I know you love being a firefighter. And I will support you. Always." She kissed him, and then said again, "I love you, Gabe. I love you so much."

"I love hearing you say it," he said, and it was so true that he was nearly overcome with emotion. "But do you think I didn't already know how you felt?"

Her eyes widened at the realization that he'd known her true feelings for him all along. "I didn't say it. I should have said that I'm in love with you. I should have told you I fell in love with you that day in the hospital when Summer ran to hug you and you hugged her back just as tight. I should have been honest about falling more in love with you every second since then." She barely paused for breath. "If anything had happened to you today, if you'd been slightly distracted because of me, because of what I wasn't brave enough to say—"

Gabe pressed one sooty finger over her lips. "I'll never get tired of hearing you say you love me, but whether you're saying it or not, I feel it every time you look at me. Every time you kiss me. You say it every time you come apart in my arms and you give your heart to me." He smiled down at her. "Do you want to know how I felt today when I was fighting this fire?"

Her eyes were sparkling with tears as she nodded.

"I felt stronger than I ever have before. I felt confident. Steady." He tipped his finger beneath her chin, made sure their gazes held. "I felt loved."

He pressed his mouth to hers and the kiss they shared was soft and sweet and passionate all wrapped into one.

"I knew you and Summer were waiting for me to come back to you, safe and sound. I'm not going to let you down, Megan. You both deserve forever this time. Let me be that forever."

Tears ran down her cheeks.

"Forever," she whispered, and then Gabe was claiming her mouth again as people watched and

smiled at the heroic fireman and the beautiful young woman embracing on a sidewalk in the middle of downtown San Francisco.

Epilogue

Sophie Sullivan sat at her mother's kitchen table, brochures spread out all around her for the various surprises she was planning for Chase and Chloe's upcoming wedding.

Gabe, Megan and Summer had joined her and her mother for lunch and now Summer was riding her bike out in the front yard, a bike similar to the one Sophie had had when she was seven, with a banana seat and pink streamers flying from the handlebars. Back in December, the last time they were all together at her mother's house, she'd felt a little bad about playing matchmaker by mentioning Gabe's plans to go skiing in Lake Tahoe to Summer.

But look how well it had turned out.

Sophie was beyond happy for her brother and her friend. They clearly belonged together, even though they'd both obviously tried to—foolishly—fight their connection at first.

The door flew open and Gabe ran inside and into

the kitchen. Megan and Summer walked inside holding hands a moment later, the little girl sniffling and limping on a leg with a bloody knee.

Sophie immediately went to them and had just given Summer a hug when Gabe returned with their mother's first-aid kit. He looked strangely pale, despite his tanned skin, as he lifted Summer onto his lap. Speaking softly to Megan's daughter, he gently cleaned, then bandaged, her knee.

He'd just finished putting on the last Band-Aid when Summer hopped off his lap and said, "Race you to the tree house."

Sophie watched as Megan put her hand on his shoulder. "You did great."

Gabe blew out a hard breath. "Seeing her fall off the bike onto the street and not knowing how badly she was hurt made me the most nervous I've ever been in my life."

Megan leaned over and kissed him and Sophie moved back to the table to give them some privacy. Her heart squeezed tight at watching her brother be so paternal. It was so sweet.

And yet, as the two of them headed into the backyard to join Summer in the tree house, Sophie sighed, trying not to compare the way Megan and Gabe looked at each other to the way *nobody* looked at her. Especially not—

"Hey, Nice."

She whirled around, shocked to find Jake McCann standing next to her mother on the Persian rug. "What are you doing here?"

Her mother raised an eyebrow at her snippy tone. "Jake has offered to help with the bar at Chase and Chloe's wedding."

Chase and Chloe had plenty of money—and contacts—to put on a wedding without any of their help. But that was beside the point. Everyone who loved them wanted to help.

Why hadn't her mother told her Jake was coming over? If she'd known, Sophie would have worn something other than the most boring white long-sleeved dress in the world.

Not, she knew, that it would have mattered what she was wearing. She could have been completely naked, spread-eagle on the table, and Jake wouldn't notice. In fact, if he did notice her nudity, he'd probably toss a couple of pillows at her to cover her up without so much as blinking.

The phone rang and her mother excused herself to answer it, leaving Sophie and Jake alone.

"Pretty crazy," he drawled as he looked out the living room window and saw Gabe, Megan and Summer playing in the backyard, "all you Sullivans pairing up like this."

His mouth was quirked up into one of those ridiculously hot half grins that turned her insides to jelly and had her heartbeat kicking into overdrive, just as it always did around Jake. It didn't help that he was wearing a short-sleeved black T-shirt that showed off his muscular, tattooed forearms and dark jeans that showed off his tight a—

No. She couldn't go there. It was too pointless.

Too pathetic.

She'd wasted enough time mooning over Jake. Approximately twenty years, to be precise. But it was one thing to be a five-year-old with a crush. It was entirely another to be a twenty-five-year-old woman who couldn't get over the one guy who barely noticed she was alive.

He thought of her as *Nice,* for God's sake.

Which pretty much summed things up in the most depressing way, considering there was no one she wanted to be naughty with more.

"I'm happy for them," she finally said, unable to quell the defensive tone in her voice. "Chase and Marcus and Gabe all deserve to be happy."

He held his hands up and she hated the way it felt like he was laughing at her. "Sure they do. You've probably got a guy stashed away somewhere, ready to pop a ring on your finger, don't you?"

God, how she wished she could say yes, that she could rub a gorgeous, hunky, successful boyfriend in his face.

Although, since he wouldn't care, the victory would be short-lived, wouldn't it?

Planting a fake smile on her face, she shrugged. "Nope. Still having fun, playing the field."

For a split second, she thought she saw something flash in his chocolate-brown eyes, but it was gone so fast she knew she must have imagined his reaction to the idea of her dating a bunch of random guys.

If anything, he was probably feeling overprotective of her in a brotherly way. He'd probably freak out if he ever realized she looked at him as anything but, if he knew the kinds of fantasies she had about him, ones that included whipped cream and blindfolds and screaming out his na—

She forcefully snapped herself out of the wicked—and pointless—daydream just as he said, "Well, don't worry. You're a pretty girl. Some guy will come along and sweep you off your feet."

Oh, my God. Seriously? Had the number-one subject of all her secret fantasies just called her a *pretty girl*...and then told her *not to worry* about some guy coming to *sweep her away?*

As he gazed at her with a double serving of male condescension, something inside Sophie snapped... breaking right in two, somewhere in the region of her heart.

Sophie knew she was attractive. Even without looking in the mirror, just judging by the way men responded to her identical twin, Lori, she knew her features and figure were put together pretty well.

Only, unlike Lori, Sophie had never tried to trade on her looks for male attention.

In the past year, she'd read literally hundreds of love stories for her library project. Suddenly it hit her: What if she put everything she'd learned about seduction to good use?

What if she made Jake want her?

What if she could find a way to make him desperate to have her?

He was a man, after all. And, no matter how rusty her feminine wiles, she was a woman.

Licking her lips, the power of her new intention had her sitting up straighter in her chair, pulling back her shoulders and crossing her legs to let her white dress ride up past her knees.

Amazingly, Jake actually looked uncomfortable, as if he were finally seeing something he didn't want to—*ever*—have to acknowledge.

And in that moment, Sophie didn't have to work for the wicked little smile on her lips. Not now that she'd decided on her plan of action. Because as soon as she figured out how to get Jake right where she wanted him, she was going to make darn sure she exacted a little revenge for her poor unrequited heart.

Oh, yes, she was going to teach him the lesson someone should have taught him a long time ago.

Namely, that he couldn't have every girl in the world.

Especially not her.

* * * * *

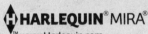

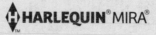

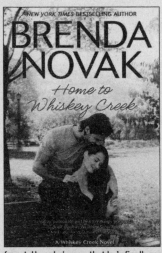

REQUEST YOUR FREE BOOKS!

2 FREE NOVELS
FROM THE ROMANCE COLLECTION
PLUS 2 FREE GIFTS!

YES! Please send me 2 FREE novels from the Romance Collection and my 2 FREE gifts (gifts are worth about $10). After receiving them, if I don't wish to receive any more books, I can return the shipping statement marked "cancel." If I don't cancel, I will receive 4 brand-new novels every month and be billed just $6.24 per book in the U.S. or $6.74 per book in Canada. That's a savings of at least 22% off the cover price. It's quite a bargain! Shipping and handling is just 50¢ per book in the U.S. and 75¢ per book in Canada.* I understand that accepting the 2 free books and gifts places me under no obligation to buy anything. I can always return a shipment and cancel at any time. Even if I never buy another book, the two free books and gifts are mine to keep forever.

194/394 MDN F4XY

Name _____ (PLEASE PRINT) _____

Address _____ Apt. # _____

City _____ State/Prov. _____ Zip/Postal Code _____

Signature (if under 18, a parent or guardian must sign)

Mail to the **Harlequin® Reader Service:**
IN U.S.A.: P.O. Box 1867, Buffalo, NY 14240-1867
IN CANADA: P.O. Box 609, Fort Erie, Ontario L2A 5X3

Want to try two free books from another line?
Call 1-800-873-8635 or visit www.ReaderService.com.

* Terms and prices subject to change without notice. Prices do not include applicable taxes. Sales tax applicable in N.Y. Canadian residents will be charged applicable taxes. Offer not valid in Quebec. This offer is limited to one order per household. Not valid for current subscribers to the Romance Collection or the Romance/Suspense Collection. All orders subject to credit approval. Credit or debit balances in a customer's account(s) may be offset by any other outstanding balance owed by or to the customer. Please allow 4 to 6 weeks for delivery. Offer available while quantities last.

Your Privacy—The Harlequin® Reader Service is committed to protecting your privacy. Our Privacy Policy is available online at www.ReaderService.com or upon request from the Harlequin Reader Service.

We make a portion of our mailing list available to reputable third parties that offer products we believe may interest you. If you prefer that we not exchange your name with third parties, or if you wish to clarify or modify your communication preferences, please visit us at www.ReaderService.com/consumerschoice or write to us at Harlequin Reader Service Preference Service, P.O. Box 9062, Buffalo, NY 14269. Include your complete name and address.

BETH ALBRIGHT

The Sassy Belles are back…and this time, wedding bells are ringing!

Seven months pregnant, Vivi Ann McFadden is busy pulling together the final details for her wedding to Lewis Heart, famous play-by-play announcer for the Crimson Tide. But with two wedding-planners-gone-wild, a psychic giving her advice and the ceremony happening on the same day as the wildly popular Crimson Tide kickoff game, chaos reigns supreme. Luckily, maid of honor Blake O'Hara Heart is on the job. She'll tackle this wedding if it's the last thing she does!

But news of the upcoming nuptials has brought Lewis's old flame back to Tuscaloosa—and she's got a secret that could mean the end of Lewis's marriage…before it even begins.

Available wherever books are sold.

Be sure to connect with us at:

Harlequin.com/Newsletters
Facebook.com/HarlequinBooks
Twitter.com/HarlequinBooks

www.Harlequin.com